Other titles by Robert Cubitt

Fiction

The Deputy Prime Minister

The Inconvenience Store

The Warriors - The Girl I Left Behind Me

The Warriors - Mirror Man

Non-Fiction

I'm So Glad You Asked Me That

I want That Job

Contents

One - The Petulant Pop Princess

"I don't care. I am not going to be filmed holding a fucking ugly baby." Cherry Versace-Laboutin shrieked at Lionel, the location producer. "You either get me a fucking better looking baby or I'm going back to the fucking hotel."

"Andy, love, can you have a word. There must be a better looking baby somewhere in this godforsaken hole."

"I'll see what I can do Lionel. Hold on for a moment. Perhaps it would be best if we got everyone out of the heat for a few minutes."

"Good idea. Can everyone go back to the cars please and wait in the cool. Thank you all." The small crowd shuffled off towards the fleet of air-conditioned SUVs that stood just out of camera shot.

I turned to Jacob, my interpreter. "I'm afraid there's a bit of a problem with the baby they've chosen. We need to get a different one."

"The baby is the grandson of the village headman. He'll be offended if we don't use him."

"Ah, I see the problem. Perhaps he has a granddaughter we could use instead?"

Jacob turned to the representative of the villagers and entered into a lengthy conversation. I glanced over to the cars in which the producer, the film crew, Cherry Versace-Laboutin, and her entourage were now sitting. A trickle of sweat ran down the back of my neck and I hated them with my whole being. The whole shoot had been one problem after another, and Cherry Versace-Laboutin was the root cause of them all.

Jacob and the man walked towards one of the huts and stooped to go inside. That looked promising, unless they had just gone to get out of the heat as well. I was left on my own in the middle of the narrow, filth strewn street. A small group of boys gathered round me, staring up, hopeful of some sweets. I was known to be the custodian of the sweets. I obliged by handing out the remainder of the sticky objects that I had in my shoulder bag. I felt a small pang of guilt about what I might be doing to their teeth, especially as we were so far from a dentist.

It seemed like an age before Jacob and the man came back out of the hut accompanied, I was pleased to see, by a woman carrying a child of about two years of age. The child was naked but for a disposable nappy.

"This is the head man's great niece. He will accept her being in the film providing his grandson is also in it." Jacob reported. "He can be shown playing, perhaps."

"Well done Jacob. Thanks. Look, the disposable nappy will have to go. Can you see if you can find something that looks a bit less "Rich West" and a bit more 'Poor Africa'." I left him to deal with that while I walked over to Lionel's SUV and he lowered the window.

"I think I have a compromise. A rather pretty little girl, as long as we also film the boy. He doesn't have to be in the final cut of course, just a few seconds of filming with him playing in the muck to keep the village headman happy."

"OK, I think I can get Cherry to buy into that." Lionel opened the car door and sauntered over to Cherry's SUV and held a lengthy conversation. His body language suggested that he was having to do a lot of persuading. That didn't surprise me, everything that involved Cherry always involved a lot of persuasion, or arse licking as I preferred to call it. She hadn't even seen the child yet.

An agreement must have been reached, because Lionel roused the film crew from their air conditioned comfort and they started to set up the shot using the child's mother as a stand-in for Cherry, who remained resolutely inside her car. With everything in position Cherry's presence was finally requested.

We waited a full twenty minutes as Cherry's make-up artist repaired the damage that had already been done by the heat. It was painstaking work, trying to make it look like Cherry wasn't wearing any make-up when she was in fact slathered in the stuff. Natural is a hard look to get right, especially with someone who normally wears more make-up than a Japanese geisha.

At last Cherry left the SUV and stomped over to take her place in front of the camera. Without looking at the mother she held her arms out to take the child, who was now wearing a torn and oversized tee shirt with a Manchester United logo. I sighed. It just wouldn't be a charitable appeal if there was no child in a Man U tee shirt.

The mother slid out of shot and Lionel held the clapper board up in front of the camera. "Action."

A smile lit up Cherry's face and she started to recite her lines.

"Hi, I'm Cherry Versace-Laboutin and I'm here in this African village to ask you to pledge just ten pounds to help children like this." She raised the child and turned her so that the camera could capture the little girl's toothy smile. "Little Angelica here" Where had she got that name? The child had an unpronounceable Tutsi name. "has nowhere to play but in the filth of this street." She paused and turned to indicate the narrow alley with the open sewer running down the middle of it.

Turning back to face the camera she continued her lines and completed them, blessedly, in a single take. As soon as Lionel shouted 'cut' the smile vanished from her face. Thrusting the child back into its mother's arms she stalked off back to her SUV, which immediately whisked her away towards the city. Lionel and the crew took some background shots of the running gutters, including the promised footage of the grandson, before packing the gear away and also returning to the city.

Jacob and I were the last to leave, after shaking the hands of the villagers and watching them get into their pick-up trucks to go back to the new, modern bungalows that they really lived in, just over two kilometres away. This run down village had been their previous home, but thanks to MOF and other charities they had been able to move into more salubrious dwellings.

As our own SUV whipped up a cloud of dust in the rear view mirror, I spared a glance back towards the abandoned huts which the weeds and scrub were already starting to reclaim.

That is how a charity fund raising film appeal is made. After dealing with Cherry the next most difficult task was getting the villagers to dress down. People won't pay money to a charity where the 'poor' look better dressed than they are themselves. Getting the women to take off their jewellery had been a major sticking point and had drastically increased the shoot's budget in 'compensation' payments.

Now I'm not knocking charity appeals. I work for a charity and without the money that is raised, an awful lot of people would starve, or die of disease, or go blind or, well you get the picture. The problem is that the places where the money is actually being spent are often hard to get to. Some of them are hundreds of miles from the nearest hotel, let alone airport. It had been hard enough getting Cherry Versace-Laboutin out of her five star suite without having to take her five hundred miles through the bush before we could even start filming.

So we cheat a little...

Yes, it came as a bit of a surprise to me as well.

Two - The Elegant Executive

Perhaps I had better start at the beginning. Well what counts as the beginning of my involvement with this project, at least.

My name is Andy Mirren, I'm twenty seven years old, born in Essex to Scottish parents. I went to my local comprehensive school, attended a university not far from my home and graduated with a 2.2 in Humanitarian Studies. I had always wanted to work with a charity so I applied for suitable posts. After a couple of years of temping, I eventually got a place with the Moses Odama Foundation, hereafter referred to as MOF or simply 'the charity'. You probably haven't heard of us by that name, but we're actually the outfit behind the annual 'Cuddly Toy Day' telethon that takes place every July. I don't know why I'm telling you that because you must know about it. It's the biggest fund raiser on the planet, well maybe the third biggest. Not to be confused, of course, with other similar telethons.

The MOF was named after a boy that the charity's founder, Jim Sawyer, found lying outside the five star hotel he was staying at in Kampala, Uganda, back in the bad old days. He was dying of malnutrition or maybe of half a dozen endemic diseases, take your pick. The only possession the child had was a ragged cuddly toy, its stuffing all gone, its eyes missing, but it was the only thing that the child had to remind him of his dead mother. Jim Sawyer couldn't save the life of Moses, who died two days later despite the efforts of the best doctors that Jim could pay for, but he decided that day to try to put a stop to the suffering of children like him and to prevent their parents from dying and leaving their children orphaned. Although now retired from active involvement he is still one of the charity's trustees. He lives in quiet retirement and declined the offer of a knighthood for his charitable work, saying that it would give out the wrong message. Having seen the sort of people who now involve themselves in the charity's fundraising, I have to say I agree with him.

How I got this gig was a bit of an accident. It came about from the previous year's fundraiser, when my boss at MOF went into a panic because one of the presenters was stuck in Dublin, with no scheduled flight that would get her back to London in time for the show. A show in which she had several pivotal parts to play. Well, I'd gone to school with a guy who was now working for one of those budget airlines, so I gave him a call to see if he knew anyone that could help us out. An hour later the presenter was the sole passenger on a BudgFly aircraft speeding towards a small airfield in Kent, where a motor bike and rider was waiting to take her the final few miles to the TV studio.

The airline, of course, received a lot of free publicity, live on air and in the popular press. Everyone agreed that they probably ended up in profit. I, for my part, was given the 'opportunity' to take on the role of Liaison Manager between the charity and the TV company for this year's fund raiser.

It wasn't until much later that I discovered that the reason the post was vacant was because the previous incumbent was currently 'resting' at a well-known clinic where she spends a lot of her time crying, especially when shown pictures of Africa. I'm starting to understand why, and it has nothing to do with all the poverty and disease she witnessed.

So, on the Monday after the latest fundraising telethon, I found myself sitting in the offices of Metro TV waiting to meet the bloke I'm supposed to liaise with for the next twelve months. That's how long it takes to make a telethon happen. Longer in fact, as the charity itself started working on the programme several weeks before the last telethon went to air.

Around me the open plan office was a hive of activity. Most of it was taking place round the water coolers or in the minuscule kitchen area. Ringing phones went unanswered until they were picked up by the automated voicemail systems. Computer screens blinked and scrolled unattended as the staff of Metro TV swapped their stories of the previous weekend's celebrity parties that are the inevitable follow-on from any sort of TV event, whether it be an award ceremony, a reality TV show finale or a charity telethon.

The staff were mainly young creative types. When I say young please remember that it is a comparison and I am only twenty seven. It was easy to see that they were creative from the range of on-trend clothing, make-up and hairstyles that were on display. The staff were so creative that they had managed to create a type of conformity all of their own.

I had been told to arrive by 9 a.m. and it was already 10.15 with no sign of the executive that I was supposed to be meeting. Eventually the lift doors slid open to reveal Igor Kasnisky, the Executive Producer. I knew it was he from the A4 sized portrait that topped the organisation chart mounted opposite the lift's doors.

Unlike his staff he was more stylishly dressed. It would have taken more than a month of my pay to shop for the chino's, cashmere polo neck sweater, haircut and sun glasses that he sported. The sun glasses rested raffishly on the top of his head, though carefully placed so as not to disturb the coiffure. I couldn't see his wrist watch under the sleeve of the sweater but I would bet good money on it being gold and very expensive.

One of the trendy young girls broke away from a water cooler group and rushed to her desk to pick up a note-pad. She didn't need to wear a sign for me to know that her job title was something like 'executive assistant'. She followed Igor into one of the few enclosed offices, securing the door behind her. It was thirty minutes before she re-emerged.

"Igor will see you now, Mr. Mirren." She spoke with a coolness that suggested that she didn't care whether Igor wanted to see me or not, looking me over and passing judgement on my off-the-peg-chain-store suit and polyester tie.

She turned back to walk the short distance to her desk, not concerned about whether or not I knew where to go. I knocked on the office door and a languid voice instructed me to enter. Igor was the sort of person who drawled and he did it in a way that suggested he was just so bored that he was surprised he was still awake. Even on show-day with divas throwing tantrums and boy scouts being sick on the studio floor, he never raised his voice or varied its pitch. He was reclining in a Captain Kirk style executive office chair. His feet were propped up on his desk as he casually flipped though some sort of document.

He ignored me until he had turned the last page, though I knew he wasn't reading the document. No one can read that fast. It was merely a pretence designed to show me how important, or unimportant, I really was.

I introduced myself and was told to help myself to coffee and to take a seat. The office was furnished in the latest trend-setting style, as was everything about Metro TV. Primary colours dominated, as did shiny surfaces. The lighting was suitably subdued. Anything brighter would have been reflected so brilliantly that it would have been a severe threat to my retinas. It probably cost a fortune. I was just thankful that the TV Licence payers weren't paying for this level of indulgence. I vowed never to buy shares in the company if they were prepared to spend shareholder funds in such a lavish style. Mind you, with my salary that was a moot point. Little did I know, at that early stage, just how both Igor's office and his wardrobe were really being funded.

"Now, Andy. May I call you Andy?" He continued without waiting for my reply. "What do you think an Executive Producer does?"

"I guess you're the man responsible for putting the show together and making sure it gets to air."

"That's about right. Anything to do with the TV side of this little shin-dig is down to me. I find the celebs, I talk them into appearing, not that it's difficult, I organise the studios, the make-up, the costumes, the props, and any outside broadcasts or filming that needs doing. I appoint the producers for the different elements, as well as the directors and other senior creative staff. So, if that is what I do, what do you think the charity does?"

I was ready for the question, having already spoken to the fund raising team. "They organise the corporate sponsors, identify the locations from which to do the celebrity appeals, provide the facts and figures that are used as part of the appeal and then collect the money that's pledged. I spent Friday night answering a phone and taking pledges."

"I'm so pleased for you." Igor drawled, clearly uninterested in the seven hours of unpaid overtime that I had put in. "In which case, what do you see as the responsibilities of the Liaison Manager? That's you, by the way."

"Well, I make the travel arrangements for the celebs and the film crew, book flights, hotels, cars, all that sort of thing. I communicate with the charity workers on the ground so that they know when to expect us, what we want to film and what facilities we need when we get to the location."

"Very good. Just one thing you missed out. You also pay the bills."

I looked a little bit nonplussed. "How do you mean, pay the bills?"

"You said it yourself: Hotels, flights, cars. Add to that meals, drinks and sundries and it all racks up. The celebs give their time for free, but they don't pay out a penny. That comes from the charity, and you're the man who pays the bills. I assume they've given you a credit card?"

"No. Not yet anyway."

"Well make sure they do. You'll probably have to start spending money before the week is out. I've got my staff contacting agents now to start recruiting this year's crop of celebrities, and they will need tickets and hotel bookings made for when they attend their meetings with me. Now, any questions?"

"A few. I know it isn't really my side of the operation, but how do you recruit the celebrities?"

"Actually it's probably more a case of them recruiting us. There are basically three groups of celebs. First there's the wannabees. They'll turn up to the opening of an envelope if it gets their face on TV. So they're the ones that came fourth on some TV talent show or got slung out of the Big Brother House after the first week and so on. They're great for doing regional OB's, that's outside broadcasts by the way, surrounded by crowds of loonies dressed as giant chickens or whatever.

The next group are the pluggers. These are the ones with the new film, CD, DVD, play or whatever that needs to be plugged. We have the PR people practically begging us to get them on air with a clip or a performance. The most desperate can usually be persuaded to record the charity single as well.

The final group are the established celebs who want to have the word 'charity' on their CV. They feel it gives them credibility, or increases their chances of getting a gong. They're usually the ones we get to do the location shoots. There's nothing quite like standing over a dying baby with tears streaming down the face to give the old credibility a boost. Of course we have our regulars. Names we can count on. I wouldn't really put them into any of the groups. They've attached themselves to the cause and if they don't appear people will wonder why, so they keep doing it."

"What about the group events, you know, like the soap stars or newsreaders doing routines from musicals and the like."

"We hardly have to do anything. One of the cast will usually be from one of the groups I've already described and they'll talk the other cast members into doing it. Once we've got that buy-in we can go to the show's producers and sell it to them as a ratings booster. They organise the script and the shooting and all we have to do is show it on the night, along with a live appearance by the cast members. We can usually get a whole ten, maybe fifteen minutes of air-time out of it. It never fails."

I was flabbergasted by the level of cynicism that Igor was displaying. It sounded to me like no one really cared about the charity and what it was doing. I plucked up my courage and said as much. Igor was un-phased by the implied criticism.

"I know it sounds like that." He replied, "but many of the celebs do genuinely care. Look at the ones who do the big stunts: The treks across polar ice caps; Swimming the River Nile or whatever. They don't do that just for publicity. It's far too much work and far too much of a time commitment. No, they're the genuine ones, and they come back year after year, either doing more stunts or as presenters on the night. I think we're running at half a dozen MBEs, a couple of OBEs and a CBE now. Anything else?"

"Only one more question, I think. Where do I work?"

"Oh yes. Well I assume that you have your own desk at the charity's offices in Southwark. But we've got a desk for you that you can use when you're over here. Sonia will show you where, and she'll arrange computer access for you as well."

The meeting was clearly over so I rose to leave.

"One last thing." I turned back at the sound of Igor's voice, expecting a good luck wish or a welcome speech perhaps. "Don't forget to get that credit card sorted."

I felt my shoulders slump and slunk towards the young woman that I assumed was Sonia.

"Igor says you've got a desk for me." She looked at me as though I had just suggested having a threesome with Jimmy Savile, before wafting an emerald green tipped hand towards the far side of the office.

"And he said you would arrange computer access."

She let out a long sigh of impatience and turned towards me with a pad of post-it notes. As I looked towards her I couldn't help but notice the important work I was interrupting. On her computer screen I could see it was a video clip of a kitten playing with a ball of wool. I was surprised that I had been able to attract her attention at all with such fierce competition.

"Write what you want your username to be, and an e-mail address where IT can send a password. They'll set you up a Metro TV e-mail address and give you access to the systems you'll be using."

"How do I get access to my e-mail if I can't access a PC?" I asked, knowing full well I could use my smart phone to open my personal e-mail account. She was annoying me so I felt justified in annoying her.

"Oh, go and see Martin. He'll let you use his PC."

I noted that she firstly didn't tell me where I could find Martin and secondly that she assumed Martin would comply. The use of Sonia's name would apparently act as the magic word.

I wrote down the username as she requested and handed the pad back to her. She placed it at the rear most edge of her desk where it was almost certain to fall down between her desk and her neighbour's and get lost. I didn't anticipate getting computer access in the immediate future.

Three - The Indiscreet Martin

I found my desk right next to the entrance to the gents toilets. Convenient I suppose, but the waft of urine scented air that emerged every time the door opened left a lot to be desired, not least a desk somewhere further away. That accounted for why the desk wasn't in current use. Still, it had its compensations. I would pretty soon get to know most of the men in the team, even if it meant also getting to know their toilet habits.

After claiming my place I went off in search of Martin, who I guessed would also inhabit this side of the office. I found him hard at work playing a computer game. He was unconcerned by my interruption. I explained my reason for interrupting his 'work'.

"That Sonia's a real bitch." He commented. "She thinks she's great because she's Igor assistant, but it's just a fancy way of saying P.A. Not that there's anything wrong with being a P.A." he added hurriedly, "but she thinks she runs the whole company, whereas in fact Igor doesn't actually trust her with any of the important stuff."

I used Martin's PC to access my e-mail and was surprised to find that my username and password were waiting for me. Perhaps I had judged Sonia a bit harshly.

"No you didn't." Martin reassured me after I had explained my concern. "She'll have bullied Cassie into organising it for her. Cassie's a saint and Sonia would sink without trace if Cassie didn't keep bailing her out."

"So what's your role in this … set-up?" I nearly said zoo but managed to divert my tongue in time.

"Well, I'm Executive Assistant to Gary Larkin. He's the set designer. That's him over there." He pointed towards a pink haired, slightly older man, seated at one of the larger desks. By 'slightly older', I meant that he was over twenty-five.

"Why do you need a set designer?" I must have seemed so naïve. "There's already a set and it's only been used once."

"You've got a lot to learn, sweetie. You don't mind if I call you sweetie do you?" Martin gushed. "I'm not gay, just bi, but I like to keep my options open." He giggled before continuing. "The set has to fit in with the themed cuddly toy of the year. Surely you knew that. The theme for last year was cuddly bunnies." He made it sound like it was twelve months earlier, rather than just three days. "And the theme for this year is pandas. That means a whole redesign of the set. Pandas are conceptually sooooo different to bunnies. You couldn't possibly use the same set again. It would just look soooo wrong."

I would have to get used to the elongated soooo and toooo (as in toooo much) and several other ways of emphasising words. I was just grateful that no one was making bunny ear quotation marks with their fingers. It meant I didn't have to kill them.

"So Gary designs and builds the set, does he?"

"Good grief no. He designs the concept. We then outsource the concept to a design and build company who draw up the design and build it in sections and deliver it to the studio in time for rehearsals."

"So Gary's only part time then?" Oh God, more naïvety.

"No, full time. It takes a huge amount of time to come up with a concept that fits the theme you know. Then of course Gary has to supervise the company we outsource the work to."

"So what do you do?" If I was at a loss to understand why Gary needed to be employed full-time I was at even more of a loss to understand why he needed an executive assistant all to himself.

"I assist Gary of course." Martin seemed surprised that I hadn't grasped the concept. For my part I was starting to wonder when the White Rabbit and the March Hare were due to arrive.

I managed to keep any sign of disapproval from my voice. While I felt that money was being wasted it wasn't my charity's money, or so I thought. I was wrong, as Martin was just about to enlighten me.

"We were so excited by last week's show. It raised a record amount you know." Martin beamed at me.

"I know, I was working the 'phones. It's great. It will help so many people in Africa."

"That too, of course, but what it really means is a bigger budget for us."

"Oh, does Metro give you more money if the show is more successful?"

"What's Metro got to do with it? Our budget is provided by MOF. The more that the show raises, the more your bosses give us to run the show. It's brilliant, isn't it?"

"I thought the TV company gave its time and resources for free."

"We do, but that's only on the day of the show. We don't charge for studio time and all the staff and technicians give their time for free, but all this," he waved his hand, "has to be paid for, doesn't it?"

No it doesn't, I thought. Not all of it at least. The words of the well-known saying rang in my head. The words every celebrity said when they made their appeal. "Every pound you give goes straight to help these poor, desperate people."

But of course it didn't, did it? Some of it came to Metro TV and paid for Sonia to watch kittens playing with balls of wool, Martin to play computer games and for Gary Larkin to sit at his desk until inspiration struck him, and then it paid for the set to be built and for the expenses for the celebs and.... what else? I wondered.

I felt slightly sick as the reality hit home. There was a whole industry behind the charity I worked for and it was sucking money away from its intended beneficiaries. On top of that, the more successful the fundraising the more money that would be sucked out.

"How much budget do you get then?" I asked, my voice a croaky whisper.

"Oh, I'm not sure. That's way above my pay grade, but I think it's about ten per cent of the amount raised." I did a quick divide by ten based on the pledges made the previous Friday. The figure was startling. Perhaps not startling to a Premiership football club considering the transfer of the latest Brazilian wonder player, but big enough to bring howls of protest from those that made the pledges, were they ever to find out the truth.

I had a mental image of the set that had been used, as I had glimpsed it on TV during my breaks between sessions of telephone answering. It was a masterpiece comparable with any of the great entertainment shows. High gloss floors and walls, plenty of gold paint, a mock marble staircase with mock gold hand rails. There were flashing lasers and pyrotechnics, enough light bulbs to illuminate a city centre and digital displays flashing up good will messages and amounts of money. There were giant faux fur bunnies everywhere and the studio audience were kept plied with food and drink so that they would cheer and clap on cue.

Then I looked around the office and saw the forty or so people that were being paid for out of the charity's coffers and did a mental calculation of the wages bill. It didn't seem too bad. I didn't know it at the time, of course, but I had grossly under estimated the rates of pay. But even factoring in the margin of error I had made it didn't account for ten per cent of the show's income.

It wasn't until I started to meet the celebs and deal with their expenses that I realised where even more money was going. Then there was the big one …but no. I'm getting ahead of myself. I must stop doing that.

Martin broke into my reverie. "Lunchtime Andy. Would you like me to show you where the cafeteria is? I always go there. You get the best gossip up there. It's the only place in the building where you get to meet up regularly with people working on other shows and in other departments."

I followed him through the office and into the lift, which whisked us up to the top of the building.

"There's only one floor above this." Martin confided. "That's the Executive level, where all the directors hang out. I've never been up there. I think Igor's only been up there once himself. If you get called up there you're either being promoted or sacked, so that shouldn't affect you, as you don't work for Metro."

I chose a sandwich and a can of fizzy pop from the chilled food display and followed Martin along the servery to the hotplate. Martin picked up a plate and began filling it with curried chicken and rice. "This is my main meal of the day." He explained. "I don't cook except at weekends and breakfast is a joke with my lifestyle." When we got to the cashier I expected him to stop and pay, but instead he flashed his ID card and walked on. The cashier rang up the bill for his food but made no comment. I put my hand in my pocket to take out some money but Martin intervened. "He's with me Beryl." He called back over his shoulder. Beryl graced me with a smile and waved me on.

"Don't tell me," I said as we sat down. "Lunch is charged to the budget."

"Of course. We're lucky. Most of the shows have to pay, and of course the admin staff don't have production budgets so they have to pay as well. Make sure that Sonia gets you a production ID like this." He swung his on the end of the lanyard round his neck. "That way you won't have to pay either."

Things were getting worse, I realised. Over in our HQ in Southwark we were too small an outfit to warrant a cafeteria of our own, so we used the local sandwich bars and cafes to buy our lunches, dipping into our own pockets to pay for them, just as most of the people who gave money to the charity had to do.

"So who negotiated the budget in the first place?" I asked.

"No idea. It was before my time. You have to remember that Cuddly Toy Day has been going for over twenty years now. Igor wasn't even with Metro then and he's ancient." For the record I would have placed Igor at around thirty.

I could see the need for a full time team to manage the annual telethon. It was a big project and there were many strands to it. The TV company would need a production budget to make it happen, even though on broadcast day the staff and technicians gave their time for free. The telethon had started out small and had been running for several years before it captured the public's imagination and started to pull in the big money and break records for charity fund raising. Most of that big money was as a result of capturing the interest of corporate sponsors. They were the ones who sold the badges and cuddly toys and all other merchandising as well as holding fund raising events of their own.

Ten per cent of a small pie wasn't an unreasonable budget, I acknowledged to myself. But it wasn't a small pie any more. Ten per cent was now a sizeable wedge, and Metro were determined to spend it, even if it meant employing staff to play computer games and stand around the water cooler gossiping for much of the day. I wondered what sort of contribution the Cuddly Toy Day budget was making to Metro TV's profits, and therefore its share price.

I made a mental note to find out who had been involved in setting up the first contract with Metro TV. I also made a note to ask why no one had renegotiated the contract to get more favourable terms.

In reality none of that was my business. I'm just a small fish in a big pond, but there was something in my Scottish Presbyterian heritage that made my hackles rise when I saw money being wantonly squandered. I may be a small fish, but even some of the smallest can administer a sharp sting if provoked.

As I sat absorbed in my own thoughts, Martin chattered away about the people in the office and passed on snippets of gossip about the various characters that entered or left the cafeteria.

"Of course she's sleeping with Igor." The use of the Executive Producer's name brought me back to pay full attention to Martin.

"Who's that?" I asked. If someone was involved with Igor then it was probably best that I was aware of who they were, just in case I bumped into them. It wouldn't do to offend them.

"Helen Spencer. That's her at the servery now." I looked across and identified a small, slim brunette standing between two men. She was as stylishly and expensively dressed as Igor. Had she been a little taller she could have taken her place on any cat walk in the world.

"What does she do for Metro?"

"Weren't you listening? She's Head of Entertainment Broadcasting. It effectively makes her Igor's boss. If they ever have a row it could end up nastily for him, I can tell you. She's got a vicious temper. I've heard her bawling out people from two floors away."

To look at her I couldn't imagine her even raising her voice if someone parked a car on her foot, but of course looks can be so deceiving. She turned, perhaps some sixth sense telling her she was being observed, and I caught a glint as her eyes met mine. Even at that distance I could sense the steel behind her otherwise placid exterior. I quickly broke eye contact in case she decided my stare was offensive. She didn't know me, yet, and I had no intention of our first meeting being in the form of a confrontation.

"I didn't realise that Cuddly Toy Day was classed as entertainment." I changed the subject.

"Maybe not to you, but that's what it is to us. The more we entertain the more money is raised. Do you know there's actually a formula for it?"

"How do you mean?"

"Well the American telethons did some research. I suppose it works for us as well. The ratio of time spent between appeals and entertainment is crucial. If the public spends too much time looking at starving people then they might change channels. On the other hand if you don't make enough appeals you won't raise enough money, which is what it's all about in the end. Apparently the optimum time is nine and a half minutes of entertainment for every three minutes of appeals. We go ten and three to make things simpler. So for a five hour broadcast we have to have two hundred and thirty minutes of entertainment, or just under four hours. Deduct an hour for news and ad breaks of course and that leaves you with just under three hours of entertainment. The appeals can be repeated, naturally, or edited to make them look a little bit different and we usually have about five or six films which we cycle through during the four hours. Of course that's where you come in."

"Yes, I'm looking forward to it." Martin gave me a slightly quizzical look.

"Be careful what you wish for, Andy. Some of those celebs can be right buggers. Have you spoken to Mellissa?"

It was my turn to look quizzical.

"Mellissa, the woman who was last year's liaison." Martin explained.

The penny cropped. "Actually, no. We haven't met. She wouldn't have needed to come into the department I used to work in."

"It might be an idea to track her down and have a chat before you go much further."

The tone of his warning struck me as ominous and I made another mental note to try to find Mellissa.

"Back to the grindstone then." Martin rose to leave, taking his tray across to the collection point. I dropped my drinks can into the recycling box next to it and placed my single small plate on top of Martin's.

"You know, I really love working here." Martin commented. What's not to love? I thought. Being paid to play computer games all day and a free lunch thrown in.

Four - Mellissa's Malaise

"On this occasion, Andy, I'm going to forgive your tirade. They say that a little knowledge is a dangerous thing, and I think that applies in this case."

I had been with Greg Jones, our Director of Fundraising, for half an hour berating him over the fact that we were lying to our donors about every penny of their donations going to support our work in Africa.

"But it's clear from the accounts that over seventeen per cent of all money donated goes in income generation and governance. From that the vast majority of the spend is on Income Generation, by which I assume it includes the budget for the telethon. I've checked the accounts on the Charities Commission website, and that's what it shows." I could see that Greg's patience was wearing thin, but I wasn't about to cave in that easily.

"But it's not quite true, the way the accounts are presented. What they don't show is the difference between the donations and the Gift Aid. You know what Gift Aid is, don't you?"

"Of course. It's the tax we claim back from the Inland Revenue on the donations we receive."

"Precisely. For every pound we get we claim back twenty pence, providing the donor gives their permission for us to do so. Some wealthier donors don't give permission, as they claim the tax back off of HMRC for themselves, but almost all the donors on PAYE do give their permission. So what we say in our appeals is sufficiently factual. Every penny we get in donations goes straight to Africa. It's the tax we claim back that pays for the show and our other income generation activities and for our running costs. All those twenty pences add up to several million pounds a year, you know. We checked with the lawyers that it was OK to say what we do, just in case anyone challenged us on it. Though I didn't expect it to be an employee who challenged us."

"In that case I must apologise, Greg, but it certainly isn't clear from the accounts where the split is between tax and donations. But that's not the only issue. I've just spent the day at Metro TV and its quite clear that the charity is being ripped off."

"Do tell." Greg sighed, clearly wishing I'd go away and leave him alone.

"Well, there's about forty staff directly employed on the telethon, and that doesn't include the work they out-source to other suppliers. From what I saw most of them are under-employed. Even the assistants have assistants, which is ridiculous." I had that confirmed to me when Martin introduced me to Henry, his assistant. "They get their lunches paid for every day, and God knows what else is included in the deal. To cap it all, the more the telethon raises the bigger the budget for the next year, which just gives them more money to squander."

"But that was the basis of the original agreement with Metro. They subsidised us by a considerable amount in the early days, because the telethon couldn't have gone ahead any other way. They had a vision that was considerably broader than ours, so they agreed to carry a loss until the amount of subsidy they provided could afford to be repaid. A figure of ten per cent of the money pledged on the night was agreed, well actually it's nine point nine seven per cent for some obscure reason."

"Has anyone done a calculation to see how that has panned out over the years? How much they paid out in the early days compared to how much they're making now?"

Greg paused for a long moment. I could see that I had given him something to think about. "Actually, no, I don't believe anyone has."

"So we could have repaid the subsidy several times over by now. Let's face it, it's not in Metro TV's interests to point that out to us, is it?"

"Hmm, I suppose not. OK, I'll concede the point on that, and I'll take it to the next Board Meeting. See what Martha and Charles think of it."

Martha Vine is the charity's Chief Executive and Charles Conway is our Director of Finance. With Greg, Faye Goodyear the Director of Field Operations, and Malcolm McKenzie the Director of Logistics, they made up the Board of Directors, answerable only to the trustees of the charity.

"Thank you Greg. Again I apologise over the other issue."

"Apology accepted, but I do suggest that if you have any other queries like that you bring them to me or Charles before you go sounding off. OK?"

"OK. Oh, just one other thing. How can I contact Mellissa Sutherland? I could do with a chat with her about what I'm actually supposed to be doing and how I should go about doing it."

"Well technically Mellissa's on sick leave. I'd rather she wasn't bothered at the moment."

"That's a pity. Can't you stretch a point on it? I'm really struggling to get a handle on things right now." I pleaded.

Greg must have taken pity on me, because he gave me the information I needed.

* * *

I followed a nurse through a comfortable looking lounge to where Mellissa was slumped on a settee staring at the TV.

"Your brother's here." The nurse announced.

"Brother? I haven't got...." She must have twigged because she changed her mind about having a brother. "Of course. Sorry, I was miles away. Yes of course. Lovely to see you. Come and sit next to me."

As the nurse left us I took the proffered cushion on the settee and introduced myself.

"Sorry about that, but they would only let me in if I was family. You recognised me though?"

"Not really, but you're wearing your MOF ID card, so I guessed what you wanted. You are my replacement, aren't you?"

"I am. How come our paths haven't crossed before?"

"I was only recruited last year, specifically for the Liaison Manager role. I spent most of my time at Metro TV so I hardly know anyone at the Southwark offices. I think I was only in them half a dozen times. Where do you work?"

"Well, until a couple of weeks ago I was down in the basement. I managed the database that records all the donors and acts as the master list of addresses for postal campaigns."

"Wow, so a big change for you then. I was never down in the basement. Are there many people working there?"

"No, just me, the post room staff and the cleaners."

"Well that accounts for us not having met. So what can I do for you now?"

As we chatted I'd had a chance to study Mellissa. The towelling dressing gown did nothing for her and her lack of make-up and tangled hair probably made her look five years older than she really was which, based on that assessment, was probably no more than thirty. There were dark rings under her emerald green eyes. A trip to the hairdresser would put the shine and shape back into her thick mane of copper coloured hair, which at the moment was pulled back into a loose pony tail from which strands had escaped and drooped limply over her forehead. I tried to visualise her as she might have appeared in the Metro TV offices and decided she would make heads turn.

"I hope you don't mind me dropping in like this, but I really needed to talk to someone who had done this job before."

"You're concerned about the set up at Metro TV, aren't you?"

Was she telepathic or was it just a lucky guess? No, she had worked with Metro for a year. She knew why I was there. "Is it that obvious?"

"Oh yes. It's the only reason I can think for you to want to come all this way to see me."

"I don't want to pry, but…."

"Yes, it's because of Metro TV that I'm in here. Well, not entirely. But they are one part of the larger whole."

"And the other parts?"

"Danny Devane, Pippa St John, Ded NuronZ, Stan 'The Man' Goodwin, and maybe another dozen so called musicians, singers, comedians, sports stars, presenters, and celebrities with unspecified and unidentifiable talents."

I recognised all the names and could guess at some of the ones she hadn't listed. "Are there any good guys at all?" I asked, hoping I had kept any sign of panic from my voice.

"A couple. Marty Webster is a sweetie and Gina Jay is easy enough to work with, but most of the rest are a nightmare. I hope you have stacks of resilience. Of course you won't know yet who they have lined up for next year's show."

"No, not yet. Igor hasn't mentioned any names."

At the sound of Igor's name Mellissa's eyes had started to fill with tears. "That bastard." She spat. "Look, it won't make any difference, but keep as much distance between you and him as possible. Him and his girlfriend are pure poison. There's nothing they won't try, and I do mean nothing." Mellissa pulled her dressing gown closer around herself, as though donning a suit of armour.

"Is there anything specific you can tell me?"

"Nothing that would stand up in court. Have you worked out the deal with the budget?"

I told her that I had.

"Well, from what I could work out they've got their hands deep into the charity's pockets. Quite a lot of the actual work is outsourced, as you'll find out. Independent film crews, location producers hired through an agency, set construction, equipment hire, you name it and it's outsourced."

"So, that's the way things are done these days. You hire people and resources in when you need them rather than paying for them all year round."

"Leaving aside the fact that some of the forty staff they have on the third floor also have some of those elements in their job descriptions, you need to look at who has shares in the companies that are awarded contracts."

"Don't tell me, Igor and Helen Spencer."

"Like I said, nothing that would stand up in court. And they're ruthless. I think they suspected that I'd worked it out, which is why they started applying a lot of pressure. When that didn't work Igor turned on the charm. Trouble is I'm gay, so when that didn't work out Helen tried her hand. She nearly had me as well, the bitch, but Martin warned me what she was up to."

"So Martin's one of the good guys?"

"As far as anyone at Metro TV is. But don't look on him as an ally. He'll cover his own arse first, you can be sure."

"But why would they be scared of you?"

"They're employed by Metro TV. Anything they do as part of their job has to be done in the best interests of their employer. So, if they're outsourcing work to contractors that they have a financial interest in then they're acting against the best interests of Metro TV. The company may already have contracts in place for all those services and at a better price, or even full time staff who could do it.

It could cost Igor and Helen their jobs and probably their reputations as well. Reputations count for a lot in the media. They might even be guilty of criminal offences, fraud or similar."

"Well, I can see that they wouldn't want any of that to become public knowledge."

"But as I said, that was only part of the story. It's the celebs that finally broke me. The demands they make are ridiculous. And what they expect you to turn a blind eye to."

"Drugs I suppose."

"That's the least of it. But some of it's really silly. You know Pipkin?" I nodded to acknowledge the name of the children's TV presenter. "Well, he's a real comic book geek. We were in Kenya and he asked me to get him the latest issue of The Green Lantern comic. Sorry, "comic book" as he insisted on calling it. Of course there was no way it was available anywhere near where we were, so I went on line and ordered it and had it FedEx'd out from the States. I took it to his room and he very carefully counted out the $2.99 cover price, entirely disregarding the $50 it cost to have shipped out. How he thought it had got there I have no idea."

She paused and took a sip of water from the glass that sat on the low table next to the settee.

"But you're right, there's lot of drugs involved. I have no problem with drugs; that's people's personal choice. If they want to kill themselves that's their look out. But that wasn't the worst. It was the girls, and boys of course, with no real concern with whether or not they're over the age of consent. Well I'm no prude, but I came close to throwing up over some of the things I was asked to make sure were on offer. It's up to you how you handle it, but I refused a couple of times. It caused a furore on both occasions but I stuck to my guns. There are lines I won't cross and I don't care how important the celeb thinks he or she is."

"Why didn't you just quit?"

"I did, twice, but Greg talked me out of it both times. He told me he would talk to Metro TV about it and they would talk to the celebs, or at least to their agents. He said that if Metro wanted to go along with those sorts of things they would have to provide their own staff to deal with it. I'm sure he meant it, but it just made matters worse. Things started happening at work, you know, sly little things. I went to the loo and got super glued to the seat. I was sent some flowers, but when I opened the greetings envelope there was a sketch of a gun pointing at a woman's head. No prizes for guessing who the woman might be."

"I'm sorry to hear that. I really am. That shouldn't happen to anyone."

"The final straw was when they sent pictures of me to my new partner. We'd been together for just a few weeks and she'd just moved into my flat. They showed me naked with another woman and a man. It was a fake, of course, but Magda wouldn't believe me and walked out. The next day I checked in here for the first time."

"So you've been here before."

"Twice before. The first time was six months ago and I was only in for a couple of days. The second time was a bit longer. It was just before the last Cuddly Toy Day show and Igor had been really over the top, then Helen had joined in. I got out after a week and managed to get through the show but then at the after party some of the celebs ganged up on me. It wasn't much at first, just a little bit of name calling. Goody Two Shoes, that sort of thing. But it got worse; Really mean stuff. My dress got torn and someone, I don't know who, put their hand up my skirt from behind. I broke down in tears and Greg had me in here within an hour. He didn't want to risk a scandal if I was seen in hysterics at the party."

"Why didn't you report it to the police?"

"I did. They came this morning to tell me that they're not pursuing my complaint. They're all backing each other up. They all say I'm nuts and making it all up, even the ones who didn't get involved. The fact that this is my third time in here tends to support that view. Check your contract. You'll find there's a confidentiality clause in it. It wouldn't stand up in court, of course, but they would use it to sack you and by the time a tribunal had ruled on it word of mouth would make you unemployable.

"So the police really haven't learnt anything from the Savile affair."

"I don't blame the police. It's my word against a dozen eye witnesses, even if they are all lying through their teeth. Who would you believe?"

"Right now I believe you."

She patted my hand. "That's sweet, Andy, but don't waste your sympathy on me. Just make sure it doesn't happen to you."

"Who's picking up the bill for this place? It can't be cheap."

"The charity. Greg insisted. I think he's worried I might sue for negligence. I wouldn't, of course. I don't want to divert the charity's money away from where it's needed. The cost of this place is cheap in comparison to what I might get in compensation, so I feel justified in letting them pay for that. I've been through hell for them."

At that moment the temptation to go and tell Greg where to stick his job was strong, but I realised that it wouldn't help me or Mellissa. What would help us both would be to turn the tables. I felt sorry for Mellissa, of course, and if I could extract some revenge on her behalf it would be a good thing, but more importantly well-known people were misusing the charity that I worked for.

They were going about pretending to be such altruistic people only interested in helping the poor, diseased people of Africa. Whereas in fact they were exploiting the charity for their own ends. Not just in gaining publicity from it, which I could understand, but in hard cash terms as well. I don't believe in much, but I do believe in what I do for a living and they were making a mockery of it. That had to stop.

"Well, thanks for your time Mellissa. I hope you get better soon. Is there any final word of advice you can give me?"

"Yes there is. I've told you about the Igor and Helen, and about the way the celebs behave, but there's one group of people that are more dangerous than any of them. The agents."

"Oh, what about them?"

"Well, they don't benefit from their clients contributions to the charity. The only benefit comes from the client's improved profile, which they will then try to turn into earnings. That means if the client looks bad there's little chance of any upside for the agent. They'll defend their clients like a mother tiger defending her cubs. There's an old saying about agents, which I only learnt last year. 'Your friends will help you move house. Your agent will help you move a body.' Personally I think that understates the case. I think some agents would be willing to create the body if it suited their purpose. If anything bad happens to you it's likely to be an agent that made it happen, unless of course it's a face to face confrontation."

"Wow. Well OK, I hear you. Anyway thanks again for your time. I doubt we'll meet again, so good luck to you."

Mellissa and I exchanged pecks on the cheek. As I walked back through the clinic I used my phone to order her the biggest bouquet of flowers that I could find. And I paid for it myself.

Five - Cassie

Armed with my new knowledge I returned to work the following day and started doing some digging. The names and addresses of the supplier companies used to create the Cuddly Toy Day programme were a matter of record, and I found all the details on the Metro TV intranet site. From there I was able to check them out with Companies House. Neither Igor nor his girlfriend were listed as directors, but that didn't surprise me. They would want to keep an arm's length relationship with the Board.

There was a clear pattern. Annabel Creech was on the Board of at least four of the suppliers and Hazel Delacourt held similar positions with four more. No other names stood out in any of the other companies, but that didn't mean that Igor and Helen didn't have people in place inside them as well.

It didn't take long to find references on the internet to both women. A gossip magazine had a picture of Annabel Creech emerging from a night club on the arm of her husband. The family resemblance to Helen Spencer was striking. I guessed at them being sisters. Hazel Delacourt was even better known, as she was married to a well-known playwright. It didn't take long to find out that her maiden name was Kasnisky.

It didn't prove anything. It isn't against the law to sit on the Board of Directors of a company, even several companies, and it would be difficult to prove that the two women's shareholdings had been paid for by either Igor or Helen. It was quite possible, probable even, that the women were wealthy in their own right and therefore as likely to own shares as anyone else.

I became aware that someone was standing beside my desk and looked up to see a vision of dark haired loveliness looking down at me.

"I was just going to make some coffee. Can I get you some?" The vision asked.

"That would be nice." I stuttered. "I'm sorry. I don't think we've met." I struggled to my feet, extending my hand in greeting. My swivel chair conspired to wrap itself around my feet and drag me downwards, but I discretely fought it and managed to remain upright. I noticed that the vision had a pale pink streak in her hair on the side furthest from me. Of course she would. She worked for Metro TV and was creative.

She gave me a generous smile, displaying her perfect teeth. Grasping my hand she told me her name was Cassie. That would be the Cassie that Martin had described as a saint, I surmised. Cassie had a heart shaped face framed by her bobbed hair style and made perfect by her tiny button nose. I resisted the urge to take in the rest of her but my initial, fleeting impression had been of a slim and rather petit woman with curves in the right places.

"How do you like it?" She breathed. I almost told her, but managed to regain my sanity as I realised she meant my coffee.

"White no sugar." I stammered.

"Strong or weak?"

"Strong, definitely strong." A caffeine fix might help me concentrate and prevent me from blurting out my undying love for this woman.

"Back in a mo." She turned and sauntered towards the kitchen at the far end of the office. If she looked back she would undoubtedly have been met by the unedifying sight of my tongue dragging on the floor as I took in the gentle swaying of her buttocks as she walked. I had a feeling she was deliberately accentuating the movement.

I realised that in geographical terms there was no reason for Cassie to have come anywhere near my desk as she went from her own to the kitchen to make coffee. That meant one of two things. She had either been visiting someone else and just happened to be passing, or she had deliberately crossed the office to my desk. I prayed that it was the latter. I allowed myself to drop back into my chair. In my befuddled state I misjudged the distance and landed on the edge of the seat, propelling it backwards. I heard a giggle as Martin saw me floundering as I struggled to prevent myself from falling to the ground. The chair was quite definitely out to get me.

I turned to glare at him but Martin was staring resolutely at his computer screen, though I couldn't help but noticing the reddening of his ears as he struggled to stifle his laughter.

Cassie returned a few minutes later bearing two cups of coffee. After handing me mine she perched herself daintily on the edge of my desk. I tried to keep my eyes fixed on a point above her head as the hem line of her dress rode up to reveal a length of green, nylon clad thigh.

"So how are you finding Metro TV?"

"Oh, you know, I turn left out of the tube station and there it is." I attempted a joke. Cassie gave a weak smile. I wondered if she was already regretting her decision to talk to me. "Sorry, old joke. It's OK, really."

"No it isn't." She whispered, lowering her face until it was close to mine. "It's an absolute bear garden. No one does any work and practically everyone has a scam going." She straightened up.

"Surely it's not that bad." I dissembled, also lowering my voice.

"I think you know already just how bad it is." Cassie whispered. "We have a mutual friend. She sent me a text last night. A long text."

"Ah. Well, in that case there isn't much I can say."

"Certainly not here. Meet me in The Greyhound after work." The Greyhound was a pub just round the corner past the underground station. "We can talk more freely there."

"Alright. What time do you finish?"

"Five normally. Depends on how much work Sonia pushes onto me." She rose to leave. "If we get on maybe I'll let you take me out one night."

With that bombshell she turned and walked away, her hips once more swaying like a metronome.

Had I just heard what I thought I heard? Was Cassie propositioning me? I very much hoped so.

A thought crossed my mind. Why hadn't Mellissa mentioned that she was friends with Cassie? Another, more sinister, thought crossed my mind. I only had Cassie's word that Mellissa had contacted her. Perhaps she had heard about my visit from another source, such as a member of the clinic's staff. I shook my head savagely. I was starting to act paranoid.

I went over to Martin's desk to try to find out more.

"Cassie seems like a nice girl." I commented.

"Oh she is. She's one of the very best."

"Does she make coffee for all the blokes."

"Never seen her do that before. Certainly she's never made coffee for me. But then we're more like brother and sister, if you get my drift."

"Did she get on well with Mellissa?"

Martin gave me an appraising look. "Halt, who goes there? Friend or foe? Am I right?"

"You see right through me."

"Years of watching my back in this place."

"You haven't answered my question."

"I told you that Cassie's one of the best. I meant it. I don't know if she and Mellissa were close. If they were then they kept it quiet. But if she said she was Mellissa's friend then she was."

"And do you think I'm in with a chance?"

Martin's broad face cracked into a smile. "So long as you keep your chair under control." He giggled. "I can tell you that her last relationship broke up over a year ago and there's been no talk of anyone else in her life since then."

"Who was she seeing?"

"It was only a rumour, but Igor's name was mentioned."

"But…."

"They have a very open relationship. They sleep with whoever they need to. It's not sex, it's business. Cassie took it very badly when her relationship ended, whoever it was with. Be gentle with her."

"I will."

I returned to my desk with thoughts rushing through my head. If it had been Igor, and he had hurt Cassie, then it would account for a lot. She and Mellissa might well have become allies.

Six - The Greyhound

The Greyhound was busy with the after work rush and we struggled to find a table, eventually wedging ourselves between a sweaty business man talking football with pals and a smartly dressed woman knocking back gin and tonics like they were going to stop making them at any moment.

"Right now you're wondering if you can trust me." Cassie opened the conversation.

"What makes you think that?"

"Because if I were in your shoes that's what I'd be asking myself. You know what's going on at Metro, and you're wondering if Igor sent me to spy on you."

"How do you know what I know about Metro?"

"As I said in the office, we have a mutual friend. Perhaps she had better vouch for me. What's your mobile number?"

I gave her the number and she rapidly composed a text message. A few seconds later my 'phone rang."

"Cassie texted me. She wants me to tell you that you can trust her." I recognised the voice at once. It was Mellissa.

"And can I trust her?"

"Yes. Absolutely." The line went dead as she rang off.

"So tell me about you and Mellissa. How did you become friends, and why didn't Mellissa mention you when I saw her the other night?"

"We did our best to keep it quiet. Mellissa was already having problems with Igor and others at Metro. I found her in the loo one day crying her eyes out. I dried her tears and brought her round here and got the story out of her. Just like you she didn't trust me at first, but I won her over by helping her out whenever I could. I liked her. Not in a sexual way, you understand. I'm straight, though if I wasn't then I could quite fancy Mellissa. But I liked her a lot and didn't like seeing her getting hurt. But we had to keep our friendship quiet so as to avoid me being shut out at work. If that happened I wouldn't be able to help her. I passed on tid-bits that I got from Sonia and others. I don't know how Mellissa used them though."

"Aren't you worried about being seen with me in here?" I waved my hand to take in the clientele of the pub.

"Metro staff wouldn't be seen dead in here. They use the private bar in the basement of the Metro building. It allows them to rub shoulders with the people who turn up to do programmes. Makes them feel they're in the same league. If they don't go there then they use the wine bar round the corner." I had passed the place a few times. Pretentious, over-priced wine and trendy food served in tiny portions. Not my sort of place at all.

"I take it you haven't invited me here just because you fancy me?" I queried.

"Well, I wouldn't rule that out." She smiled coyly at me, "but you're right. I understand from Mellissa that you're taking up the good fight and I thought I'd offer you the same support as I gave her. Since Mel left I've picked up some knew information. It's red hot stuff as well."

"You have my undivided attention."

"You know Greg Larkin?" The set designer, I reminded myself.

"I know of him, certainly."

"He's on the fiddle big time. I'm sure Martin must have told you how he works: coming up with the concept for the set and then putting the work out to contract?" I nodded that I understood. "Well it turns out that he's earning at both ends of the deal. He has his own design consultancy. Nothing wrong with that in itself, but when he puts the work out to contract he insists that the contractor uses his consultancy for the design of the set. He then rents himself out at £1,500 a day to do the design, and spends his working hours at

Metro actually doing the work, so he's being paid twice for the same thing really. When the contractor puts in the invoice to Metro it all shows up as a single line entry for consultancy fees. It doesn't even mention Greg's company. And, just to rub salt in, it's Greg's job to sign off the invoice and put it through for payment."

"Does Igor know about this?"

"Given that the contract always goes to one of the companies that Igor has an interest in it's impossible to imagine that he doesn't know. He probably gets a slice of the action as well." Cassie emptied the last of her wine into her pretty mouth. "Now, in exchange for that, you can buy me a pizza." She stood up and I levered myself out of my corner and rushed to catch up with her.

* * *

"Of course Greg Larkin isn't the only one with a scam." Cassie added as she took a bite out of a wedge of pizza. "It's happening at every level. Even Sonia's in on it."

"How does that work. She's an executive assistant, not a mover and shaker. Surely HR would spot it if she was on the fiddle."

"She doesn't work for Metro though, she's on a personal contract so her invoice goes through finance, not HR. Igor gets an allowance in the budget for an assistant. It's about sixty grand a year. So he told Sonia to set herself up as a private company. He then pays her company to provide him with an assistant. She pays herself minimum wage, then makes up the difference with expenses and other tax deductibles. At the end of the year she then pays herself a dividend from the company's profits, which means she only pays tax at twenty per cent and also avoids a whole wodge of National Insurance contributions. It's quite a common scam in the entertainment business. Sonia probably nets about fifty grand a year, which isn't bad for a job that would pay her only thirty gross if she was a Metro employee."

"You said Igor advised her to do it."

"Of course. He takes a slice of the action of course. And Sonia's besotted with him."

"Are they having a relationship?"

"Put it this way, she goes into his office for meetings and comes out half an hour later without having written anything on her note pad and with a satisfied smile on her face. You join the dots."

"And what about you? What's your scam?"

Her eyes hardened at the accusation, but she didn't deny that she had anything going on. She took another bite out of her wedge of pizza and gave me a studied look.

"I suppose I shouldn't be surprised at that remark. After all, if everyone else is on the take then I must be too. Is that the idea?"

"I'm sorry," I hurried to apologise. "It was a low blow and totally unjustified."

"Maybe not totally. Igor said he could get me on the same sort of deal as Sonia if I played ball. It made me want to vomit, just the thought of it. So no. I haven't got a scam going. At least nothing that Igor has a stake in."

"That's not the same as not having anything going at all."

"True. Let's just say my overtime claims wouldn't stand a close examinations." Cassie looked at her watch as she wiped pizza crumbs from her fingers. "In fact I'm just finishing work about now."

Seven - First Blood

My investigations into the goings on at Metro TV had to be put on the back burner for a while as my work rate started to pick up. Igor called me in and gave me the schedule of meetings that were due to take place with the celebrities and their agents in order to get them on board. Until that happened there could be no thought of putting together a shooting schedule for the location work, which was Igor's biggest problem. Trying to schedule a dozen or more celebrities for film work when they had tours to do, filming, recording, promotional work and, finally, holidays to take would be a nightmare and I knew that Cassie was involved in much of that, delegated by Sonia who in turn had been set the task by Igor himself.

I realised how difficult it was when I got an irate call from the agent of Ded NuronZ, the latest and biggest of the crop of boy bands. Apparently sending a taxi to collect them was an insult to their artistic integrity. They expected a stretch limo at the very least. Until that arrived they wouldn't be setting a foot outside their five star hotel. Oh, and the agent expected a limo for himself, though he would make do with something more modest, a Mercedes perhaps, but taxis were definitely off the agenda.

I checked the arrangements that had been made for the previous years and realised that most of the celebrities and their agents had been driven around town in ostentatious splendour. Even the one who was the biggest campaigner on green issues and made a great point of being photographed on buses and underground trains. I cancelled the taxi bookings and started again from scratch, after first sending the required limo to pick up Ded NuronZ.

A few minutes later I received another call.

"Are you trying to wind me up, you little shit?" The voice snarled down the 'phone at me. "Where was the limo for their entourage?"

"I'm sorry, but why do they need an entourage with them? You will be here to represent them and they will be looked after by Metro staff while they're here."

"Now, let me make myself very clear. Ded NuronZ go nowhere without their entourage. That's security, hair, make up, their PAs and PR reps. They have one of each of those. That's fifteen people at the last count, so you're going to need three more limos at least."

This was the moment, I decided. This request, no, demand was stupid. It was a one hour scheduled meeting. No cameras and no press. So why did they need hairdressers and make-up artists? They wouldn't need PR people and their PAs, all five of them, would have nothing to do. As for security, well, if Metro TV couldn't manage to protect them inside their own offices then something was badly wrong. No. This had to stop and it stopped here and now.

"I'm afraid we won't be paying for the entourage to attend." I informed the agent.

"What? You can't do that."

"Yes I can. I'm the man who signs off the bills, so I can do that. In fact I am doing that. No entourage."

"In that case no Ded NuronZ." He snarled.

"If that's the way you feel, then I'm sure the fans will understand." I carefully replaced the phone in its cradle.

I looked up to find Martin staring at me, aghast.

"What have you done?" he asked, his jaw hanging open.

"Drawing a line in the sand." I replied. My knees felt like jelly and my guts were threatening to explode. What *had* I done? Ded NuronZ were big. Probably the biggest group taking part in the most recent appeal. I had just told their agent we would do without them.

It hadn't been on a whim though. I had done my research. The band were in the group that Igor had called the 'pluggers'. By the time the appeal show went to air the band would have a new album out with a single ready to be downloaded as soon as they had sung it during their spot on the show. No doubt tickets for a stadium tour would go on sale the next day.

My research had shown that their album sales before the show had been on the slide, but had boomeranged back up following their appeal. They needed publicity to keep them in the consciousness of the teenagers that were their fan base. That is the audience that is probably more fickle than any other. They would have a hard core of fans of course, but most of their sales would be spur of the moment and made on the back of the publicity that Cuddly Toy Day gave them. I hoped I was right.

My relief didn't last long. Five minutes later Sonia appeared beside my desk.

"Igor wants to see you. He's spitting fire." She smiled gleefully at my evident misfortune. She had probably pulled the legs off spiders when she was a child. Maybe she still did. I rose and followed her back across the office.

I hadn't even got the door shut when Igor opened up with both barrels.

"What the fuck do you think you're doing?" Despite his obvious anger he still spoke in the same, bored drawl. "You have no idea what this is going to do to the production."

"What are you talking about?" I asked, giving him my most innocent look.

"Don't play coy with me, you little shit. I've just got off the phone with Damian Ellis."

"Oh, him. Well, what of it?"

"You can't go treating the talent like that. They have expectations."

I had expected this and was ready for it. "The people who donate to the charity have expectations too, Igor. They expect their hard earned money to go to Africa to help poor, starving, disease ridden people. To help them survive and to live happy, fulfilled lives. They don't give their money so brats like Ded NuronZ can have hairdressers accompany them around London in luxury limo's. It's bad enough that we have to pamper the band. We don't have to pamper the hangers on and I, for one, have no intention of allowing the charity to be ripped off in that way."

I had no doubt I would pay for that little speech in the longer term, but if I didn't make a stand now then tomorrow would be too late.

"We do this for you, you know." Igor replied. "If there are no acts then there's no show. If there's no show then there are no donations."

"I know that, Igor. But there are limits. The Charity is being ripped off because no one will say no to the acts. Well, I'm here to say no to them. I know how it works. We'll pamper the acts, if that's what it takes, but that doesn't justify indulging them and pampering the hangers on as well. Now, if you want to take that to my boss then that's fine. But I have last year's figures and I'm quite happy to show them to him to support my argument. I think he'll back me when he sees how much money is being wasted."

It was a gamble and a big one, but I had an ace up my sleeve. Igor wouldn't want the charity looking too closely at how the budget was being spent. If they started to take a close look at one aspect of the show's budget then they might start looking at other parts of it. Of course Igor didn't know about the conversation I had already had with Greg, or the reassurances I had received that our Finance Director was already going over the contract with Metro TV with a fine tooth comb. That would come as a nice surprise for Igor.

Igor, I could see, was pondering my response, calculating the options and the potential cost for him of each one. At last Igor's face split onto a broad, insincere smile.

"OK, Andy. I see where you're coming from. So long as you know we have to look after the talent."

"Fair warning, Igor. I'm going to be taking a good look at the riders and location expenses as well." The riders were those things that artists asked to be put in their dressing rooms. It had started out years ago when theatres had started to provide refreshments for acts to keep them going between shows. It was a way of preventing them from nipping out to the pub between shows and perhaps not getting back in time for the next one, or worse still, arriving back the worse for wear. According to legend, however, the riders had grown into all sorts of extravagances. Well not on my watch.

"Be careful Andy" Igor counselled, this time apparently sincere. "Don't rush in where angels fear to tread."

I assured him I would take care and returned to my desk. Round one to me.

Martin was waiting for me, along with Cassie. I told them what had happened.

"I hope you're right about this Andy." Cassie said, concern in her voice.

I was. My phone rang.

"Andy Mirren." I announced myself.

"Andy. Hi, it's Damian Ellis again."

"Oh, hi Damian." I said for Martin and Cassie's benefit.

"Look, I think we got off to a bit of a bad start. Can we forget about it and start again?"

"It's forgotten." I stated magnanimously. Igor must have rung him back straight away and spelt it out for him. "What have you got in mind?"

"Well, let's say we do without the PAs and the PR. And I think you're right about not needing hair and make-up. So just security eh? That means we only need one extra limo."

"I just don't see any need for security staff. If you want security then they travel with the band or you pay for the transport." The line went silent. Had I pushed him too far?

"They need security when they leave the hotel. You see that, don't you? The place is alive with paparazzi and hormonal teenagers."

"That's fine. But you don't need a limo for them at the hotel. Unless the band are followed through the streets then there won't be any fans or paparazzi at this end, so no need for security."

"People will see them. They'll be Tweeted all over the place. By the time they come out of the meeting the place will be awash with teenage girls. They need security."

"We have basement access. They can leave that way. We aren't going to pay for security to be driven round London in luxury." I bit my fingernails. It's an old habit and one I only indulge in when I'm under the greatest pressure. I realised that if he banned the entourage entirely then it would upset the band, damaging their childish egos, so I needed to give him something to save face.

"OK. I'll meet you half way. We'll pay for security to travel with the band, but in an ordinary taxi. No more than will fit in a London cab. They're not the talent, so why treat them like rock stars?"

"It's in their contracts." Damian objected.

"Their contracts are with you, or with Ded NuronZ, not with Cuddly Toy Day. It's a taxi or nothing."

I could almost hear Damian Ellis grinding his teeth at the other end of the 'phone, but he guessed correctly that I wasn't going to give any more ground. He gave in with little grace and I hung up the phone. I slumped in my chair with relief. The line in the sand was established.

Beside my desk Cassie and Martin gave me a round of mock applause.

* * *

Ded NuronZ arrived an hour later and two hours late for their scheduled appointment, due largely to the extended negotiations regarding their travel arrangements. They were all teen attitude and drooping jeans. Two wore baseball caps set at angles that were designed to make them appear non-conformist and cool, but as with all such cool it made them seem to conform even more. The remaining three sported hair dos that made me realise why they required hairdressers to be ever present. One gust of wind would require hours of repair work. The pimples that lurked beneath their make-up also provided an explanation for the presence of make-up artists, and security guards to make sure that no fan got close enough to see the blemishes.

Behind me there was an outbreak of whispered conversations as staff members spotted the arrival of the band. Necks were craned over partitions to get a better look. I saw at least one phone being pointed towards the boys to sneak a photo that would appear on Twitter within moments.

I showed them into the larger conference room while the security guards, complete with black designer sunglasses, were shown into a smaller one. One of them removed his shades and treated me to a venomous glare. I fervently hoped that I would never meet any of them on the door of a night club. Not that it was likely. These guys didn't do door security. They were the elite and they knew it.

Ded NuronZ were no more pleasant. I had deprived them of their status symbols and that meant I was their enemy. In the world of music the size of one's entourage is more important than the size of one's penis. I suspected there was an inverse ratio between the two. Entourages are a visible sign of high level success. Their mock disdain for the world, typical of most of the teenage bands, was genuine when it came to their opinion of me. They refused to shake my extended hand and sat themselves around the long table in attitudes of boredom. Damian Ellis also ignored me and went straight to indulge in theatrical man hugs with Igor. The battle lines were clearly drawn.

The first part of the meeting was routine and handled mainly by Igor and Damian Ellis. It related to the group's performances on the next show, the amount of promotional activity they would be required to participate in and how repeats would be handled, especially edits of the show that would appear on the internet. With agreement reached they moved into my domain.

"The boys won't do Africa again." Damian announced.

"Well, that is rather the point of the show." I commented.

"Ain't goin' to Africa again Bro." One of the boys, CrayZee I think, spoke for the first time.

"The boys didn't enjoy the experience last time."

"It's not about enjoyment, Damian." I observed. "It's about raising money for the charity. The public need to see the work we do out there, and who better to show them than a well-known band like Ded NuronZ."

"Cray's right." Another of the group spoke up. "We ain't going again. Maybe if you hadn't…" He fell silent as Damian shot him a warning glance that I wasn't supposed to see.

"Ah, I get it." I commented. "So, if I don't indulge every whim then the band don't go to Africa to do the appeal. OK. That's fine with me. There are no contracts in place yet. I'll give Suite 2X a ring and tell them they can have the gig."

I rose and stepped towards the door. I didn't get halfway before Damian called my name.

"Andy, Andy. Don't be too hasty. I'm sure we can work this out." Damian had to work hard to try to hide the note of panic in his voice.

Suite 2X were the up and coming female equivalent of Ded NuronZ and competing for the same market sector. In other words they were a real threat, as I knew. Their last album had outsold the boys by two to one. An appearance on the Cuddly Toy Day show would put them streets ahead in their much rumoured feud.

"But I've already got the agreement of the girls." I lied. "They're really up for it."

"Look, I'm sure we can work it out. Africa I mean." Damian almost pleaded.

"Here's the deal. Same as last year or no deal at all."

Damian looked beseechingly at his band, willing them to say a word of agreement.

"OK. That's what I thought." I turned to leave the room again. I noticed that Igor wasn't saying anything. Maybe he thought I really had spoken to Suite 2X.

Damian spoke at last. "OK, We'll do it."

There was a hubbub of protest from the band. He was clearly going against what had been agreed with them. He glared at them and one by one they fell into a sulky silence.

"You drive a hard bargain, Andy." Damian said, almost admiringly.

"Oh, you ain't seen nothing yet. We haven't even started to look at the band's rider."

His smile faded as I re-took my seat.

* * *

Damian Ellis caught up with me in the gents. As I washed my hands he stood at the urinal, addressing me over his shoulder. "You're playing a dangerous game, Andy. You could get your fingers burnt."

"Is that a threat." I struggled to keep my tone relaxed.

"If you like. There are many ways a band can screw you around, you know."

"You mean like sexual assault?"

He turned suddenly, realised what he was doing and turned back again. "What are you implying?" He growled.

"Gossip gets around, you know. There have been rumours, both about what happened when the boys were in Africa and also what happened at the after-party."

I was bluffing, of course. Mellissa hadn't named names, other than that of Pipkin and his over-priced comic book.

"You can't prove anything."

"So, there's something to prove, is there?" I gave a smirk, though I wasn't feeling very humorous at that moment.

"No. Nothing. Nothing at all."

"Good, I'm glad to hear it. Because if there was I'd have no option but to go to the police and tell them what I know."

He had finally finished at the urinal and joined me at the wash basins. He gave me an appraising look in the mirror before speaking again. "You may have won a battle, Andy, but don't for one moment think you've won the war."

He turned and stalked out of the room. I leant forward, relief flowing through me. It was several minutes before I had composed myself enough to return to my desk.

Eight - The Nashville Proposition

The routine continued with each artist, group and wannabe celebrity being metaphorically beaten into submission in order to enjoy the privilege of appearing on Cuddly Toy Day and travelling to Africa to film an appeal clip. I didn't win them all of course. Word got round quickly and the bolder agents called my bluff. We lost Stan "The Man" Goodwin and had to settle on terms I wasn't happy with to retain Jesse James the singer song-writer. I wasn't too bothered about losing an over-the-hill comedian but Jesse James had a considerable amount of credibility with trendy middle class viewers and to lose him would have damaged the show. Besides he was quite a nice bloke, even if his agent could give great white sharks a good name.

But I won more than I lost and by the end of the fortnight of meetings I had cut at least a hundred thousand pounds off the previous year's budget. That was money that would have come directly from MOF, not via the Metro TV budget. I gave myself a metaphorical pat on the back and started to make my Friday evening preparations to end the working week.

My phone rang. That was unusual at that time of day and even more unusual on a Friday. I glanced around the office to see if anyone there might have been ringing me. Many of the calls I took were internal. The office was as uninhabited as the Marie Celeste as far as I could see. Just me and the dim glow of my PC screen. No doubt the bar in the cellar was packed. So, if it was an external call I would have to take it. Unlikely as it seemed it might just be important.

"Andy Mirren." I spoke into the mouthpiece.

"You don't sound too cheerful about it." A soft American voice drawled into my ear. I sat bolt upright in my chair. I knew that voice. Or at least I thought I did.

"I'm sorry. Just a bit tired after as long week."

"Too tired to buy a girl a drink?" The voice dripped into my ear like warm honey.

"No, not at all. Am I speaking to who I think I am?"

"I don't know Sugar. Who do you think you're speaking to?"

"Charleese Morgan." I breathed, hardly daring to hope that it was.

"You got that just from my voice?" Through the 'phone lines I could sense that she was smiling.

"You have a very distinctive voice."

"Well, it helps in my business. Look, I've got a flight to catch in four hours. I can give you an hour if you want to hear why I'm calling."

"If you've taken the trouble to call me then it must be important. Of course I'd love to meet up with you."

"I love your English pubs. Is there one near your office?"

I gave her the name and address of The Greyhound and we agreed to meet there in thirty minutes. Her presence would undoubtedly cause a stir. The pub would be packed at that time on a Friday evening. I hoped she had good security. I realised that I hadn't been asked to provide the ubiquitous limo and wondered if I would receive an invoice when I met her. Time to worry about that later. I closed down my PC and hurried to wait impatiently in the pub.

She arrived without any fanfare and without security. She was dressed modestly in a checked shirt and jeans, with a beige leather bomber style jacket draped across her shoulders. Her mane of blond hair was pulled back and tied at the nape of her neck with a plain black scrunchy and her face was devoid of make-up. She was as unlike a country music goddess as it was possible to be. Heads turned to look at the pretty lady then went back to their conversations without a second glance.

"That's probably the best disguise I've ever seen." I said, shaking her hand. Had I not been expecting her I would never have recognised her.

"Dress like a country singer and everyone will see a country singer. Dress like the girl next door and they see the girl next door. Nice to meet you Andy."

I offered her a drink and she accepted a sparkling mineral water. "I thought you would ask for Jack Daniels." I commented as I set the glass on the table in front of her.

"Five years ago I would have, but that was the old me. The new me drinks mineral water and no longer wakes up in a pool of her own vomit."

"I'm sorry, I was prying."

"Don't apologise. I was what I was and now I am what I am. Now, how are the preparations for the next telethon going?"

I made light of the subject with a 'going-as-well-as-can-be-expected' sort of answer and she smiled knowingly at me.

"The business is alive with rumours about you playing hard-ball, Andy. I'm impressed. You've given the industry a good shake up. It needed it."

"Well, I'm just trying to keep the most amount of money possible for the charity, rather than for the hangers on."

"I thoroughly approve. Which is why I'm here."

"I was just about to ask about that."

"Well, no need to. I want to be a part of the next show. Can you fit me in?"

"Of course. You're a big name. Britain isn't as big on Country music as the USA, of course, but you're still a household name. But you should really be talking to Igor Kasnisky. He's the Exec Producer."

"If I wanted to talk to Kasnisky it would be him sitting here, not you. I want to deal direct with the charity as much as possible. I have a feeling that your interests are much more closely aligned to mine."

That puzzled me, but It had also aroused my curiosity.

"So, what sort of thing did you have in mind?" I asked.

"I want to do one of those big spectacular journeys. But I want to do it for real."

"What do you mean 'for real'?"

"Well, you've heard of Merle Walker?" I nodded. "Well, he was supposed to have canoed along the Orinoco river for one of the US telethon shows. But he didn't. Oh, they showed footage of him doing it and it looked real enough, but he hadn't really. The telethon people said it was a six week trip, but I'd seen him on a live TV show one Sunday and then met him at an awards ceremony the next Friday and he told me he'd just got back from doing it. That means he'd been out of the country for less than a week. I asked him about it again, after the telethon was broadcast, and he laughed and said that he spent most of the week in a luxury hotel and shot the canoe scenes on location just a few miles upriver. It was all faked. Even the alligator swimming alongside his canoe was a fake."

"So you want to do it without faking it."

"Maybe not canoeing but, yeah, maybe something else."

"Got any ideas?"

"I sure have. An old school friend of mine was on the US Olympic cycling team. She thinks she can get a few other team members. Maybe we could all cycle through Africa visiting some of the places where the charity spends its money."

I did some quick mental arithmetic, or math as Charleese would have called it. "That would be very expensive. Even if we found you a route that took only a couple of weeks it would mean a film crew, food, hotels. You'd have to have armed guards in some places. It would need quite a budget."

"Look, I'm really serious about this. I think that all the charities that work in Africa do a really great job. I'm considering setting up my own foundation to work over there. A trip like this will serve two purposes. First it will raise money for your charity, which is great by me, but second it will help me to work out where the most help is needed, so I can target my foundation properly."

She paused and sipped at her water. I could see she was thinking hard. "OK. I understand your concern about the money. You haven't worked hard the last few weeks cutting the budget just for me to blow the savings on some mad enterprise. I'll fund the whole expedition myself, so long as I can use the MOF expertise to help me when I'm out there. You get to use the film but I'll hold the copyright. I can use the footage myself when I'm back home. How does that sound?"

Well, I could see how film of her helping starving Africa would help sell the sort of music she made, so her wish to protect her use of the film made sense and if we weren't paying then she had every right to retain ownership. I'm not great with horses, but I know that you don't look a gift one in the mouth. This was too good an opportunity to pass up. Charleese Morgan was one of the biggest names in Country music and to get her for the Cuddly Toy Day show would be a spectacular coup.

"There's one other thing. We're a UK charity and we raise our money in UK and Ireland. It would work better for us if at least some of the other cyclists were British or Irish. Could you manage that?"

"It doesn't sound like too big a deal. I'm sure these gals all know each other. I'll look into it and get back to you."

"OK. You've got a deal." I extended my hand across the table and she took it and gave me a firm handshake.

"You're an easy man to work with Andy. Of course it helps that I'm paying." She laughed. She finished off her drink.

"Part of the deal will be having you in Africa with me." She gave me the sort of smile that could have melted ice.

My hearty skipped a beat. It was like being offered a front row seat at one of her concerts, only better.

"I'm not sure I'd be available for the whole trip." I stammered. "I've got other people to work with."

"Just so long as you spend a bit of time with little old me, that will be cool. Now, I've got that flight to catch, so I'd better be going."

I stood up and walked her to the door of the pub, so elated my feet barely touching the ground. I held the door open for her. Sat at the kerb was a gleaming Mercedes with a uniformed chauffeur behind the wheel. He leapt out and held the rear door open and Charleese slipped onto the pale grey leather upholstery of the seat. She smiled and gave me a little wave as the driver re-took his seat and guided the car out into the evening traffic. I watched the car until it disappeared around a corner.

I smiled to myself and returned to the pub to reward myself with another pint of beer.

Nine - Spider and Fly

With all the celebrities we needed on board I was able to spend more time on checking out the way Metro TV spent the Cuddly Toy Day budget. 'Follow the money' the police always say when investigating fraud or drugs, so that was what I did.

A thick wad of evidence began to grow as I traced the labyrinthine route through the ordering process to the final bills, via the companies that provided the services. I had Gary Larkin, the set designer, bang to rights within a few hours. He was sole owner of the design consultancy that the design and build company had employed, at Gary's own insistence. There was no way he could talk his way out of it. By waiting until Martin was out to lunch I had managed to get access to Gary Larkin's personal e-mails and copy the one in which he insisted on his own consultancy being employed. It proved that Larkin was getting paid twice for effectively doing the same work.

Of course Larkin was just the tip of the iceberg and several names from Metro's production team were beginning to attract my attention. There was Igor himself, of course and his girlfriend Helen Spencer but they were intertwined with a number of others who had scams like Larkin's going. There was the catering franchise for the rehearsals and the day of the shoot, the studio facilities, the camera and lighting rental companies and a whole raft of other service providers that the event needed if it was to run smoothly.

I have to say that I did feel a bit like a private detective in the Sam Spade mode, tracking the criminals to their lair. Little did I know that there was a storm brewing.

I was eating my lunch one day when I saw the elegant form of Helen Spencer approaching. Her power was obvious in the way that people stepped out of her path as she approached. She looked neither to her left or her right but focused directly on me, sat alone at the Formica cafeteria table with my sandwich and my Kindle.

I stood up to greet her, which I had seen others do in her presence. It wasn't an act of chivalry or good manners but one of obsequiousness. I hated myself for doing it but couldn't stop myself.

"Ah, Andy Mirren. I've heard a lot about you. perhaps you might stop by my office after lunch. I think we should have a little chat."

The way her ice blue eyes bored into me I felt like a goat being assessed by a tiger as a possible meal.

I took a deep breath. "Certainly Helen. Where will I find your office?"

She pointed upwards to the 'floor of power'. "We have our own reception desk up there. They'll direct you."

She turned on her heel and strolled away, queen of all she surveyed. The summons didn't come as a surprise. I knew that our Finance Director, Charles Conway, had been taking a close look at the budget and I guessed that some sort of approach was being made to renegotiate. As the charity's man-on-the-inside, so to speak, I was the natural choice to pump for more information. The only surprise was that it was Helen that wanted to speak to me and not Igor. The penny dropped. Helen was the brains of the outfit. She wouldn't want Igor stumbling about and giving away more than he found out.

After being eyed up by a hungry tiger I found that I had lost my appetite, so I made my way back to my desk and dropped my Kindle into my shoulder bag. I took a few minutes to pop into the gents and get myself tidied up then made my way to the top floor.

The receptionist was so imperious that she managed to make Sonia look like the very essence of charm. She pointed to a chair in a small waiting area and telephoned news of my arrival to Helen. I knew how this worked, of course. I would be kept waiting until Helen felt that I understood the power relationship, then I would be allowed into The Presence. I bet myself that I would be left to stew for ten minutes; it turned out to be fifteen.

I was shown into a spacious office. Helen relaxed in a large swivel chair behind a lacquered desk that reflected the sunshine that streamed through the windows that made up one entire wall of the office. At the other end was a seating area consisting of a modern L-shaped sofa and two arm chairs. There was nowhere in front of Helen's desk for me to sit and no spare chair that I could drag over so I had no choice but to stand. Another demonstration of power.

"Thank you so much for coming, Andy" Helen smiled sweetly, as though I had a choice in the matter. Technically I did as I wasn't a Metro TV employee, but we both knew that in reality I could hardly refuse. "I should have taken the time to meet you when you first joined us, but you know how it is. The demands on my time are many."

I noticed that there were no 'in' or 'out' trays on her desk, neither was there a PC screen or keyboard. Whatever work she did came to her through other channels. There was a single telephone sat on one corner of the desk, but otherwise it was as smooth and empty as a sheet of ice. No doubt there was a tiny little laptop tucked away somewhere for when she felt the need to record something.

"Charles Conway contacted me this morning." She searched my face for any sort of reaction but I kept it deadpan. I couldn't control the pupils of my eyes, so any reflexive action might have shown up in them, but I hoped I was too far away for her to register that.

"Oh. What did he want?" I asked as innocently as I could manage.

"He wants to discuss our joint financial arrangements. It occurred to me that you may have some sort of inkling as to what that might mean."

"I'm sorry, Helen, but I've no idea. Your financial arrangements with MOF are far too far above my pay grade for me to be consulted." In Metro the term "above my paygrade" meant just about any decision that was required to be made. Except when it came to me. Nothing seemed to be above my pay grade until the need for obfuscation arrived.

She gave me a long, searching look, trying to read my expression. I hope I radiated puzzlement at her question. From her reaction I think I may have been suggesting constipation.

"Do you like working here Andy?" She suddenly changed the subject.

"It's very … interesting." Having decided that obfuscation was the best tactic I stuck with it, but she had registered my pause.

"You don't sound too sure. Is there something bothering you?"

Lots of things, I wanted to scream at her, but I metaphorically bit my tongue. Instead I kept to my plan. "It's all very strange to me. I've never worked in such a … creative environment before. I'm an IT man at heart. Databases, facts and figures. You know the sort of thing."

"Yes, I can see what you mean. Creative people are so… creative is the only word for it really. You're not getting any hassle, are you?"

"No. Everyone is being very helpful." I lied. "It's just a little unusual to find that no one seems to be prepared to haggle about money with the people who come on the show." She must have realised that I was referring to Igor, but she didn't react to my accusation.

"Why does that bother you?"

"At the end of the day the show is about raising money for MOF. I feel that everyone should be focusing their efforts on maximising the return from the donations. If no one is prepared to haggle a little then the acts can ask for anything they want and the charity loses out. I don't think that's right. It's a matter of principle, really."

"I see what you mean. Can you give me specific examples?"

I told her about the negotiations with Ded NuronZ and the end result. No doubt she was as aware of the details as I was. Either that or she and Igor never spoke to each other while they were at home. "It saved us nearly a thousand pounds just for them to attend the meeting." I concluded.

"We have to be careful, Andy. If we screw the nut too tightly then the talent won't play ball." She mixed her metaphors. "No talent means no show and no show means no donations."

"I accept that, but there is a happy medium. I thought Damian Ellis was using the band to take us for a ride, so I challenged him on it. In the end he backed down."

"You may have won the battle, Andy, but that doesn't mean you won the war." I noted she used the same words as Damian Ellis and that made me wonder about their relationship. That might be an area worth closer scrutiny. "There's a long way to go before show night." With the benefit of hindsight her words proved to be more prophetic than even she realised.

"In terms of production, I spoke to some people I know at other TV companies and they suggested that the studio hire, set design, camera hire and a whole range of other services all seemed a bit on the high side." I knew no one at any other TV companies, so I was making a calculated guess, but everything I had learnt so far pointed to me being right.

She stood up and came round to my side of the desk, resting her buttocks on the gleaming black edge, folding her arms across the crisp whiteness of her blouse. I noticed that she wore a pencil line, knee length skirt that seemed to cling to her legs and show them off.

"How do you know so much about our costs, Andy?" her tone was low, like a lioness letting out a warning growl.

"Last year's budget is on your intranet. I didn't realise I wasn't supposed to look at it."

What I said was true, but both she and I knew that I wasn't supposed to have access to the more confidential pages and to the financial data in particular. Her eyes hardened into shards of blue glass.

"You're in a very privileged position here, Andy. You get to participate in a lot of the decision making. But that also means that you get to see and hear a lot of things that are confidential. Do you understand me?" She placed a manicured fingertip on the middle of my shirt and pressed the point of the nail into my chest. "It wouldn't do to be telling tales out of school."

"I'm sure it wouldn't Helen." A waft of expensive perfume hit my nostrils as she leant forward and levered herself off the desk, brushing past me and returning to her seat.

"If you play ball with us... well, I'm sure you know the rest. But be aware, there are consequences for those who don't respect our privacy. Do I make myself clear?"

"I think so."

"Do more than think, Andy, be certain. We'll talk again, I'm sure."

I took the hint and left as quickly as I could without actually breaking into a run.

I felt I had just escaped from a spider's web and knew how those dwarfs must have felt in The Hobbit. This was not the sort of woman one tangled with if it could be avoided. Unfortunately that was exactly what I planned to do. But not yet. I wasn't ready yet.

I hurried to the toilets, the receptionist giving me the sort of stare that was supposed to stop me dead in my tracks, but my need was urgent. Once inside I splashed water over my face, cooling myself down and at the same time giving my nervous system time to get my body back under control. I don't know if Helen Spencer had been aware of it, but I had been trembling like a leaf for most of the interview. She was one very scary lady. What worried me was that I had met her when she was only warning me off. God knows what she would be like when she found out what I'd actually been doing.

Ten - Ded NuronZ

So there I was in Africa and heading back to my hotel in the air conditioned comfort of my SUV, with Jacob driving. I wish I could say I was going to rest, but I had an evening of pre-shoot meetings to sit through with the location producer, Lionel, the drivers, the security guards and, of course, Ded NuronZ' PR rep. I had managed to cut the group down from five personal reps to one for the whole band but Damian Ellis had insisted on that one. He needed someone to babysit the band in his absence. His agency provided the PR rep, of course, and charged the band for her services. I could see that the group of teenagers were really just a milk cow for the agency, but they thought they were running the show and Damian let them think that, for the most part.

Cherry Versace-Laboutin, her make-up artist, hairdresser and PA had already checked out by the time I got back to the hotel, so I had avoided the fake sincerity of seeing her off. Ded NuronZ would fly in on the aircraft on which she would fly out. The celebrities only stayed "in country" long enough to film their appeals before jetting off to do whatever else was in their crowded schedules. It was a good job too, as they could work their way through a mini-bar and room service menu quicker than a swarm of locusts through a lettuce patch.

After Ded NuronZ I would get a little bit of a break. Jesse James was next on the schedule and I didn't anticipate any problems from him. After that I had five days off, which I would be using to accompany Charleese Morgan along some of her cycle route.

Igor had been impressed that I had got her for the show and of course I had been called in to participate in the conference call with Charleese's agent in Nashville. She hadn't let the grass grow under her feet and an e-mail arranging the call had been in Igor's in-box when he arrived for work on Monday morning. No doubt the time difference between London and Nashville had helped, as the agent would still have been working when Charleese left The Greyhound.

The music side of things was going to be the hardest to arrange, as Charleese was due on stage in Los Angeles at about the time she would also be required to perform on Cuddly Toy Day. Eventually it was agreed that her performance would take the form of a live satellite link from the stage of the theatre she was performing at, timed for just before her audience were due to arrive. Igor said it would allow us to promote it as a surprise guest appearance which would keep people in their arm chairs late into the night. The later it got the bigger the donations that were pledged; the 'alcohol effect' as it's known. The edited highlights of Charleese's cycle trek would be played in just before and just after her performance and more extensive coverage would be used in a one hour "special" the following evening, if the networks could be persuaded to play ball.

The cycle trek, and the arrangements for it, were down to me to organise. Igor was cynical about the way Charleese wanted to play it. "Just not the way it's done." He opined. Well it was the way Charleese wanted to do it so that was the way it would be done. With her she brought Mary Tennant, the US cycling gold medallist and, as promised, two other cyclists: Scotland's Sandy Phillips who had won a bronze in one of the Olympic road races and Bridie MacAleesh who had represented Ireland. She would be worth several thousand Euros in additional pledges from the Irish viewers of the show.

The route had been the hard thing on which to agree. MOF had over a hundred projects running in a dozen countries but they were scattered across the continent from Cairo to Cape Town and from the Horn of Africa to Cap-Vert in Senegal. Some countries were relatively safe and easy to travel through while others were significantly more dangerous. We quickly took West Africa and its recent Ebola crisis off all our plans as well as Nigeria because of its terrorist threat and, of course, the Horn of Africa which included Somalia amongst other hot spots.

A quick search of the Foreign Office website revealed some of the dangers involved and that wasn't even taking into account the risk of disease. In the end we decided to start in southern Uganda close to Lake Victoria, then go through Rwanda and into Tanzania to avoid Burundi and then continue to Victoria Falls in Zambia. It was over two thousand miles and would take six weeks at fifty miles a day. Twice a week the schedule would be increased to seventy five miles to allow a day off which would be used to allow the cyclists to rest and also to do some additional filming at selected projects. I was glad I wasn't doing it, but Charleese was pretty upbeat and optimistic. Fortunately they didn't have to do it against the clock so they could take as much time each day as they needed. Charleese had even built in a two week buffer so that she didn't have to worry about missing any music or business commitments.

For the professional cyclists the distances involved meant nothing. They would do twice or three times that distance each day just as part of their training schedule, but for Charleese, and me when I joined them, those sort of distances would be more of a challenge in Africa's heat and dust.

I was to meet them in Tanzania for one of the middle sections of the journey and would ride with them for a while on one of the spare bikes. Before leaving the UK I had spent hours in the gym preparing, but I don't think it had prepared me well enough. The big prize wasn't the few pounds I would bring in from sponsorships for my small effort, it was the several million pounds in pledges that Charleese had attracted. Not just private sponsors but big, corporate American ones with a strong foothold in the UK and Ireland. After rows over their UK tax status, some of the corporations needed a bit of positive PR and Charleese had turned that screw for all she was worth. By screening the whole trip over several evenings during the run up to Cuddly Toy Day we would almost certainly double the corporate sponsorships with personal pledges.

In the meantime I had Ded NuronZ to deal with. They came into the hotel lobby looking hot and frazzled. This puzzled me as they had the ubiquitous air conditioned SUVs available to them. Unfortunately their PR rep had decided that they didn't fit in with the image of the band doing charitable work so she had sent the SUVs away and made the boys travel in battered old airport taxis, the worst she could find on the rank. Rank was an appropriate word for them as well.

I took her to one side. "What are you playing at?" I demanded. "The last thing I need is five sulky teenagers blaming me because they feel like they've been through a sauna."

"It was Damian's idea." She protested. "I filmed it on my phone and it'll go on YouTube tonight."

There wasn't much I could do about it now. It did make for good PR for the band to be shown roughing it. But there were dangers involved.

"So, what about this hotel? Are you going to show the boys eating their dinners in the Michelin starred restaurant?"

"Of course not. We did some research and we've found a shanty restaurant where I'll film the boys eating the local food."

I slapped my forehead in despair. "Are you trying to get these kids killed?" I shouted at her. In the busy foyer conversations stopped as people turned to stare. I lowered my voice.

"The shanty towns are pretty lawless. Anything could happen there. And as for the food, if a drop if it touches their lips they'll spend the rest of the trip and probably the next fortnight, sitting on the toilet. Don't even think about it."

"What about Crayzee and Hipster. They're black. They'll fit right in."

I couldn't believe this woman's stupidity. "Just take a look at those boys. The price of their clothes alone would feed an African family for a year. Look at all the gold they're wearing. They're practically sweating it out of their pores. I'm surprised you got them from the airport in one piece. If you take them out looking like that you'll get them killed. Now do you understand me?"

"So you don't think it's a good idea?" Her look said she didn't believe me almost as much as her tone of voice. She had been present for the security brief that all the performers got before travelling but she didn't appear to have taken in a single word. Come to think of it she had seemed to spend most of her time texting rather than listening. Personally I couldn't have cared less if this bunch of talentless, over-indulged teenagers were eaten by cannibals (not that there are any in Africa) but unfortunately their insurance company might see things differently.

I resisted the urge to grab the woman by the throat. "No. I don't. This isn't Hounslow or Tooting." I named the places from where two of the band originated. "You follow the plan I've put in place for tomorrow. You'll get plenty of opportunities to film what great things the boys are doing and if you want to put them on YouTube and Twitter then you can. But don't let them out of the hotel unless they're with the security team. You understand that?"

She told me she did, but with very bad grace. At that point I should have given the boys the same warning, but instead I left the PR woman to do it. What a mistake that was.

* * *

I was just getting into the shower when the phone rang. I was tempted to ignore it, but some sixth sense told me there was trouble brewing. I turned the water off and grabbed a towel, tying it round my waste as I dripped my way to pick up the phone beside the bed.

"Andy Mirren." I growled into the handset, annoyed that what little 'me time' I was due had been interrupted.

"It's Vicky Mitchell." A panicked voice sounded in my ear. It took me a moment to recognise the voice and name of Ded NuronZ' PR rep. "Crayzee and Hipster have gone missing."

My heart sank. Although there were a dozen places the two teenagers could have gone to without placing themselves at risk I had a strong sense of doom and little doubt that wherever they had gone it wasn't to one of those dozen places.

"How long have they been gone?" I asked, trying to keep the panic out of my own voice.

"I'm not sure. We finished eating at about nine and the boys said they were going to go up to one of their rooms to play computer games. Apparently you can hire them through the hotel's system." I knew that you could. Many of the younger celebs amused themselves that way in the evening, with the charity picking up the tab. I had even played a couple of times, though I wouldn't be charging the cost to expenses.

"So how do you know they're missing?"

"I was doing a late night phone round to see if they were OK or if they needed anything. I couldn't get an answer from either of their rooms and none of the other three knew where they were. I checked with Reception, who checked with hotel security and they were seen leaving the hotel at about eleven. The guard saw them get into one of the taxis that was waiting on the rank."

"Did he hear where they told the driver to take them?"

"No, but they headed north. He didn't sound too happy to have to tell me that. What's north of here?"

I really didn't want to answer that question. All dozen locations where the boys might be safe would have required the taxi driver to make a U turn onto the broad thoroughfare and head south towards the city centre just a few streets away. North headed out of town, into the maze of shanties that had grown up along the road that led out into the African savannah. There was nothing except danger for the boys in that direction.

Don't get me wrong. There were plenty of law abiding people living in the shanties. In fact they make up the majority. We had two different projects running there to help to educate the children and keep them healthy. But the shanties were also the refuge of the criminal gangs that prevented the city from being a centre for tourism. The one decent hotel, the one we had based ourselves in, remained a safe haven by employing armed guards and by paying protection money to the criminal gangs.

"Stay calm. There's nothing to worry about. It's probably nothing. I'll make a few calls and they'll be back here before you know it." I lied. I hung up before she could ask any more questions.

As I towelled myself dry I rang Jacob's number. According to the payroll Jacob Chikawe was employed as an interpreter, but he was far more than that. He was my local fixer, the man who knew everyone and everywhere. He also had charge of the security team that we employed. If anyone could locate the two members of Ded NuronZ, who appeared to be living up to their name, then it would be Jacob.

The conversation was a short one. Jacob didn't need to be told of the danger the boys were in. He told me to meet him in the foyer in fifteen minutes. I finished drying myself, threw on some clothes and went to wait for him.

He arrived in an SUV with a second vehicle close behind. I recognised the driver and the front seat passenger of the second vehicle as members of our local security team and had no doubt that there would be two more in the back seats, concealed by the darkened window glass. I climbed in beside Jacob and nodded to the two guards in the rear of the vehicle. Good; six security men in all, plus Jacob. I would be useless in a fight, but I was very much hoping it wouldn't come to that.

"I managed to trace the taxi driver who took them. My cousin runs the taxi franchise for the hotel so it wasn't hard. The boys said they wanted to go somewhere with women and alcohol, so he took them to a shebeen that he knows."

"Why didn't he just take them to the Country Club? They would have been safe there." The Country Club wasn't in the country, but it did attract the sons and daughters of the wealthy locals and also the foreign workers that lived in the city. It was lively enough without being dangerous. No doubt a share of its profits went in payment for protection, just like the hotel.

"They didn't want European drink or nice safe westernised girls, according to the driver. They wanted to experience Africa. The shebeen is one of the safer ones, but that isn't saying very much out there."

"Do your team have guns?"

"It's better if you don't know."

I could see his point. If I thought the guards were armed I might end up talking them into a shooting war. On the other hand not knowing made me feel more nervous. Besides, MOF had very strict ethical policies with regards to firearms and it would be wrong of me to suggest to Jacob that his team infringe those.

He drove at a steady but not excessive pace. Expensive foreign cars attracted the attention of police patrols and we could do without that at the moment. There was no guarantee that the police were the peacekeepers that they might be in other countries.

Turning off the main highway we entered into the maze of dirt tracks that wound through the wooden, corrugated iron and sheet plastic structures that half the city's population called home. With no thought given to layout the houses were thrown up on any scrap of empty land so steering the cars around the maze was a task that required a lot of concentration. Raw sewage sprayed up from the wheels as they splashed through the rivulets of water and sludge that ran down the middle of every alleyway. An appeal aimed at improving the way sewage was disposed of in the shanties had already been filmed.

Jacob pulled the car up outside a brightly lit structure, obviously profitable enough to run its own electricity generator. Figures spilled out of the doorway holding bottles of beer or jam jars filled with whatever rot gut the owners had managed to get hold of that week. Heavy jazz rhythms pulsed loudly through the air making the car vibrate in sympathy.

"Stay in the car." Jacob commanded. I obeyed, the employee-employer relationship reversed in the face of the situation. The two guards got out of the car and followed Jacob as he pushed his way into the shebeen. The four guards from the second car took up positions that discouraged any encroachment on the vehicles, but they did their best to adopt relaxed attitudes. Just four guys not wanting their cars to get scratched.

A couple of bolder spirits did approach and try to engage in a conversation, but the guards did nothing to encourage them. The men lost interest and returned to their friends.

Jacob returned a few minutes later and the guards took their seats as he quickly drove us out of the area.

"They're not there." He filled me in on the situation. "The barman said they hooked up with a couple of girls, maybe twenty minutes ago. They went off with the girls but he doesn't know where."

"So what do we do now?"

"He didn't know the girls, but he says they were prostitutes. If so there are two brothels where they might have gone to."

"Well, that's good."

"No it isn't. If they're in either of them then they're in great danger. They're both notorious for men going into them and not coming out again. Sometimes the bodies turn up a few miles away. Sometimes they don't turn up at all."

I felt a lump form in my throat.

The shanties thinned out as we got further from the city and we suddenly found ourselves in a patch of open ground. One shanty stood apart from the rest. Candles or oil lamps flickered behind thick plastic sheets. Outside the door stood two men. They made no attempt to conceal the guns stuck in the waistbands of their trousers. Gold glittered at their wrists and necks, meaning they were either very stupid to wear their wealth so visibly in the shanties, or that they were the sort of men that had nothing to fear in this area. I didn't have to be a genius to work out which of the two was true; the guns told me everything I needed to know.

Once again Jacob left the car accompanied by his two guards. The other four took station again. Jacob approached the two sentries and started talking to them. The men made head shaking gestures. They didn't know anything. Or if they did know then they were denying it.

I saw Jacob rub his thumb and fingers together; The international mime for a bribe. They shook their heads again. To me it meant they knew nothing. If they did they'd have taken the money and then mocked Jacob for being unable to do anything with the information.

Would Jacob take a gamble and try to disarm the two men? After all he had six men backing him up. On the other hand who knew how many more armed men there might be inside the brothel. Jacob returned to the car and climbed in, though I noticed his colleagues remained outside. He voiced the options I had been considering.

"What do you think boss?"

"You said there were two places the boys might have been taken. Shouldn't we try the other one before we start a fight?"

"OK. We may as well."

Jacob started the engine of the car and the security team got the message and returned to the cool of the interiors. It was well past midnight but the heat of the day still lingered, though now with an accompanying humidity.

We bounced and twisted our way back through the shanties to the second location.

"This one is run by a rival gang. That's why it's on the other side of the slum." Jacob informed me. "The other one is owned by the same gang as owns the shebeen. That's why I went there first. But the girls from both gangs work at all the clubs. They come and they go, so no one knows who works for whom at any time, so they get away with it." He applied his brakes and the car slid to a dusty standstill once again.

This was a more impressive building by the standards of the shanties. It was built of mud bricks which had once been painted white. The roof was of rusty corrugated iron, but there were proper plastic gutters and down-spouts. Lights glimmered from behind what might reasonably be called curtains. Again there were armed men at the door.

Jacob repeated his negotiations and again was met with denials of knowledge. In the car's headlights I could quite clearly see the smirks on the sentry's face as he spoke. He knew something and wasn't too bothered about hiding it from Jacob. The second sentry said something and the two men laughed. Jacob shook his head and returned to the car.

"The boys are here. I'm pretty sure of it."

"What did he say? The one on the left. It made the other one laugh."

"He said that if the two British boys were lost then someone would find them and give them a good time."

"Meaning?"

"Meaning I didn't tell them that the boys were British, only that they were foreign."

"So what do we do?"

"The only thing we can do. We go and get them out of there."

Jacob started the car and drove away. He didn't go far before he switched the headlights off and turned the car round. He drove back towards the bungalow by a different route. Thankfully the hot night time breeze made the shanties bang and creak with a constant noise that would cover up the sound of the engines. He stopped the car before it would be seen by the sentries and held a counsel of war with his colleagues. Two of them slipped into an alley and disappeared from view.

"I've sent Joseph and Thomas to take a look around the back to see if there's another way in. They will also try to see inside to see if there are more guards.

It was ten minutes before the two men returned.

"They're having a bit of a party in there." Thomas reported. "Five men, maybe seven or eight women. The two boys you're looking for are in another room. They're tied up." He paused, clearly nervous about saying anything more, but he took a deep breath and looked directly at Jacob. "Akeem is one of the men."

Jacob sucked air through his teeth.

I looked at him, "I take it that's not good news?" Jacob shook his head.

"Akeem is the top man on this side of the shanties. He runs the biggest crime gang in the city. We will be taking a big risk if we go in there. If he knows that a European is involved in rescuing the boys he'll come after you. If he recognises any of us he'll come after us and if he can't find us then he'll go after our families."

"Is it possible," I asked, "to just get in, untie the boys and get out again without them seeing us?"

"Maybe." Joseph said. "If we can do it without making any noise. There's no glass in the window and there's no one else in the room. They're all having too much fun next door." Joseph's face split into a big toothy grin. I decided not to ask him to go into more detail.

"Look, why don't we just call the police and let them do it?" I feared I knew the answer, but had to ask the question anyway.

"First we have to find a policeman that isn't being paid off by Akeem. Then we have to wait for daylight. The police won't come in here at night. By then it will be too late. Akeem will want the boys gone before the sun comes up, just in case the police do come."

"So it's now or not at all."

Jacob nodded his head glumly.

"This is your patch, Jacob. I'll take your advice."

"Thanks boss, but it's up to you. They're your people. If you want them back then we have to do it now."

"And what of the others?" I asked. I would be putting ten lives at risk, all told, including my own and those of the two teenagers. I didn't want to shoulder that burden without consulting those that I could. I had no doubt about which way the two band members would vote.

"We're all related, one way or another." Jacob told me. "we're bound by family honour to help each other. If I go then they go."

"And do you go?"

"Your call." He insisted again.

I'm not known for my bravery. In fact until I went to work at Metro TV I was more known for my timidity, but I had changed a lot in the past few months. I'd 'grown a pair' to use a term often heard on American cop shows. But would my new found bravado get me or someone else killed? Could I risk the lives of these men?"

"There's one other alternative to explore. Would they accept a ransom?"

"I told the two guys we spoke to that there was a reward for the boys return and they didn't bite. It's too risky for them to hold the boys while they negotiate. If they could get them out of the city and into the country they might have considered it, but the boys were snatched for robbery I guess, so they didn't think of it and it's too late to move them now, at least alive it is.

"In that case, we do it." I made up my mind. It was after three in the morning and sunrise wasn't too far away. We had to get the boys out before the gang decided to kill them and hide the bodies.

"OK. It will be me, Joseph and Thomas. The others will stay here to look after the cars and to protect you."

"No. I'm going as well. I can't ask you to risk this while I stay here in safety." I was surprised to hear myself say it, but I meant every word.

"No boss. It's too dangerous."

"No Jacob. Either I go or nobody goes."

It would have been easy for him to say that nobody goes, but he had already committed himself and his pride wouldn't let him change his mind. He owed the two stupid teenagers no loyalty, but he didn't say that. He just smiled a rueful smile and nodded his head in acquiescence. The four of us climbed out of the car and Jacob went off to brief the other four members of his security team.

* * *

The rear of the house was much darker than the front, which was a good thing. Loud music pulsated through the darkness. Again good, it would cover the sound of our approach. Joseph led the way with Jacob right behind him, then myself and Thomas bringing up the rear. We scurried from one patch of shadow to the next. A rat ran across my path, big as a cat, and I almost leapt out of my skin. Jacob placed a reassuring hand on my arm and led me forward again.

We crouched below a window. The blast of music from it was an almost physical force. Other sounds were mixed in, moans and groans interspersed with the odd cry of passion, or perhaps pain. I resisted the temptation to see what was going on. It would only need one pair of eyes to glance at the window and see my shining white face for the game to be up.

Joseph led us to the next window.

"You come in with me." Jacob whispered, though the music would have drowned out the voice of a parade ground drill sergeant at full bellow. "If the boys see your face they're less likely to panic."

I nodded my understanding, not trusting my voice not to betray my terror. I risked a look into the room to try to work out the layout. Opposite the window stood a door. A thin sliver of light showed that it stood slightly open. To the left was a single bed, bare except for a mattress that glowed unnaturally white in the blackness. I craned my head and saw a small wash hand basin in the corner, below which sat two figures, heads hanging disconsolately. I ducked back and nodded to Jacob that I was ready to go.

Joseph made a step by linking his hands. I placed my foot into it and he raised me up so that I could squirm across the window ledge. Splinters snagged at my clothing and I felt something tear. I made a mental note to lodge an expenses claim for the damage and it would be the band that would pay, not MOF. I think what I was currently doing would count as being above and beyond the call of duty. I slid forward until my hands touched the floor and then dragged myself into the room. It had a foul, fetid smell despite being open to the night air. I realised that the source of the smell might well be the two boys sitting tied to the iron drainage pipe below the basin.

Their eyes were wide with terror, but there was no risk of them calling out as they both had gags firmly wound round their faces. Nevertheless I raised a warning finger to my lips. They nodded their heads.

Jacob slid through the window behind me and joined me in struggling with the knots that secured the boys' wrists.

We both froze as the door to the room slammed open. A body fell heavily onto the bed just inside the door, causing the springs to twang in protest. There were girlish giggles and then a second body hit the bed. The pair were too engrossed in what they were doing to notice us, but that could change in an instant. The room was in deep darkness, but it's hard for four people to remain concealed by darkness alone. Besides, whoever the two were they would know that the two boys were in the room with them and might well decide to check on them.

My worst fears were realised as one of the figures swung itself upright on the bed. Whoever it was it wasn't the source of the girlish giggling. The shape was massive. Two feet were planted heavily on the floor and the figure levered itself upright, seeming to fill the room.

The woman let out a stream of words in Swahili and the man sat down heavily on the bed once more. I had no idea what she was saying but her tone suggested she was trying to persuade him to lie down again. He did as he was told.

Jacob wasted no time. He swung his arm and even above the noise of the music I heard something hard crunch against the man's head. As Jacob's hand was drawn back I saw the hard outline of a hand gun. The girl screamed and I threw myself across the man to grab a hold of her. Her sweat soaked body made her slippery but I managed to get a grip of one wrist and drag her across her unconscious lover and onto the floor beside me. I clamped one hand across her mouth as I used my body weight to pin her to the floor.

She was naked and it was difficult to secure her without placing my hand somewhere indecent. It took a moment to work out that the girl's modesty wasn't my first priority at that moment.

She bit hard on the palm of my hand and I nearly cried out in pain.

"Stop fighting or I'll kill you" I snarled an empty threat, not knowing if she would understand or not but hoping my tone would be enough to silence her. It seemed to do the trick. There was no way I would actually harm this woman, but I hoped she wouldn't work that out for herself.

Jacob worked furiously to untie the knots that secured the two teenagers before we were disturbed again. At last the two boys were free and he helped them through the widow to the waiting Joseph and Thomas.

"What about her?" I asked Jacob.

"We tie her up, just like the boys." There was a moan from the bed as the man started to recover from the blow that Jacob had inflicted. "Him too."

The girl struggled against us but between Jacob's threats and my boy scout knot tying skills we managed to get her secured to the drain pipe. The still dazed man was easier. We tied his hands to the bed rail and gagged him as well, not that he was conscious enough to cry out.

There was no one outside when we climbed back out through the window. Joseph and Thomas had sensibly decided to get the boys out of danger without waiting for us. Jacob and I half ran, half scuttled our way back to the cars. We had just about reached them when the sound of the music was cut off and we heard shouting. Jacob wasted no more time in getting us out of the shanties and back to the safety of the hotel.

When we returned to the hotel the police were called, along with a member of the consular staff from the British Embassy. It was a long night. At the end of it I e-mailed the charity with a request for a bonus to be paid to Jacob and his security team, along with a report on the night's events.

Eleven - A Premature Departure

The aftermath of our little escapade took far longer to sort out than the actual rescue. It started with my interrogation of Hipster, aka Gary Smith. He was sandwiched into the back seat of the SUV between Thomas and Joseph. Crayzee was travelling in the second vehicle. I was right, the fetid smell was coming from the boys and it was necessary to eschew the air condition in exchange for the fresher air blown through the open windows.

"Whose idea was it to go to the shanties?" I asked. The kidnap, my brusque tone and the sight of Jacob's gun had combined to knock the arrogance out of the two lads and their teen attitude had evaporated.

"That was Vicky. We talked about it over dinner. She really wasn't happy about you not letting us go out to be seen around the town. She suggested that we sneak out and go and find somewhere to party then film it on our 'phones. She reckoned that you wouldn't miss us so long as you knew she was still in the hotel."

I knew Vicky had been panicked when I had spoken to her, and didn't credit her with being a good enough actress to fake it, so I wondered what had brought about her change of heart.

"Did she tell you where to go?"

"No. Just to ask the taxi driver to take use somewhere where the Europeans didn't usually go. So we did."

"Why didn't you stay there? Why go off with those women?"

"They said they knew somewhere better. They said it was OK. There would be lots of people our age. So we thought we would be OK."

"What were you really after? Sex?"

"Yeah, I guess so."

"Have you ever heard of AIDS?"

"Yeah, that's the thing the gays get, innit."

The Good Lord save us from the British educations system! "Yes, gay people can get it, but so can anyone else. Out here in Africa it's endemic. Do you know what that means?"

"No, not really."

"It means that it's a common disease and just about anyone can get it. Prostitutes are almost certain to have it, and that's the main way it's spread. If you'd had sex with just about any woman tonight you would have been at high risk." In the rear view mirror, I saw Hipster's eyes widen in fear. "You didn't, did you?"

He shook his head violently. "No. We was just about to when those men came in and grabbed us."

"You may not believe it, but they may have saved your life." It was ironic of course, given that those same men were probably going to shoot them before morning, but irony works that way sometimes.

Back at the hotel, I discovered that one of the hotel's security guards had queried the direction that the taxi had taken the boys and reported it to the night duty manager. I realised that that was when Vicky Mitchell must have panicked. Why she didn't just phone them and get them to come back, I had no idea. Well, I had some idea. If they hadn't obeyed her she might have had to admit it had all been her idea in the first place. Better to play dumb and pretend to know nothing about what the boys were up to.

After dealing with the police I re-organised the day's filming. There was no way any work could be done that day. We could have managed without Crayzee and Hipster, but not without Jacob and the security detail and I had sent them home to get some sleep. Fortunately the band didn't have to rush to get back to London so I re-booked their flights for two days later. Jesse James was on a much tighter schedule so he would be my priority for the next day's filming. It meant I would lose a day with Charleese Morgan, which

I was less than happy about, but there was nothing that could be done about it. There was no way I was going to leave Ded NuronZ unsupervised. They may have learnt their lesson, but then again maybe not. I was pretty sure Vicky Mitchell had learnt nothing from the incident. She wasn't the learning type.

With the administration out of the way I managed to get up to my room to try to sleep. I lay on my bed fully clothed, too tired to undress.

The trembling started first. My hands, then my feet. As I replayed the night's events in my head it became worse. I found myself flying towards the bathroom. I made it just in time to avoid vomiting over the bedroom carpet. Some might say it would have improved the look of it, but that wouldn't have justified it.

After spending half a lifetime with my head stuck in the toilet bowl I eventually managed to crawl back to my bed to get some nightmare filled sleep. I won't bore you with the details as other people's dreams are never as interesting as they think they are. I woke in a pool of my own sweat sometime in the mid afternoon. After a refreshing shower I started to tackle my e-mail backlog.

The first was from Igor thanking me for the great publicity that I'd given the telethon. I was at a loss to understand what he meant until I clicked on the link he had included that took me to a shaky video clip of Crayzee and Hipster telling their story of the kidnap and rescue. Jacob and myself didn't feature much in the telling and the inference was that the other members of the band had ridden to the rescue. This was bad, I knew it in my gut and not because the credit wasn't going to the right people. I hastily clicked onto the next e-mail, which was from the charity's head office.

It was as bad I thought it might be. The insurance company that provided all risk cover for Ded NuronZ had cancelled the contract. If the band ran into trouble now then it would be down to the charity to cover their costs. I couldn't take the risk. It only needed one of them to go down with some sort of fever and it could costs hundreds of thousands of pounds to get him back to Britain for medical treatment. I daren't even think about what might happen if Akeem and his friends managed to kidnap them again.

I hurried up to Vicky Mitchell's room and pounded on the door. I heard the security chain rattle and she opened up.

"What the fuck do you think you're doing." I demanded, barging past her into the room before my shouting could attract the attention of the other hotel guests.

"What do you mean?" she placed her hands on her hips in the gesture that the male of the species learns to fear by the time they're three years old.

"Posting that video of the band on the internet."

"Great, isn't it." She beamed her satisfaction at me. "It makes Cheryl Cole's bout of malaria look a bit limp, don't you think?"

"No. I don't think. Her medical treatment was covered by her insurance."

"So? We've got insurance…..." She stopped talking as she saw me shaking my head from side to side. "Oh shit." She finished limply. The enormity of the problem hit her between the eyes.

"So what do we do now?"

"You pack your bags and get the band to pack theirs. You're out of this country on this evening's flight. I can't risk anything happening to them."

"What about something happening to me?"

"You can think that through on the ride to the airport and hope like hell nothing goes wrong. The charity would have to pay out for the band. They don't have to pay out for you." It was a cruel jibe, I knew, but I had no sympathy for her right then.

"Downstairs in the lobby in one hour, packed and ready." I commanded as I stomped out of the room.

"But the boy's appeal films?" I heard her protesting.

"Not my problem anymore." I yelled back, slamming the door behind me. A PR coup had just turned into a disaster for Ms Mitchell and she knew it.

Back in my room I made the calls to re-book the band's flights. Fortunately they were flying Business Class and there were just enough empty seats. I took great pleasure in bumping Vicky Mitchell into the last remaining seat in economy. I then made another call to the long suffering Jacob.

* * *

I found Jacob waiting for me in the lobby as arranged.

"It's all sorted boss." He pointed through the plate glass to the hotel forecourt where two SUVs sat between a pair of HUMVs; not the civilian versions favoured by macho movie stars but the full military spec ones, though painted plain white and sporting a company logo. Standing around were several security men.

These weren't the overweight guys that Jacob brought with him, more intended to act as crowd control than to provide a physical deterrence. These men were lean and fit looking, dressed in jeans and leather jackets, black mirrored sunglasses covering their eyes. Their hands were folded loosely in front of them and I suspected it was so that they weren't far from concealed guns. Coiled wires emerged from their ears and snaked down into the collars of their shirts. Most of the men were black Africans, but there were three white faces in view.

"Who's in charge?"

"Jan de Kok." Jacob pointed to a white man standing close to the lead HUMV.

"South African?"

"Yes. Professional. A lot of the European businesses use his company to provide security. No one messes with them, or if they do they don't do it twice."

"Thanks Jacob." I walked out into the heat of the late afternoon and approached Jan de Kok.

He took my proffered hand without taking his eyes off the road in front of the hotel, scanning back and forth unceasingly.

"Did Jacob brief you?" I asked.

"Ja. Get the passengers to the airport safe and sound. Don't leave them until they're on the aircraft and the door's closed. Don't stop for anyone or anything."

"That's about it. Will you have any problems with airport security?"

"Any costs in that area will be added to your bill." He didn't have to elaborate. This was Africa.

"Do you know who you're babysitting?"

"Makes no odds to me, man."

"Well, it does to me. They're a band called Ded NuronZ. The name just about sums them up."

"They the ones that were all over the internet today?" I told him they were.

"Figures. So, no insurance then?"

"That's right."

"No problem, man. We're the best insurance they can have right now anyway."

I thanked him, reassured by his calm confidence and went back inside the hotel lobby, the ice cold air making goose bumps rise on my arms. The band were standing around a heap of their luggage.

"Right you lot. I can't say I'm sorry to be seeing the back of you. You see them?" I pointed out of the window. "They're your security escort and they don't mess around. I've told them that if you so much as cough at the wrong time they can dump you at the side of the road and you can take your chances walking to the airport."

It was the sort of threat that a father will make when his children are misbehaving in the back seat of the car. Well, they had behaved like children so I would treat them as such. Just as the father's threat is empty so was mine, but they knew I'd had enough and they weren't prepared to call my bluff. I called the hotel porter over and asked him to start loading the luggage into the back of the SUVs.

As the boys left to take their seats Vicky Mitchell hung back to talk to me, a smug self-satisfied smile playing on her lips. "I've just spoken to Damian Ellis." She informed me. "He's got the band lined up to do just about every TV and radio chat show in the UK. He's been on the phone to LA and there's talk of a film."

"Well, looks like you won't need Cuddly Toy Day after all." I said somewhat bitterly. "I can tell you now those brats will never appear on it again so long as I have anything to do with it."

She laughed at me. "So, it won't be long before they're back on the bill then. Not if Igor has his way."

"You've spoken to him as well?" It wouldn't be that much of a surprise if she had.

"No, but Damian has. I doubt you'll last long once you're back home."

That may be true, but she wouldn't know about the amount of evidence I had gathered on Igor and his girlfriend and all the others at Metro TV that had been milking the budget with their scams. Patience, I told myself. It wouldn't do to give myself away by going off half-cocked just to get back at Vicky Bloody Mitchell. I said nothing but went back outside to supervise the loading. It wasn't necessary but it got me away from her and her smirking.

Jan de Kok attracted my attention and I went across to see what he wanted.

"Do you know him?" he asked, indicating a figure standing in the shadows of an alley on the other side of the wide boulevard. It was a tall, well-built man, his face puffed up around one eye and with an ostrich egg sized lump on his forehead.

"I'm not sure, but that lump on his head makes me think it's one of the men from last night. One of Akeem's men."

"I thought as much." He took out his phone and used it to take a photo of the man. "Always good to know who's on the opposition team."

De Kok spoke into his lapel microphone and two of his men started to walk across the road to challenge the man. He turned and as he disappeared deeper into the alley de Kok recalled his men.

"No point in sending two men into an alley with no idea what might be there." He commented. "So now they know we're here and they know that we know they're watching us. I doubt they'll try anything if they know we're ready for them."

With the last of the band safely on board the SUVs Jan de Kok pulled his men in from their perimeter and they boarded the HUMVs. Just as he was climbing into the front of the lead vehicle he turned to me.

"I know we're expensive, Mr. Mirren, but if you need us just give us a call. Jacob's boys are OK, but you may find us a little bit more effective if things get a bit sticky."

"Do you think they will? Get sticky I mean?"

"Who knows. You've upset a very dangerous man. He won't like that."

With those ominous words hanging in the air Jan de Kok slammed the door of the HUMV and it roared off towards the airport, the other vehicles staying close behind.

My shoulders sagged with relief at getting rid of Ded NuronZ and their loose cannon of a PR rep. I went back into the hotel looking for the location producer. With the band gone there would need to be more changes to the shooting schedule.

* * *

After the nightmare of Ded NuronZ, Jesse James was a dream to work with. OK, we'd had our differences over his expenses, but it was nothing personal. I met him in the hotel lobby after Jacob collected him from the airport. He was dressed in jeans and tee shirt, carrying only a small ruck sack and a battered guitar case. There wasn't a PA, hairdresser, stylist or agent in sight. I expressed my surprise to see him alone and he rewarded me with the smile that made a million housewives go weak at the knees.

"I took on board what you said about the need to spend the charity's money wisely, so I cancelled my agent's ticket; his hotel room as well. He wasn't happy, but I don't pay him to be happy."

Over coffee I filled him in on what had happened. He was very sympathetic.

"So I guess that leaves you a bit short on film." He observed.

"A bit. The band were supposed to provide three appeals. One at a clinic for sight impaired people, a second at a school and the last one at a project to provide clean water. We can cover the first two with stuff we filmed earlier and what we'll get from Charleese Morgan, but we've no fall back plan for the water project. It was a one-off shoot."

"Hey man, maybe I can cover that." I could have hugged him.

"Are you sure?"

"Well, why don't you tell me what's involved then I can tell you if I'm sure."

I filled him in on the detail. It would mean an early start the next day if we were to reach the project location and complete the filming before we had to be at the other locations at which Jesse was due to film. The important one was a school project for five year olds, where he was supposed to teach the children a nursery rhyme and then be seen playing his guitar and singing along with them. It was a real feel good piece aimed at showing the sort of thing the charity spent the public's donations on. "It means you won't get much sleep." I finished.

"I can sleep when I'm dead. This is more important. Now, I'd like to wash the travel off me and get an early night. Is it OK if I order room service?"

I'd been trying to cut back on the room service bill because the food was so much more expensive when compared to the hotel's restaurant. It also covered a multitude of other, less salubrious indulgences. I'd told all the celebrities and their entourages that any room service charges would have to come out of their own pockets. But after what Jesse had just agreed to do I could hardly refuse him the indulgence. Besides, I didn't think that Jesse was the type to order in hookers or watch the X rated TV channels. I wished him a good night and told him I'd arrange an alarm call.

Twelve - On Safari

The helicopter lifted off in a cloud of dust and I made my way across to a shade tree at the edge of the village. A small group of children had gathered to see the excitement.

The irreplaceable Jacob had arranged the lift for me. The Parks Department had an anti-poaching patrol going out to one of the game reserves and they agreed to give a lift to a charity worker who needed to be at a village not far off their flight path.

I searched the side pocket of my rucksack and pulled out a bag of sweets. Each child was ceremonially handed a cellophane wrapped morsel of boiled sugar, which they examined with interest. One small boy turned and scampered off into the village and the others turned and followed, their excited voices dwindling into the heat filled afternoon.

The children were soon back, this time accompanied by an adult. He was tall and thin, dressed in a brightly coloured cape affair and pair of khaki shorts that had seen better days. In one hand he carried a spear, which he leant on while he took a long look at me. I have no idea how old he was. From the lines on his face I'd have said probably sixty, but he could have been younger or older.

I felt a little uncomfortable under his gaze and wished he would say something, even if it was only "boo", but he was determined to take his time. The children gathered around him, silent in the presence of someone who they must have considered to be important. Eventually he spoke.

"Have you brought TV?" he asked in heavily accented English. I realised that his delay in talking may have been the result of him searching his memory for half-forgotten words in a language he learnt a long time before and not spoken much since.

"No. I don't have TV." I replied, indicating all my worldly goods which were stored in the rucksack.

He said something to the children in Swahili and there were cries of disappointment.

"Women are coming with TV." He stated. It took me some moments to realise that he probably meant Charleese and her party. Right on cue two trucks appeared in the distance kicking up a cloud of dust from the unmade road. The support team from Charleese's expedition. She couldn't stay in five star hotels, but she could do her best to take her home comforts with her and that was what the trucks were needed for. Behind each truck a water bowser was hooked up. Charleese was determined that she shouldn't have to call on the meagre resources of the local population to provide support for her. The bowsers would only be filled at places where there was a reliable water supply

The trucks ground to a halt and the children gathered around them chattering loudly and calling up to the drivers and men seated in the cargo beds. The men shouted back and the children cheered. They ran back to the thin man and gathered around him, all seeming to speak at the same time. The man's face broke into a toothy grin.

"TV comes." He announced to me, before turning and walking back towards the village. The children trailed after him.

A man clambered down from the cab of the lead vehicle and strolled towards me.

"It's the same wherever we go." He announced. "How they know we're coming I have no idea, but they certainly know." he stretched out his hand for me to shake. "I'm Musoke. I am the support team leader."

"What's all this about TV?" I asked, my curiosity piqued. Musoke laughed.

"We have TV and DVD with us, so we have some entertainment in the evenings. Word has got out and now every time we stop we have children coming from miles around to see a show. Not just children but adults too."

That explained it. Somehow word had got out and travelled ahead by whatever mysterious means was available. It certainly wasn't by mobile phone. Mine was resolutely showing that I had no signal. I was pleased. A few days without having to dance attendance on the celebrity world suited me just fine.

"So when will Charleese and the others arrive?" I returned my attention to the reason for which I had given up the luxury of my hotel.

"Maybe an hour. We passed them about fifteen miles back. They are on schedule."

After the cyclists started off each day on their scheduled journey Musoke and his team broke camp and then followed them down the road until they eventually caught and passed them. The half dozen men from the lorries were already working hard to establish a new camp for the night, with tents and other camping equipment being lifted down from the vehicles.

"Is there anything I can do to help?" I asked.

Musoke shook his head, smiling indulgently. "I don't think so. My boys know what they're doing. We've had lots of practice now. I'll call you when your tent is up."

And that was that. For the next hour I sat in the shade as Musoke and his team quickly erected tents, dug latrines and assembled a field kitchen. A rudimentary shower was established on one side. Just a canvass screen surrounding a pole with a water tank sitting on top of it. A chain hanging down from the tank told me that there was some sort of flush system that controlled the flow of water. Beside the assembly were stacked Jerri cans of water.

* * *

The first to arrive was Charleese, leading her three woman team of cyclists off of the road and into the camp. Close behind was the camera truck with the cameraman faithfully recording everything just as it happened from his position perched in the cargo area of the pick-up. Behind that was the command vehicle, bristling with aerials and towing a trailer on which spare bicycles were racked up.

Last of all came a stripped down Land Rover carrying four Dolph Lundgren lookalikes; all square jaws and cropped hair. Each had shoulders like a bull and biceps that stretched the boundaries of physical probability. I suspected the men would have names like 'Hank' and 'Brad'. There was no doubting their reason for being with the expedition.

I waited for the dust to settle a little before leaving the marginal coolness of my shade tree and walking over to greet the cyclists.

I could hear Mary Tennant's nasal Brooklyn accent as she lead the cyclists in stretching exercises, helping them to cool down their bodies after the gruelling fifty miles they had just cycled in the heat of the African sun. I watched their lycra clad bodies twist and turn before realising that my close attention might be misinterpreted. I quickly took an interest in the bikes instead.

They were sturdy mountain bikes, or trail bikes as the Americans called them. I picked one up and tried it out, but the saddle adjustment was wrong for me and it felt uncomfortable. I looked up to find Charleese watching me with some amusement.

"We'll get yours adjusted for your leg size." She announced. I was to use one of the spare bikes. It would leave them one short if they had any breakdowns but I could always retire to the command vehicle if necessary.

"How's it going?" I asked by way of a reply.

"Pretty good." She reached her hand behind her back and returned it with a thermally protected water bottle. She took a long pull from the bottle and replaced it in its pouch, belted into the small of her back. "We're on schedule and we've got all the film we wanted in the can. So far that is."

"Where did you get the muscle?" I nodded towards the security detail who were hefting their packs out of the back of their vehicle.

She gave me a wry smile. "When you've sung for the President in the White House then getting the phone numbers for a few retired Navy SEALS isn't too much of a problem. Don't worry, they don't violate the weapons policy."

The charity had a very strong policy against the carrying of weapons by any of their employees. Guns and charitable work don't go well together, even if it means the charity's employees being at risk. However, technically, the four man security detail weren't in the employ of the charity and I suspected that there was a loophole there that the four men might be exploiting. I decided it would be better not to explore the issue any further. I had taken the same approach with Jacob a few nights earlier. If you know that you won't like the answer then sometimes it's better not to ask the question.

"How are the legs holding up?" I asked instead.

She laughed. "It isn't the legs that are the problem. My butt glows in the dark."

"I'd like to see that." I laughed before realising what I'd said. "Er, sorry. I didn't mean that to come out like it did."

Charleese waved her hand dismissively. "The other girls are used to it of course. They do more miles than that each day just in training, but it's new to me, and I didn't get that much time to work out before we left."

"You're managing quite well, though, apart from…." I tailed off, not wishing to return to a closed subject.

"Well, I keep myself fit, but these girls are the superstars. They keep me going." The other three women had now joined us and introductions were made. I noticed that the camera kept on rolling, capturing every word and action. I was more used to the cameras being pointed everywhere but at me. It was something I would have to get used to over the next few days.

"OK, whose turn is it to use the shower first?" Charleese asked the girls.

"Oh, that would be me." Bridie MacAleesh raised her hand, like a schoolgirl asking to be excused. The pale Celtic skin of her face glowed red from the heat and over exposure to the sun. She turned and headed towards the tiny canvas cubicle, where a ladder had been propped up against the cistern. Two of the labourers were manhandling the Jerry cans up and emptying their contents into it.

"We sometimes get a bit short of water, so we take it in turns to go first just in case it runs out, but we should be OK for the next few days. This village has a good well, or so I'm led to believe, so we'll top up the Jerri cans with bathing water. You can't drink it without boiling it, but it's OK for washing in."

"So what's the usual end of day routine?" I asked, anxious to fit myself into the team as quickly as possible.

"Well, after our showers we normally check the route for the next day, then we talk over any filming that will be done with the film crew. They're good guys, the best I could find in Kampala. Then I check in with the folks back home. We've got full satellite comms if you want to contact anyone. That takes us to supper time. Then after supper it's time for the movie show to start."

"Yes, I've heard about that."

"We've discovered that word travels fast out here." Charleese laughed again. I could see that her spirits were high despite her obvious fatigue. "So we have a routine worked out now. Half an hour of cartoons for the children followed by half an hour of soccer for the Dads. We managed to get an edited copy of the national team playing in the last African Nations Cup. After that I give them a couple of numbers from a recording of one of my shows, then we finish the evening with whatever film we haven't watched too many times before. I hardly ever stay awake long enough to see the end credits though."

"What's the food like?"

"Not bad, considering it's all cooked on a charcoal fired field kitchen." She pointed to one of the young men fiddling with a large metal contraption which I guessed might be a cooker. "That's the cook, Kizza. I may take him home with me just to cook my bar-b-ques." I wasn't sure if she was joking or not.

Charleese stretched upwards with her arms, going up onto tip toe. It gave me a more than was appropriate view of her lycra clad body. I quickly looked away, anxious not to be caught again. "OK, I have to go and get out of this sweat suit and into something less clingy. I'll see you later."

She turned and walked away towards the row of tents that had appeared along one side of the square that had been created by the support team. There were three small tents, about large enough to accommodate two people in each, a medium sized tent that probably slept four. I guessed that was used by the security team, plus two larger, military style tents that were for the support team and film crew. An open sided dining tent had also sprung up next to Kizza's kitchen area. Musoke saw that I was no longer in conversation and headed in my direction.

"Miss Charleese and Miss Mary are in the first tent." He informed me, pointing to the small tent on the left. "And Miss Bridie and Miss Sandy are in the middle one. The third one, the smallest, is yours. You have a camp bed and a mosquito net. You must use the net if you wish to avoid sickness, you understand."

I told him that I did understand. I had watched enough celebrities make appeals for malaria vaccine and mosquito nets over the last few weeks to be sure that the message had been well and truly driven home.

"Can anything get into the tent? You know, like snakes or lions."

Musoke laughed, a big booming sound. "There is no need to worry about lions, but if you are concerned about snakes just make sure the zipper on the tent is fully closed. There is no other way for anything to get in. If you are worried about wildlife I would be more concerned about elephants. They don't see well in the dark."

With that ominous remark Musoke turned and walked off towards the kitchen, chuckling to himself.

Thirteen - Charleese's Plans

After dinner the crowd began to assemble to watch the TV show. Saul, the driver of the command vehicle, had set up a large screen on its tailgate and connected it up to a small generator. He'd connected up the DVD player and applied power to that as well. He organised the villagers into a semi-circle, with the children sitting on the ground at the front, mothers behind them and the fathers at the back. As Saul began the show, Charleese beckoned me over to the shade tree where she had positioned two canvas chairs. The deep night time shadow hid us from casual observation.

"I've seen this stuff a thousand times already." She smiled at me. "I hope you don't mind giving it a miss, but I wanted to chat about my plans for my new foundation."

"Yes, that puzzled me a bit. I mean, there's plenty of poverty in other places where you could do some good."

"You mean the Good Ol' U.S. of A."

It was what I meant but I hadn't wanted to be rude towards her native country.

"Well, you have to remember that in the USA any form of welfare spending is seen in some quarters as a commie plot, so I have to be very careful. I do have a foundation running in the USA already, which works in some of the most deprived areas, but I'm careful to keep it at arms' length. A large part of the audience for my music tends to be very conservative and it wouldn't do me much good to kill the goose that lays the golden eggs.

I also have a second foundation that works in Central and South America but some of the places where it operates wouldn't be seen as friends of Uncle Sam, so again I have to keep it at arms' length. The same will apply here in Africa. If I want to do something in a country that isn't favourably disposed to America then I'm going to have to keep pretty quiet about it back home. But that isn't going to stop me from doing what's right."

I admired her forthrightness and also her vision. If we don't help our enemies then they're pretty much destined to remain our enemies. I said as much and Charleese nodded her agreement.

"Don't let my home spun country girl image fool you, Andy. Most of that was made up by a PR team to create an image that would sell records. According to my official biography I grew up in the Ozarks and never had a pair of shoes on my feet till I went to Nashville, but that's a complete load of bull. I graduated from Tennessee State with a first class degree in business management. Music had just been a way to pay the bills while I studied. The only reason it turned into a career was because I got lucky one night. You ever heard of Kentucky Bob Wild?"

"Who hasn't. He's one of the biggest names in country music. I'm not that big a fan but I'd heard of him by the time I was ten."

"Exactly. Well he and his band were flying to LA in a chartered plane when it developed engine trouble. They made an emergency landing at Nashville Airport. While they were waiting for a replacement aircraft to arrive they took a cab to the nearest bar to have a few drinks and the band I played in was performing there that night.

Well, Kentucky Bob didn't say anything to us, but he got his manager to take a look at our next performance. He liked me, but didn't like the band much. So I was offered a spot on Bob's tour during the Summer recess. Two duets with Bob and a solo of my own, six weeks work. Of course I grabbed it with both hands, not least because the money was good. In the Fall I went back to college and didn't think much more about it, but then I got a call asking me to record a few songs with Bob, in return for which I would be able to record a couple of songs of my own and have them released as singles. Again they paid me well but I didn't hold out much hope for the singles, but one of them went straight to the top of the country charts and the rest, as they say, is history."

"So if Bob's plane….."

"Exactly. I would have gotten a job as a manager in an office or a factory just like regular folks and maybe sung a little bit in the evenings for pocket money and that would have been that. But thanks to a stroke of luck I've got more money than I know what to do with and I want to use most of it to give other people a bit of the luck that I had. Now, that's what I wanted to talk to you about. It's why I wanted you to come along on this trip."

My heart sank. I realised that her plans for me weren't what I had hoped.

"I've seen a whole new level of poverty out here and I'm guessing that I haven't seen the worst of it because it's too dangerous for me to go to some places. If I start up this new foundation, what do you think I should focus it on? What's the best way to spend the money to have the greatest impact?"

I puffed out my cheeks and let a blast of air demonstrate how daunting that question was. "I'm not sure I'm the best person to answer that, Charleese. Until six months ago I was a database manager. This is my first visit to Africa, just like it's yours. There are a whole lot of people better qualified than me who could give you a better answer."

"I'm sure there are, Andy, and rest assured I'll be asking them as well. But I want your gut feeling on this. If it was your money, how would you be spending it?"

It was a big question and it deserved some thought, so I looked at the dust on the ground for a long while, dragging my toe through it to make some pretty patterns while I got my thoughts together. At last I was ready.

"We've done a lot of filming in clinics and hospitals while we've been here. In fact you'll be filming at another one tomorrow. Images of sick people bring in a lot of donations for some reason. The hospitals do great work, but in the end you finish up with people who are well but still poor because you can't cure poverty with an injection the way you can cure disease.

The same applies with the clean water projects and the food aid. In order to end poverty you have to give people a way of getting out of poverty for themselves. Look at these people here," I indicated the crowd enjoying the TV show, "They live in one of the most fertile countries in Africa yet they're barely able to grow enough food to live on. If the monsoons fail they will be at risk of starving to death. But how do they get out of that trap?"

I looked at Charleese, offering her a chance to answer what was essentially a rhetorical question, but she just nodded for me to continue.

"Big farms, mainly western owned, grow cash crops on the best land and the produce is exported for western consumption. It provides some jobs, but not enough and what they do provide is poorly paid because we westerners aren't prepared to pay top dollar for our fruit and vegetables. So people like these villagers are pushed out to the margins, where the land is poorest and the water hardest to come by. They grow what they can in a few fields, ploughing it by harnessing oxen. They can't use tractors even if they could afford them because there's no regular supply of fuel. You know that because you've had to bring your own fuel supply with you.

They graze a few cattle if they can, but in reality the cattle just create competition for the water supply. They would like to farm more land and graze more cattle, but they can't because of the wild life reserves. Wildlife brings in tourism, and of course a lot of it is protected species, so the people take second place. Where the land is worse and the water is scarcer, such as Somalia and Sudan, the poverty is greater and the risk of famine is greater too."

Charleese nodded her understanding. "So how do we break the cycle."

"If you provide education you can make sure that the next generation aren't trapped in the poverty cycle. The children gain the knowledge that will allow them to grow up and take control of their own businesses, their own farms, their own politics and their own lives. You educate engineers who can build dams, irrigate fields, build roads, bridges and hospitals. You educate doctors so the people aren't so reliant on western volunteers. You educate scientists so they can find the cures for diseases for which there is insufficient profit for western pharmaceutical companies to invest in. It isn't a quick fix though. It will take time and patience. Of course this isn't the only place where that applies. Wherever you find poverty you will also find the most poorly educated people. That applies in Britain or America just as much as it does here."

"So you're saying that you think I should focus my attention on education?"

"If you want to deal with the long term problems then yes. That doesn't mean you can't help with some of the shorter term issues as well, such as clean water, access to medical care etc, but that's all sticking plaster stuff. Putting a Band Aid on it, as you Americans would say."

Charleese smiled her acknowledgement at my attempted wit.

"Where would you suggest I start?"

"You need teachers before you can open a school, so I suggest a teaching academy in the country you're operating in. In many parts of Africa there are common languages shared by a number of countries, like Swahili is used in this part of the world. That means you can probably set up a single teacher training college to cover several countries' needs. Then you can set up schools at different age levels and finish up with scholarships to African universities for the most promising students and maybe at some American colleges for the elite students."

"That's all going to cost, isn't it?"

"I'm sure there are other charities that would be willing to work with you on some of it. We have schools projects operating in a number of countries already, as do other charities. You don't have to start from scratch everywhere you go.

A school doesn't have to cost a lot of money out here. You need a building which is weather proof, some books and other teaching resources and you're ready to go. The expensive part is always teachers. They need to be paid and they need somewhere to live. It's also useful if you have some boarding facilities for the children. You can't ask a child to walk two hours each way to get to and from school and then expect them to study when they get there. The hard part will be getting IT in place. Not only is there no internet access, but in many places there isn't even any electricity. Like here. You're only able to show these people TV because you brought your electricity supply with you."

"How about government assistance?"

"Depends on the country. Some places will welcome you in with open arms and some will try to shut you out. A lot depends on what you're actually going to be teaching and who's going to do the teaching. You may have to work through some intermediaries in some countries simply because you're American. In some countries you won't be able to educate women, at least not openly."

"I hadn't thought of that. Good point, Andy. That doesn't sit well with a woman like me."

"Wherever you go, whatever you do, you have to do it with the co-operation of the local people and whoever the local authorities are, be they civil, military or religious. You can't force things down their throats. You'll just end up with schools that have no pupils because everyone will be afraid to send their children there. You do what you can and it won't always be perfect. Sometimes you won't be able to do anything at all, no matter how hard you try and how much money you throw at the problem."

"It sounds like I'll have quite a challenge on my hands." She gave a rueful grin.

I smiled. "Africa is the greatest challenge anyone will ever face. You'll get used to it. Hire the right people; the people who know the countries you want to operate in and listen to them. That's what MOF does and it's what all the other NGOs (*non-governmental organisations*) out here do."

"Thanks for your advice, Andy. That's the reason why I wanted you to come on this trip."

"And here's me thinking you were just after my body." I quipped. I immediately wished I hadn't said that, but Charleese didn't seem to take offence. In fact, she smiled at me. The sort of smile a doting mother might give to an unruly but otherwise lovable child.

"Well, I'm going to turn in now. We've another fifty mile stretch to cover tomorrow."

I stood up at the same time as she did and we walked side by side towards the tents, only parting a few feet from them. I noticed the other cyclists breaking away from the group of newly created TV addicts and head towards the sleeping quarters as well.

* * *

For hours I lay on my uncomfortable camp bed fantasising about Charleese, until guilt got the better of me and I started to think about Cassie instead.

We had been out together a few times, but weren't 'going out'. She was seeing other blokes and had made it clear that if I wanted to see other girls then that was my business. Such was the hip and trendy world of Metro TV, apparently. Unfortunately, I'm a little more old fashioned about relationships so I hadn't taken advantage of my 'free pass'. But if Charleese offered, what then?

With that disturbing thought I drifted into a fitful sleep.

Something woke me; I don't know what. I'm not usually a light sleeper but the threat of being trampled to death by night blinded elephants had made it difficult for me to get into a proper sleep. I'd be a wreck in the morning, I knew.

I looked at my watch and the glowing green hands showed me it was a little after four a.m. I heard it again. A distant rattling, like rifle fire. So distant that I couldn't be absolutely sure I was hearing anything at all. It didn't sound like any sort of animal that I knew of. For ten more minutes I strained my ears but the sound wasn't repeated. I fell back into my restless sleep once again.

Fourteen - Elephant's Teeth

The first day of my cycle ride through East Africa; well, about one hundred and seventy five miles of East Africa, anyway. There was a fifty mile stretch that day followed by seventy five the next. Day three would be a rest day and then a final fifty for me on day four. After that I would rendezvous with a light aircraft at a mining camp airstrip for the journey back to the big city.

My backside was already burning and we had only covered fifteen miles by the time we took the first scheduled break to take on water. The girls had been kind to me, dropping the pace to fifteen miles an hour rather than their normal twenty. Despite our crack-of-dawn departure the temperatures were already climbing and sweat soaked my skin tight lycra. I have to say there are some people who should never be allowed to wear lycra and I'm one of them.

At Mary Tennant's lead the small convoy pulled onto the side of the road next to a wildlife viewing platform. A twelve foot high structure of ropes and poles with a rudimentary platform and a rail around the edge, perhaps to stop anyone falling off. One of the Hanks or Brads climbed up and started to scan the surrounding area while the rest of us gulped cold water from the cooler installed on the passenger seat of the command vehicle.

A loud hiss caught our attention and we turned to see Hank or Brad beckoning us up onto the platform. Curiosity got the better of me first and I climbed the shaky ladder, closely followed by Charleese and the other girls.

Hank stretched out his arm to point and passed me his binoculars. I trained them in the general direction he had indicated and adjusted the focus. I scanned back and forth until at last I saw them. Three lions; A male and two females, basking in the sunshine, all but invisible in the tall grass of the savannah. I smiled my appreciation for the privilege of being allowed to see them then passed the binoculars to Charleese.

The girls took turns to view the animals, passing the binoculars back and forth as they whispered excitedly. After three weeks in Africa these were the first big cats they, or I, had seen. There had been plenty of zebra, buffalo, antelope and a few giraffes, but no predators that we had been able to detect.

Hank's head snapped round to the left as he reacted to something only he had heard. The women didn't register his alertness but I strained my ears to try to catch whatever it was that had made him so tense all of a sudden. Out of the corner of my eye I saw the huge male lion also stand, alert to the same sound that Hank (or Brad) had heard. The two females also stood and the little pride sauntered off to find a quieter place to snooze.

It took a couple of minutes but I eventually heard them. Voices, several of them, and getting louder.

Hank tapped Charleese on the shoulder and told her to get the other three women into the relative safety of the command vehicle.

"You too, Sir." He commanded.

"Not enough room for five of us plus the driver." I shook my head. I didn't know what was coming, but I was damned if I was going to be trapped inside a metal box when it got here.

Hank shrugged his shoulders and spoke quietly into the microphone clipped to the lapel of his combat jacket. The other three security men, who had been gathered round the bonnet of their Landover, sprang into life.

Assault rifles appeared from a trunk in the bed of the Landrover. One of the other security men jogged to the foot of the viewing platform and threw a weapon up to Hank, who caught it one handed. A satchel of magazines followed, then the three men on the ground simply melted into the tall grass of the savannah.

"Sorry, what's your name?" I asked the one I had been thinking of as Hank. I hadn't been introduced to any of them as they seemed to prefer their own company to that of the rest of the expedition members.

"Colin." He replied, pronouncing it Co-lin. I was disappointed at such a mundane name. "Can you use one of these?" He pulled a hand gun from under his shirt where it hung over the waistband at the back of his trousers.

"Only to shoot my own foot off. Perhaps I'd better not." Colin shrugged and returned the weapon to its hiding place before lying prone on the platform and sighting along the road in the direction of the voices, which had grown louder in the last few seconds. He signalled to me to lie down as well, which I was happy to do. If whoever it was making all the noise couldn't see me, it would make it harder for them to kill me.

Figures appeared around the bend in the road that had been concealing the approaching party from us. There were a dozen of them. Two in front, another eight in pairs carrying what appeared to be logs, one log between each pair, then another two at the rear. All had AK-47 assault rifles in their hands or slung over their shoulders. They saw the small convoy parked alongside of the road and scattered into the grass as the leader shouted in alarm. The logs were dropped in the haste to seek cover and to free up hands to use the rifles.

Now free of the hands that had carried them I could see that the logs were actually curved and tapered. I realised what they were; elephant tusks.

"So what do we do now?" I asked Co-lin.

"We can take them easily enough, but I know Charleese doesn't want that. So we try and talk our way out."

"You seem very sure about being able to take them. You're... er ...we're, outnumbered."

"See how they've positioned themselves?" I looked and saw that they were lined up in the ditch along both sides of the road; six either side as far as I could make out. "The ones at the back can't fire their weapons without hitting the ones in the front. But me and my guys can hit a fly on a hog's back at two hundred yards. We'd have four of them dead before they could even work out where we are and another four as they panic and start shooting at anything that moves."

"What about the vehicles. They might hit them and kill someone."

"The Command Truck is armoured. That's why I sent Charleese and the others to take cover inside it. The film crew will be safe enough in the pick-up so long as they stay in the back. But as I said, that's not the way we're going to do it. We're going to buy our way out of here."

Co-lin muttered something into his lapel microphone. A few moments later Saul climbed out of the command vehicle and took a cautious step towards the poachers, raising his hands to show he wasn't armed. He stopped about half way between the vehicles and the place the poachers were hiding. One, probably the leader, rose up out of the ditch and levelled his rifle at Saul. Saul placed his hands behind his head but otherwise remained still. The poacher walked slowly forward, perhaps suspecting a trap. He came to a stop a few paces away from Saul and kept his rifle levelled, making it clear to anyone watching that he would kill Saul at the first sign of trouble.

There followed a long period of negotiation. Both Saul and the poacher did a lot of gesticulating, but after nearly a month in Africa I knew that was part of any sort of discussion and meant nothing in itself. After what seemed like an eternity an agreement was obviously reached and Saul turned and walked back to the convoy.

In order not to give away Colin's position Saul climbed back into the command vehicle and spoke on the radio. Colin acknowledge the message and turned to smile at me. "They've settled for fifty dollars each. I expected more so they must be worried about how many of us there are."

Out of the ditch climbed another one of the poachers and made his way towards our position. As he got closer it became clear that he was no more than a child; perhaps twelve or thirteen years old. I guessed he was the youngest; the most expendable. His AK-47 was almost as big as he was.

"It's funny." I whispered to Colin. "I thought I heard gunfire. It was the early hours of this morning. It must have been these guys shooting elephant."

Colin turned and gave me a hard look. "You ever hear anything like that again you tell me, you hear? If I'd known about that we could have been better prepared. Maybe not stopped here at all."

I considered myself chastised for my small omission. When the boy reached us Colin climbed down from the platform and I followed. Saul returned to tell the boy what to do, and the girls and the film crew also joined us.

"OK, here's what we're doing." Colin addressed us. There was no question of Charleese being in charge of the expedition now and she didn't challenge Colin's authority. "The pick-up with the film crew will go first, with Mike on board to take point." Mike, I guessed, was another of the security team. "Then Charleese and the cyclists follow." They looked a little apprehensive at that news. I know I was. "Sorry, but we've no room to carry the bikes and carry you as passengers at the same time. But don't worry. Those guys want their money so they won't try anything. Besides, we have a hostage." Colin indicated the surly looking boy.

"Behind the cyclists will be the command vehicle, then the Land Rover with Todd and Grant plus the hostage. We drive past the poachers and continue for a mile, then we stop to drop the boy off with the money. Then we carry on. With us all on wheels they'll not be able to catch up with us even if they wanted to. Now, any questions?"

There weren't, so we got into position and the film crew's pick up led us off, the camera pointing ahead to capture images of the poachers as we passed by them. Beside the cameramen Mike kept his rifle trained on the poachers who now stood alongside the road. As I pedalled alongside Charleese and Mary Tennant I wondered how much of the incident had been captured on camera and how it would be used when Charleese returned to America.

The small convoy passed between the two lines of poachers. Their expressions varied from aggressive, to fearful, to lascivious as they caught sight of the four women for the first time. The good news was that even though they still held their weapons there was no indication that they planned to use them.

We kicked up a cloud of flies that had gathered to feed on the blood and gore that marked the root of each tusk. So much destruction for such a small reward. Oh, I knew there was big money in ivory, but it wasn't people like this sorry bunch of men and boys that made it.

As they disappeared into our dust trail I turned to Charleese. "Colin seemed well prepared for that." I called across to her.

"Before we even left the States we discussed the possible risks and how they would be handled. Encounters like that seemed to be a possibility, so Colin planned for it. It worked well. I hate violence. I don't even own a gun, which is pretty rare where I come from, so I wanted to try to deal with these things peacefully. A couple of thousand dollars is a small price to pay."

That might be true, but we had just announced to some very desperate people that we were prepared to pay for safe passage. I wondered how long it would take for news of that to get around.

* * *

The remainder of the day's journey went without incident, with one exception. We dropped off the boy the agreed distance away from his friends and he stood in our dust cloud and watched us go, his hand clutching the wad of dollar bills that had been the price of our safe conduct. Meanwhile we wanted to put as much distance between ourselves and the poachers as possible.

It was about an hour later that we found them. It was the smell that tipped us off before we saw them. As we pedalled around long bend in the road carrion eating birds lifted ponderously into the air. A long, lean figure scampered away and then turned to watch us from a safe distance. A hyena or a jackal I guessed, not sure what the difference was between them.

The great grey bulk of the dead elephants lay a little off the path of the road. We stopped, looking at the dead animals in dumbstruck silence. The smell of death hung in the air as flies buzzed around the bloody wreckage where the beast's tusks had once been.

"Males, I think." Charleese whispered. I noticed that tears were streaming down her cheeks. I couldn't blame her. The sight had brought a lump to my own throat.

"How do you know?"

"I read somewhere that adult males and females don't travel together. Judging by the size of the tusks we saw these would have to be males. Actually that's good. It means there won't be any orphans."

Good, I thought, was a relative term. I felt anger rise within me. It's one thing to be back in the UK carrying on an intellectual argument against the ivory trade and those who benefit from it, but it was another thing entirely to view the real cost that was levied against the magnificent animals that gave up their teeth to feed the demand.

It was tempting to try to bury the elephants but it would have been a major task and Colin dissuaded Charleese. "Besides," he added, "There might be others from the herd still around. If there are wounded amongst them they won't be well disposed towards humans."

We cycled onwards in sombre silence, the elation felt by our earlier escape sapped by the tragedy we had just seen. It was a convincing argument.

Our next stop was shortened to allow just enough time to gulp down some water before we were on our way again.

By the time that we arrived in Kigali, the small town that was our destination for the day, my backside felt like it was on fire. I longed to get out of my lycra cycling gear and into a tub of cold water but suspected that such a luxury would be hard to find.

We stopped at the small town's police station to report the presence of the poachers; Charleese insisted on that for the sake of the elephant population. Colin suspected it wouldn't result in any sort of investigation. This was a small town and the police would be unlikely to want to stir up trouble by chasing after poor Africans who would get paid a pittance for ivory worth thousands of pounds. That done we continued to the clinic on the outskirts of the town where we would set up camp and also film a short appeal.

While the clinic was supposed to treat any form of ailment it had effectively become a hospice for AIDS sufferers, most of whom were women. When I had told Charleese about that during one of our conference calls she had insisted on visiting, even though it took her off her main route and added to the length of the cycle ride.

We were greeted by one of the two African nurses that helped to run the clinic. The only other member of staff was Gunther Reiner, a young German doctor who was working for MOF. Realising that we had arrived, Gunther hurried to join us and took us on a guided tour of the facility. It didn't take long.

The clinic was housed in a low building made of mud bricks with a roof made of corrugated metal. Inside was a single long ward containing a dozen beds. All the beds were occupied by women suffering from various diseases all contracted during the terminal stage of AIDS. The only other rooms were a small treatment room, a toilet and shower facility and a poky office. A separate building housed the staff accommodation, which was no more luxuriously appointed.

"Do you like football?" Gunther asked somewhat unexpectedly, when he had finished the tour.

"Well, I watch the odd game on TV." I replied. Charleese had followed the nurses across to the staff accommodation to make use of their bathroom facilities.

"Come with me." Gunter urged. I followed him around the back of the clinic, where the sound of children's voices could be heard. As we turned the last corner I could see a full sized football pitch laid out. A dozen or so boys were chasing a ball up and down, shouting and squabbling the way boys do throughout the world.

"My pride and joy." Gunther explained. "I started with just the children of the women who came here. It helps to keep them occupied. Then some of the boys from the town came out and joined in. Now I have four full teams of boys and two of girls. They play each other each week."

"Who built the pitch?"

"That was me. In the evening I would come out here and clear the stones and flatten out the bumps. It isn't perfect, but it's the best pitch within two hundred miles."

"Do you coach the boys as well?"

"Of course. I was a very keen player when I was a student. I played for my university team."

"What will become of the teams when you go home?"

He smiled. "I'm not going home. I intend staying here, for a few years at least."

The reason for this soon became apparent. One of the nurses came round the corner and headed towards us. Gunther reached out as she got near and held her hand. "This is Chiku. We're engaged to be married."

"Wow." I could see that the two of them were very much in love. "Well, the German health service's loss is our gain."

"Chiku's sister died here. She's totally dedicated to the work we do and I'm totally dedicated to her. There's no way I could leave. Now, you and Charleese will join us for supper tonight? Chiku is a very good cook and I am a perfect kitchen hand."

I could hardly refuse, so I accepted for myself and promised to ask Charleese to come along.

I knew a little of Gunther's history. Soon after he qualified as a doctor he was due to enter the army to do his National Military Service. As a pacifist he was offered the chance to undertake voluntary work instead, for the same period and at the same salary. He agreed to come and work for MOF. That had been in 2010 and National Service in Germany had been ended in 2011. Gunther, however, decided to stay on and continue to work for us. The charity agreed, but of course they felt they could no longer pay him the pitiful rate he had been entitled to as a conscript. But Gunther being Gunther he waved away the offer of a pay rise, asking instead that his budget be increased by the same amount. Apart from a couple of short holidays Gunther had never returned to Germany.

Dinner wasn't a grand affair. We shared some of our tinned rations and Chiku supplemented them with fresh vegetables from the clinic's small garden. She turned a modest meal into a very passable feast. The conversation, as might be expected, centred around the work the clinic did and the constant need for more funding.

"With just another two thousand Euros a year I could treat half as many patients again. With the right drugs I could even help some of these women to live longer."

"So what's stopping MOF providing the drugs?" Charleese looked pointedly at me.

"It's the cost of them. We have to buy proprietary drugs from the big pharmaceutical companies. There are cheaper, unlicensed copies but if we were caught buying them we would get the arse sued off us. We can't afford to take that risk. It would jeopardise our work. Not just here, but across the whole of Africa."

"Is there anything I could do?"

"If you know any Presidents that could influence the American pharma companies it would help." Gunther chipped in.

"Persuade them to let you buy the drugs from unlicensed sources? I doubt I would have much luck there." Charleese gave a wry chuckle.

"No, to sell the drugs more cheaply in Africa." Gunther gave a tart response. "They don't have to charge the same as they do in Europe or the USA. They choose to."

"They're worried that the cheap drugs would be traded on the black market and would end up back in Europe or the USA." This argument, I knew, had been going on for years between the charities and the pharmaceutical companies. I had even written a paper on it while at University.

"So how do we break that deadlock?" Charleese asked, switching her spotlight gaze between myself and Gunther. I was just about to admit that I had no idea when a knock came at the door. Looking round I saw Colin framed in the doorway.

"Sorry to break up the party, but I've just been visited by the police. They've had a report of a bunch of ivory poachers heading in this direction. They're on foot at the moment but the police chief thinks they may be meeting up with another group who have transport. He suspects that they're not out hunting elephants this time."

Fifteen - The Bridge

We couldn't travel safely at night, but we advanced the timing of everything so we could set off at the first hint of daylight. The appeal for the charity was filmed under floodlights, and I suspect that the harsh lighting added to the drama of it. Charleese paced from bed to bed holding hands with the sick women and looking sadly into the camera to provide a short summary of each woman's story and telling the viewing public how a small amount of money could help to alleviate the suffering of the women and others like them.

As dawn broke Gunther, his fiancé and the other nurse stood on the veranda of the clinic waving their farewells and we cycled off into the dim early morning. A couple of the patients had even shuffled out to stand in the background, staring curiously as these strange westerners who chose to ride bicycles when there were perfectly good trucks that they could use.

Even the two support team trucks had been packed up early and were tagging along behind the command vehicle.

"Won't you be in danger?" I had asked Gunther just before we left.

He smiled grimly. "No more so than on any other day. Besides, one of the chief of police's cousins is one of our patients. I suspect that as soon as you have left he will decide to visit her, and will bring a couple of his constables with him when he does so. It will be enough."

I considered the possibility and realised that the poachers would be no more willing to upset the status quo with the police than the police would with them. Gunther and the two nurses would be safe enough for the moment.

As the daylight grew in strength I couldn't resist taking the occasional glance over my shoulder to try to see if we were being followed, but there was no sign of a dust cloud that would indicate a vehicle.

"It's not what's behind us that worries me." Colin commented when we took our first water break. "It's what's in front. Those poachers have had all night to circle around and get ahead of us. I'm thinking that if we put the bikes in the support trucks we could take a short cut." It was a pity that we hadn't had the support trucks the previous day, but that was then and this was now.

Colin unfolded a map and spread it across the bonnet of the command vehicle. "See how the road takes a long curve to get to the next stopping point. We could take the vehicles across country." He dragged his thumb nail across the map, making a straight groove that joined the two ends of the arc of the road. "They might see our dust, but they wouldn't be in a good position to give chase."

"What if they head straight down the road. With us going over rough ground they'd travel faster and be able to get ahead of us again. We can't cross that river." I tapped the blue line that cut across our path. "We have to return to the road to use the bridge. It's the perfect place to block the road."

"You've got good tactical sense. Were you ever a soldier?" Colin grinned at me before returning to pour over the map again.

"We'll just have to take that chance, I think. We can't totally out-think them. The bridge is close to the town and the town has an army barracks. I don't think they would want to get that near to us in case their presence is reported. If they've set up an ambush it will be somewhere around here, I would think." He indicated the centre of the arc, about half way between our current position and the river. "It's too far from Kigali for us to turn round and try to make a run for it and even if we do they would bank on being able to catch us before we got there. What do you say Charleese? It's your expedition."

"I pay you to look after us Colin. If you think we should go off road then I'm not going to overrule you."

Colin looked relieved. "OK then. Let's get the bikes on the trucks."

While the support team loaded the bikes Colin stood at the rear of the command truck using the satellite link to report our situation to the back-up team in Dodoma, Tanzania's capital city. They weren't in any position to help, but if anything went wrong they would know where to start looking. When he had finished, Saul and I man-handled the big cool box from its usual place on the front seat of the command vehicle and shoved it into the back. The girls drew lots and Bridie MacAleesh took the coveted front seat while Mary Tenant sat in the back on the floor of the command vehicle. That left Charleese, myself and Sandy Philips to hunker down with the film crew in the back of their pick-up truck.

The security team's vehicle took point and led the convoy off the dirt road and into the bush. With tall grass screening everything there was no way for the drivers to spot the rocks and holes that were hidden. Progress was slow and every lurch jarred my bones as I clung onto the side of the pick-up. The lack of seats in the back of the truck meant shots of pain went searing through my already tender buttocks and I wondered why I had volunteered to come along on this trip. Then I saw Charleese's piercing eyes staring out across the savannah, pretending to try to spot game. She turned and bestowed one of her most shining smiles on me. That was why I had volunteered, I told myself.

I looked back and was dismayed to see the size of the dust cloud we were sending up behind us. It hung in the still morning air pointing towards us like an accusing finger. The poachers would have to be blind not to see it.

Colin was guiding the convoy on a compass bearing so that we wouldn't get lost and he was keeping a pretty straight line, so far.

The two lines of crushed and bent grass we left behind us were as straight as an arrow. According to the map the furthest we would be from the road was about three kilometres; too far to see if anyone was waiting alongside the road, but close enough to see a dust trail if anyone was in a vehicle.

After about two hours of rattling through the bush the small convoy reached the top of a low hill and Colin brought us to a stop. He climbed onto the roof of one of the supply trucks and scanned the ground ahead of us, and also to the side where the road ran, hidden from us by the scrub and grass.

I stood up and screwed my eyes tight to shut out the glare of the early morning sun, adding additional shade by holding my hands across my brow. I could see no sign of a dust cloud that would indicate that the poachers were on the move. I heaved myself onto the top of the cab and stared south. In the extreme distance I thought I could just make out the angular shape of the framework of part of the bridge. It seemed to be a long way away.

Colin dropped to the ground and walked back to the pick-up truck.

"I can't make out much, I'm afraid." He informed Charleese. "They could be ahead of us, behind us, or maybe even given up and gone home."

"You could do a recce." I suggested.

Colin looked puzzled for a moment. "Oh, you mean a recon. No, not a good idea. If we split up now then we weaken both the recon party and this party. A weak recon party could be cut to pieces if it stumbled into an ambush. Likewise if the poachers attack this group then you wouldn't have enough guns to mount a defence. We can't take the risk of splitting up."

"So what do you want to do?" Charleese asked. She looked worried for the first time that day.

"There's not much we can do but keep going forward."

A thought struck me. "Would it help if there was someone else who could do the recce, I mean the recon, for you?"

"Of course, but who?" Colin looked sceptical.

"Give me a few minutes." I answered. I lowered myself to the ground and trotted to the command vehicle, where the satellite telephones were kept. I returned to the pick-up truck a few minutes later with a smug smile on my lips.

"I think we might have some help in a few minutes."

"What kind of help?" Colin asked.

"Just wait and see." I answered. I do like to tease. "Give it thirty minutes or so."

The group used the time to answer calls of nature, women into the grass on one side of the vehicles and men on the other. We also took on more water to offset the effects of the increasing daytime heat.

We heard it before we saw it; the unmistakeable thrum of helicopter rotors approaching from the south. We all strained our eyes for our first sighting.

At first there was nothing but a tiny dot, low above the trees. It appeared just above the place where I thought I had seen the bridge. Gradually it grew in size until its shape was quite recognizable. It roared low over our heads and circled back again. In the open doorways on either side game wardens sat with their legs hanging over the edge, each with a rifle held casually across his knees. The words painted on the side of the chopper were broken and unintelligible as a consequence of the open doorways, but had they been closed the logo and title of the game protection service would have been visible. Good old Jacob. He'd come through for us again.

"They're based next door to the military barracks." I yelled to Colin. "They'll act as scouts for us."

The helicopter, an antique Bell Iroquois, better known to generations of American soldiers as a Huey, settled onto the ground a few yards from us. Clouds of dust were blown about forcing us to cover our eyes, noses and mouths. Saul was despatched to talk to the pilot. The rotors were kept turning so Saul would have to shout to make himself heard.

He returned after a few minutes. "The pilot said to keep going on your present course as far as the river, then there's a track that will take you to the bridge. There's no sign of anyone waiting for you there." Saul informed Colin, raising his voice to shout above the continuous clatter of the helicopter blades.

Colin raised his thumb to the pilot to indicate that he understood the instructions. The roar of the chopper's engine increased and the helicopter lifted into the air and swept off in the direction of the road.

"How did you manage that?" Colin asked, admiration clear in his voice.

"I have friends who have friends. That's the same chopper as brought me up here a couple of days back. I'm surprised it took me so long to think of it."

"Well, you got there in the end. OK. We get going, and let the chopper flush out any trouble ahead of us. What happens if they find it?" Colin looked directly at me for an answer.

"I'm guessing they'll radio back to base and their boss will get the army to come out and give us an escort." I replied.

"Can we be sure of that?" He asked.

"My influence doesn't spread that far I'm afraid." I conceded. "But the army and the game department work closely together. I asked Jacob to tell them we were dealing with poachers rather than straightforward criminals, so I'm guessing they'll want to try to capture these men if they can."

"I wish you weren't doing so much guessing." Colin retorted.

I shrugged, but let the implied criticism slide. At least I'd come up with more than he had.

The convoy got moving again, maintaining its southward course to reach the river. It took a further hour to get there and we continued to hear the drone of the chopper at intervals as it swept up and down the road looking for the poachers.

The water of the river flowed deep and dark. Colin had been right. There was no way of crossing unless we could find a ford or used the bridge.

We turned left onto the track. It was no three lane highway, but it was better than the broken ground of the savannah. We increased our speed and the angular framework of the bridge appeared ahead of us.

Colin brought the convoy to a halt about 100 metres short of the bridge and climbed up onto the support truck again to scan the road on either side of the river. I didn't have binoculars so I used the zoom lens on my camera. The road was tarmacked where it approached the bridge, presumably to prevent it from being washed away in the rain. A single monsoon season could wash away enough soil to leave the bridge high and dry with its ends connecting to nothing but a couple of concrete foundation blocks and lots of fresh air. To prevent the road itself being washed away there were deep drainage ditches on either side which carried the rain water away and expelled it into the river.

I felt some dust catch in my throat so I placed the camera on the roof of the pick-up's cab and reached down for a bottle of water from my pack. As my head descended below the level of the cab the camera exploded in a shower of plastic and electronics, followed a microsecond later by the crack-bang of a gunshot.

Colin was quick to react. He shouted down to the driver of the supply truck to get the vehicle across the road in front of us. The lorry lurched forward spraying up dust and stones which would help to conceal us. As the driver passed the security team's vehicle he jerked his hands and the lorry broadsided to provide us with a 30 foot long defensive wall, though there was still an ominous three foot gap between the chassis and the track. The porters, driver and Colin all dived over the vehicles' sides and headed for cover, sliding down the dried mud of the river bank, where over the eons floods had dumped rocks of all sizes.

As Sandy Philips and the film crew leapt over the side of the pick-up truck nearest to the river I grabbed Charleese by the shoulder and we slid over the other side and shimmied underneath it. I saw the booted feet of the security detail as they headed out into the bush to try to find firing positions. Nearly everyone else headed straight for the river bank.

"Fuck, that was an expensive camera." Was all I could think of to say. I realised we'd become separated from everyone else, but I didn't fancy breaking cover once again to try to reach them. Besides, we were probably safe enough where we were for the time being.

"Lucky it wasn't your head. Curiosity nearly killed the cat. Where are they firing from?" Charleese sounded very calm considering that we had just been shot at, but that sort of thing takes people in different ways. If I hadn't focused my mind on my busted camera I would probably now be whimpering in terror.

I shuffled forward on my knees and elbows until I was between the front wheels of the pick-up and able to see past the security vehicle and under the supply truck towards the road. I felt Charleese slide up beside me. Peering ahead I spotted a couple of heads bobbing about in the drainage ditch on the nearest side of the road.

"There." I pointed.

"I see. Two, no, three of them."

"There'll be more close by. Maybe further along the ditch. Maybe hidden in the tall grass."

I knew that Colin and his pals were waiting somewhere to pick out targets. They wouldn't waste bullets just on the fleeting appearances of heads. They would wait for clear shots.

A figure appeared above the ditch's parapet and let off a long burst of fire before ducking down again. My bowels turned to water and I shrank down so close to the earth that an anorexic worm couldn't have wriggled beneath me. But I tried not to show the abject terror that I felt. If my fear transmitted itself to Charleese then she might panic and try to get out from beneath the pick-up truck, leaving herself exposed to the poacher's weapons. Bullets pinged off the side of the support truck and it sank down at one corner as a tyre was burst.

"Hope we've got a spare" Charleese breathed. For some reason I was finding myself getting a little bit turned on. I think it must have been the warm proximity of Charleese's body combining with my terror. I shifted my hips to try to find a more comfortable position.

The same man popped up again and let off another burst of fire, but this time most of it was directed into the sky as he was hit by a single bullet and fell backwards into the ditch. One of the security team had decided it was time to hit back.

"Oh my God." Charleese's hand went up to her mouth as she reacted with horror to the man's death. I placed my arm around her and pulled her towards me. She buried her face in my shoulder, blocking out the image.

I heard the thrum of the helicopter as it returned towards us, completing another leg of its patrol pattern. Shots were fired from the ditch, straight up towards the belly of the aircraft. I don't know if any hit but the pilot reacted quickly and it veered away and circled round behind a stand of trees on the far side of the river, disappearing from view.

"Are they OK?" Charleese whispered into my armpit.

"I think so. If they'd crashed we would have heard it." I hoped I was right.

My opinion was confirmed a few seconds later when the helicopter soared upwards once again and took a long arc to pass out of range of the poachers and along the road to the north. I wondered what the pilot's plan was. He clearly wasn't running away, because he was going in the wrong direction to be returning to his base.

"It's OK. You can let go of me now." Charleese pulled away from me slightly. After a moment she must have had second thoughts about it because she inched back closer to me again. "Thanks. I needed someone close right then." Me too, I said to myself.

"My pleasure." I replied out loud. Damn. Wrong thing to say. Too flippant.

Charleese gave me a curious look, but didn't respond.

They tried again. This time two heads appeared above the parapet, one firing towards the long grass to the left of the convoy while the other fired along the river bank, sending stone chips flying off the boulders. Between them two more poachers scrambled over the parapet and made a dash towards the trucks. One made about ten metres of ground before he was hit by a single round. The other managed slightly more, perhaps fifteen metres, before he too was struck down. The two in the ditch disappeared from view as they realised how perilous it was to have their heads visible.

"Oh my God." Charleese repeated, turning her face and pushing it into my lycra clad shoulder. "I know Colin's men have to do it, but I just so hate violence."

"I think we have something of a stalemate situation developing." I commented.

"How so?" She lifted her face to look at me.

"They're in the ditch but they can't get out to attack us without risking being hit by Colin's men, as we've just seen. On the other hand we only have four guns. They will know that from yesterday's encounter. So there's no hope of attacking them and driving them out; maybe making them run away."

"What does that mean?"

"I'm no tactician, but if they wait until dark they can keep us occupied in front with the occasional burst of gun fire, while some of them circle round behind us. They're poachers. They work mainly at night so they'll be well used to the dark. I didn't notice any night sights on the guns Colin and his chums are using. Even if they have them in their vehicle they can't get back to it to get them. All the poachers have to do is sit tight and wait till it gets dark. I wonder how long it will take them to work it out."

"That doesn't sound too promising." She pause for a moment before speaking again. "What do you think they want?"

"You and the other three women, plus anything they can steal. We paid for safe passage yesterday. It won't have taken them long to work out that you'd be worth a lot in ransom money. More than they'd make in a year of poaching ivory."

I was just about to explain how perilous it made our position when a shot rang out, this time from our right, the far side of the river.

"Oh no. They're over there. Even if we get across the bridge they'll be waiting for us." Charleese tried hard to keep any hint of panic out of her voice but she was clearly on the edge. I saw a tear spring to her eye before she cuffed it away angrily.

I wasn't so sure about this new development. The bullet hadn't hit anything close to us. No metal had clanged, no windscreen glass had shattered and I hadn't heard an impact of a bullet on the ground. I slid forward so that I could see past the right hand front wheel of the pick-up truck. There was another shot and I saw the puff of smoke from the muzzle of a weapon, concealed behind trees on the far bank of the river. I looked quickly to my left. Not quickly enough to see the bullet strike, that would have been humanly impossible, but the puff of dust close to the ditch showed me where the bullet had hit. Then I heard the crack of the shot as it caught up with the visual images.

"I think it's one of the Game Wardens from the helicopter." I explained. "The pilot must have dropped him behind the trees and he's worked his way forward until he has a line of sight along the drainage ditch. It will give the poachers something else to think about for a while, but he's too far away to do more than keep their heads down. That explains where the pilot's gone."

"How so?"

"I reckon he's gone to drop the other Game Warden along the road a bit, out of sight of the ambush. He'll work his way back until he can start taking shots from the far end of the ditch."

"Will they give up?"

"I doubt it. We still don't have enough guns to force them out and no means of communications to tell the two wardens what we intend doing. That makes it confusing for everyone and confusion causes accidents. I can't see Colin taking a risk like that. In addition we don't know how many of them there are, or where they're all hiding. This might only be a few of them, sent ahead to try to cut us off from the bridge. The gunfire may bring more of them here."

"And we daren't turn back."

"No. That would expose us and it'd be suicidal. For the same reason we can't make a break for the bridge either."

There were more shots from the far side of the river as the Game Warden picked out a fresh target, but no sign that he had hit anything. Colin used the distraction to dash up from his position and dive under the pick-up truck to join us, his rifle clattering against the underside of the vehicle as he rolled in.

"Your friends are being very helpful, Andy. Are you both OK?" Charleese told him that we were.

I told Colin what I thought the helicopter pilot had done and he nodded his agreement.

"What's the plan?" I asked, not confident that Colin had one.

"The helicopter pilot will have radioed back to his HQ when he got shot at. I think we just have to wait here for the cavalry to arrive."

"Can we be sure they will?"

"Nope, but we know that just a few klicks away there's a barracks full of soldiers so we can only hope that they're willing to help a few civilians in distress. Let's hope they're Country music fans, eh Charleese?"

Charleese gave a weak smile.

"And what if they're not?" I asked, a bit more tetchily than I had meant to be. My nerves were getting pretty shot.

"We wait till dark and then change position. We can't start the vehicles engines, but if we can move back along the track we can maybe tempt them out of the ditch. We've got everything we need to light the convoy up. Trip flares and that sort of thing. Once they're out of the ditch they'll be easy pickings for my lads."

"And what if they get the same idea and try to work round behind us?" I persisted.

"We'll be ready for them. Let's face it, we haven't got a lot of options, have we?"

With that gloomy news Colin slid to the edge of the pick-up, waited until the Game Warden took his next shot and sprinted back to the river bank. One poacher tried his luck, letting loose a burst of fire from his AK-47, but another shot from the Game Warden sent him back into the safety of the ditch once again.

Something caused one of the poachers to raise his head above the parapet of the ditch and look back along the road. He ducked back again as the Game Warden loosed off another shot at the same time as a second shot rang out from the side of the road where Colin's men were concealed. I strained to see what the poacher had been looking at, but it was my ears that gave me the first clue, the laboured growl of a diesel engine. There was a vehicle approaching the bridge along the road behind the trees.

"Fuck. It must be their truck with the rest of the poachers." I swore under my breath, but not quietly enough to prevent Charleese from hearing. She gave a small whimper of fear, quickly bitten back. "What the hell are they doing over there?"

"What can we do?" I could hear the tremor of near panic in Charleese's voice.

"I don't know. They'll almost certainly stop and take out that Game Warden in the trees, then I guess they'll spread along the far bank so they can shoot at Colin and the people hiding there. That will keep their heads down. Some of them can cross the bridge and work their way along the bank. The rest of the security team are stuck in the long grass on the other side. If they want to tackle this new bunch they'll have to move and if they do they'll show themselves and the ones in the ditch can fire at them."

"Looks like we're fucked then." I had never heard Charleese swear before, but I had to admit that right then, she had every reason to.

Sixteen - Decisive Intervention

The sound of the engine grew louder and I realised that there was more than one vehicle behind the trees. There was the heavy throaty roar of a big engine, and the higher pitched sound of others, probably travelling slowly in a low gear. They would be in sight within seconds.

The heavy blunt snout of an armoured vehicle crept forward towards the edge of the bridge. I assumed I was hallucinating and squeezed my eyes shut to remove the image, but when I opened them again it was still there. Several tons of armoured car sat at the far end of the bridge. I saw movement and the Game Warden ducked from cover to cover till he reached the rear of the vehicle, where he disappeared from view.

"It's an army convoy." I blurted, my brain finally unfreezing to tell me what I was looking at."

"Are you sure?" Charleese wasn't in as good a position as I was.

"I don't think ivory poachers are rich enough to afford armoured vehicles. Besides, the Game Warden is sure and that's good enough for me. He's gone to talk to them."

With that the vehicle's machine gun opened up with a burst of automatic fire. Bullets clattered and pinged off the metal superstructure of the bridge. It was clear even to me that the gunner couldn't bring his gun to bear on the poachers in the drainage ditch from that angle.

The vehicle reversed a few feet then swung sideways and lurched across the drainage ditch at the far end of the bridge, the vehicle's big wheels preventing it from falling into the gap. It came to a stop astride the ditch and the turret swung through ninety degrees. From where we lay I could hear the whine of the hydraulics above the puttering of the idling engine. Everything had gone quiet, the whole savannah waiting for what would happen next.

The machine gun fired again, an extended burst raking its way along the drainage ditch on our side of the bridge. Concrete chips flew up as the bullets ricocheted from the sides. There would have been carnage inside the ditch itself.

Silence fell once again as the gunner decided there could be no one left alive in the ditch. He was wrong.

A rifle was thrown over the parapet and a pair of hands appeared, followed tentatively by a head and then a body as one of the poachers, probably the last one still alive, attempted to surrender. With a start I recognised the youthful figure. It was the surly teenager who had sat in the Land Rover and ridden with us as we passed his comrades standing on the side of the road.

I turned as I heard booted feet thunder on the metalled surface of the bridge. A dozen soldiers were jogging across, their rifles held at the high port, relying on the armoured car's machine gun to provide cover if it might be needed. Reaching the far end the leader levelled his weapon and shouted at the boy.

The boy hurried to obey and climbed out of the ditch and threw himself face down onto the road. The two soldiers standing behind knelt on his back and secured his hands.

That done two more of the soldiers lowered themselves into the ditch and started to hand weapons up to their comrades standing above them.

Finally came the bodies, limp and dripping blood. Five of them in all, they were laid side by side next to the road. The two that had been shot earlier were gathered up and laid alongside of them.

Colin walked forward to join the soldiers. Rifles were hastily levelled but the Game Warden said a few words into the leader's ear and he gave an order. The rifles were lowered once again.

One by one we crawled out of our hiding places. I felt myself starting to tremble with relief as the shock of what we had witnessed, and had been a part of, made itself felt.

The support truck was eased to one side so that its tyre could be changed while the rest of our convoy started up again and we finished the short journey to the bridge, jolting along as fast as the track would allow.

As we arrived beside the drainage ditch the armoured car was just crossing the bridge. It travelled on for a further fifty yards and drew to a standstill astride the road. Its turret whined around so that its stubby machine gun was pointing away into the distance, the most likely direction of attack if one were to be made. Behind it two lorries followed. The lead one was empty, its troops having been the ones to run across the bridge. The second lorry still carried its cargo of twelve soldiers. I did a quick count. Twenty four soldiers in all, a full platoon fully armed and with webbing pouches stuffed with spare magazines of ammunition. Finally a camouflage painted four wheel drive Humvee pulled to a halt close to the bonnet of the truck holding Colin's small security force. The passenger side door opened and a smartly dressed officer climbed down.

Diplomatically leaving his weapon in the cab of his vehicle Colin stepped out to join the soldier. He gave Colin a polite if casual salute and they started talking. I strained my ears but the quiet murmur of our own vehicle's engine was enough to drown out any conversation. Charleese lowered herself over the side of the pick-up and walked up to join Colin and the officer.

This time the officer was far more punctilious. He snapped smartly to attention and gave a parade ground standard salute, before returning himself to a more relaxed pose. He smiled broadly and I felt relief coursing through me. A smile like that is never threatening. Whatever the soldiers' orders were I knew that they weren't going to harm us. I decided the meeting would benefit from my presence so I too climbed over the side of the pick-up truck, jumped across the ditch and walked up onto the road.

"Of course, officially I am just carrying out a training exercise." The officer was explaining in slightly accented English. "But if the helicopter were to identify any more ivory poachers then I would be duty bound to try to apprehend them."

"Well, Captain, we're pretty sure that there are more poachers in the area. We saw them yesterday and there were more than can be accounted for here and the police told us that they joined up with a larger party that went through Kigali last night." Colin explained.

"Thank you, Sir. That is also my understanding of the situation."

At that moment there was a shout from the officer's vehicle and we looked across to see the driver, half out of the cab and brandishing the handset of a radio.

"It seems I'm needed." The office excused himself and made his way back to the vehicle.

The four women gathered around the dead bodies, their hands to their mouths and tears streaming down their faces as they contemplated the loss of life that had happened. I was just glad I wasn't lying there with them. Sandy Philips turned and vomited into the ditch. Charleese bent to hold and comfort her.

"Well, that makes me feel a darn sight more comfortable." I could almost feel the tension oozing out of me. I had stopped shaking at last but could still taste the harsh coppery taste of adrenalin. Suddenly I felt tired and recognised that I was starting to come down off an adrenalin high.

By now the rest of the party, including the support team of cooks and porters, were gathered around the security vehicle, waiting for news. It wasn't long in coming. The Captain approached us once again, his pace a little more urgent.

"The helicopter pilot says that he has found the rest of the poachers. They're about three kilometres down the road. He missed them before because they had camouflaged their truck and were well concealed. But he spotted one going to get water and that gave the position away. They would have heard the shooting so they must have been waiting to hear from the ones here at the bridge before coming up to join them."

"So what will you do now?" Charleese asked.

"I will leave some men here to guard the bridge and will take the rest forward to see if we can take them by surprise. If they try to run the helicopter will keep them under surveillance. They won't get far. Now Madam," the Captain gave Charleese another broad smile, "I will radio back to the barracks to make sure you are given a safe place to set up your camp. I trust that you and your friends will join me for dinner this evening."

Charleese gratefully and gracefully accepted. A barracks suggested proper showers and toilets for the second night running. Luxury as far as the cyclists were concerned.

The Captain led most of his soldiers away with the armoured car following the marching men. One of those left behind took some tentative steps towards us. He proffered a tatty slip of paper and a ball point pen to Charleese. With a smile she signed her autograph and the soldier returned to his comrades with a triumphal smile on his face. A few moments later we heard the refrain from one of Charleese's best known songs being sung in Swahili.

We collapsed in giggles, not because of the singing but because we were relieved to still be alive.

Colin finally gathered us up, borrowed perforated steel bridging plates off one of the soldiers' lorries to allow us cross the drainage ditch and the small convoy set off for the safety of the barracks.

* * *

I was sitting on the edge of my camp bed readying myself for bed when Charleese found me. She scratched her finger nails against the canvas to attract my attention and I invited her in. I offered her the edge of my camp bed but she shook her head and sat cross legged on the floor.

"Thank you, for this afternoon I mean. I don't think I could have held it together if you hadn't remained so calm."

"Don't be fooled, I was bricking it." I could see that she didn't understand my colloquialism so hurried to explain. "I was as scared as you."

"Well you took care not to let me see it, and I'm grateful."

We sat in silence for a moment, neither of us really sure what to say. It was Charleese who finally took the initiative.

"Forgive me if I'm wrong, but I get the feeling you have a bit of a crush on me."

I could feel myself blushing and was glad of the dim light offered by my battery powered lantern.

"Is it that obvious?" I stammered.

"You've done well to hide it, but even the girls spotted it. They've teased me about it a bit."

"I'm sorry. I didn't mean anything by it. But, you know, you are a very attractive woman and a very nice one as well."

"That's sweet of you to say so." She paused, unsure of what to say next. "Look, Andy…"

"It's OK, Charleese. I understand. After tonight I may never see you again, except when you're on TV. There's no future for us, even if you felt the same way about me as I do about you."

"Thanks Andy. You seem to have taken a very pragmatic view."

I shrugged my shoulders. "Let's face it, you're the big country star and I'm just the errand boy for a charity."

"It's not like that Andy. You're a very sweet guy, and under different circumstances…." Her voice trailed off before she rallied once again. "I have a guy back in the states and we're pretty serious. Keep it to yourself, but we're getting married next year. We'd probably be married already if I hadn't taken it in to my head to do this bike ride."

"Congratulations." I muttered, all hope draining away.

"Thanks. Look, it's been great having you here with us, and like I said, this afternoon…"

I shook my head dismissively.

"Anyway, maybe you'd like to come to the wedding. Be my guest at my ranch. I owe you that much. Maybe there's a girl you could bring."

I could feel myself colouring again and I looked down at my hands, clasped in my lap.

"I thought so." Charleese's voice sounded triumphant. "See, it didn't take you long to get over me, did it?"

"It's not like that. We're just friends."

"Pretty good friends, if that blush is anything to go by. Your glowing enough to read a book by. And by next year I'm hoping you'll be *very* good friends. The ranch will be pretty full so you'll have to share a room."

I could feel my face burning. Charleese gave a chuckle and stood to leave. Bending over me she planted a kiss on my cheek and then turned to leave. I thought I had felt a touch of dampness as her check had brushed mine, but perhaps I had imagined it.

Seventeen - Stampede

I was towelling my hair dry when Jacob arrived to greet me. His broad grin was as welcome as a cold beer on a hot day.

"How was your trip?"

"Not bad, thanks. And thank you for all your help. If you hadn't been able to persuade the Game Warden service to come to help us I might not be here having this conversation right now."

"My cousin works for them. I helped him to find a good wife, so he owes me."

"You seem to have a lot of cousins."

He laughed. "In Africa everyone has cousins. It's how we do business. We have a saying. 'Me and my brother against my cousin, but me and my cousin against the world.' "

I let out a chuckle and went back to getting dressed.

"So how are things here? Are we ready for the rest of the shoots?" We still had two location shoots to complete and then I could go back to London and the safety and security of my little flat.

Jacob's face fell. "The film crew are ready, but it may be dangerous."

"Akeem?"

"Yes boss. We've seen a lot of his men hanging around near the hotel. They're watching everything we do."

"You think they'll try to kill someone?"

"No. That would serve no purpose for them. They want money. I think they'll kidnap someone."

"Could we just pay them to go away?"

Jacob shrugged. "You could try, but I don't think you could pay enough. They have worked out who you are and what you're doing here. When the next celebrity turns up they will take a photo and find out who they are. That will set the price and it won't be cheap."

The next celebrity was a big name. The biggest we could get for this year's show aside from Charleese Morgan. Dareen Debussy had had a dozen number one hits and four number one albums as well as a sell-out stadium tour across four continents. Not even Ded NuronZ could match her celebrity status. Her third appearance on the Cuddly Toy Day telethon was her bid for respectability and 'national treasure' status.

"She's arriving tonight." I stated flatly. Jacob said nothing but I could see the concern in his eyes. His boys would be no match for a concerted attack by Akeem's gang.

"I think we need Jan de Kok." I told him.

"Can you afford him?"

"Two days. That's all we need. Once Dareen's film is in the can and we get her on the flight home we can relax." I pulled my phone out of my pocket and dialled a number.

The negotiations were hard and long, but London understood the problem. We couldn't risk Dareen's safety and at the same time we needed her appeal to round off the telethon. Her participation alone was worth an estimated million pounds in donations. London agreed to the budget to pay for Jan de Kok's team.

I gave Jacob the go ahead and he hurried off to make the arrangements.

* * *

Dareen Debussy walked into the hotel foyer and every head turned to look at her. She had that effect on people. She was tall, nearly six feet in the flip flops she was wearing. It was her legs most people seemed to focus on. If you started at her ankles and worked your way up you felt as though you might get a crick in your neck before you reached the hem of the tight fitting shorts that she wore. Her long blonde her hung loose around her bare, suntanned shoulders, stopping just above the tube top she was wearing.

I leapt to my feet and hurried across to greet her. She gave me a full two hundred watt smile and shook my hand with a delicate grip. I felt my clumsy hand might crush hers, even though physically she was a giant by comparison to me.

"Where's your entourage?" I enquired. That had been the focus of our meeting with her agent. Ms. Debussy didn't go anywhere without a string of hangers-on and it had been a difficult negotiation to talk the old harridan down to just a hairdresser stroke make-up artist, plus the agent herself.

"I ran into Jesse James in Chinawhite last week and he told me that he managed quite well without anyone with him. If it's good enough for him then it's good enough for me."

"But your hair and make-up…."

"My hair looks fine like this, far more natural. And as for make-up, let's just let nature look after me. If I need a little bit of slap to hide the shine on my nose then I think I can manage that for myself."

"Well, OK, it was just that your agent…"

"I know. She thinks she's looking after me by surrounding me with a posse, but really she's just looking after herself. She means well, but I'm here to make an appeal, not the re-make of Gone With The Wind."

"Well, thank you. The charity really appreciates it when people think about the costs involved."

"Quite right. Now, what have you got lined up for me?"

I had already decided that I had to tell Dareen the risk she was taking just by being here. If I wanted her to co-operate with Jan de Kok and his boys then she had to understand that the danger was real. I led her over to one of the settees that adorned the foyer and made her comfortable.

"I'm afraid I have a little bit of bad news for you before we get onto the itinerary."

She cocked an eyebrow but didn't interrupt.

"I'm afraid that we've attracted a bit too much attention from the wrong sort of people. They may try something while you're here."

"What sort of something?"

"Er, possibly kidnap."

Her expression didn't change. She showed no sign of alarm.

"How big a risk is it?"

"You'll have seen the news coverage of Ded NuronZ when they were out here." She nodded her assent. "Well, since then the local criminals have worked out what they might have been worth. When they originally snatched them it was just a straight forward robbery. They would have killed the boys and dumped their bodies. But they're savvy enough to be able to use the internet and when the news got out back home and the newspapers and TV went wild with the story the local hoods realised they had missed a trick and ransom would have been far more profitable for them."

"And now you think I'm at risk because of that?"

"Yes. A well known gang leader has had his people hanging around the hotel keeping an eye on us. I'm guessing your photo has already been taken and is being compared with images on the internet. You're very attractive and very noticeable. It won't take them long to identify you."

"Well, the risk of kidnapping is always present, and I've toured in some places where there is a problem. My record company sent its security people to give me a briefing all about it. All the do's and don'ts. Are things any different here?"

"Not as far as the basics are concerned, but the problem we have is that we're going out into the bush and there's no police around out there if we run into trouble. I've hired a local security company to look after us. Well, to look after you mainly. They're good but even they might not be good enough."

"Are they the hard looking guys that met me at the airport?"

"Yes."

"I thought they didn't look like TV people. Too many muscles and not enough Armani. They looked professional."

"They are, but the risk is still there. The criminals are quite determined and they want to get back at us for snatching Ded NuronZ back from them."

"Snatching them? According to the press they cut themselves free, overpowered their guards and got away in a car they hotwired."

"They couldn't overpower a rice pudding. My local man Jacob found them for us and me an' him managed to get them out when the guards were otherwise engaged. But I guess their version makes for better press and to be honest I don't want the charity too closely involved."

"So these local criminals want to get their revenge? That's not good news for me."

"Look, if you don't feel safe then I fully understand if you don't want to do the filming on location. We can get you into a local clinic and do some filming there and then get you on the next flight back home."

"But that won't show how badly the charity needs the money, will it?"

"No, but your safety comes first."

"I appreciate that, but I came here to do a job and no local hoodies are going to stop me doing it."

"They're more than just local hoodies. The danger…"

"I grew up in Moss Side in the bad old days. If I can survive that I'll take my chances here. You get your security people to stay close and I'll do what they tell me to do. You do the rest and we'll all get out of here in one piece."

The big thing about that speech was that it didn't involve any bravado; just cold, hard, determination. I decided then and there that

I was a Dareen Debussy fan for life, no matter how bad I thought her songs were.

* * *

We left the hotel before dawn, exactly on schedule. There were no diva like displays of power from Dareen to show us how important she was by keeping the whole circus waiting for her to appear. She settled into the back of her SUV, pulled her script out of her bag and immersed herself in it. I took my place in my own vehicle, the ever patient Jacob at the wheel. The HUMV at the front of the convoy revved its engine and we were off.

The journey took us out along a tarmacked road for about a hundred kilometres before we branched off onto a well-worn dirt road. After a few minutes I glanced over my shoulder, but the dust cloud we were putting up didn't allow me to see if there was anyone following us. We had seen no signs of pursuit while we were on the main road, but that could just mean that anyone who was following had stayed back out of sight. Here on the dirt road they wouldn't be able to conceal themselves so easily.

"Do you think we were followed?" I asked Jacob. He shrugged his shoulders.

"Probably. But they don't have to stay with us all the way. This is the only road we can take to get back to the city. They can sit anywhere they like and wait for us to come back."

I realised that it would have made more sense to use helicopters, but I doubted that I would have been given the money to hire them as well as Jan De Kok's security team. Still, so long as no one upset the shoot there was hope that we would get back to the hotel without incident.

Despite Dareen's determination I had re-booked her onto the evening flight back to England. It meant that we had to finish all the filming in one day, hence the early start, but it put my mind at ease to know that she would be in the country for only half the time. I wondered if Akeem had access to the airline's booking information. If he knew about the change of plan it might force him to act today. But then, he had no idea how long Dareen was scheduled to be in the country for in the first place. If he checked with the hotel, bribed someone for information, he would find that Dareen was booked in for a second night. My brain started to hurt as I tried to work out all the possible permutations so I stopped thinking about that and thought about Charleese instead.

We had spoken on the phone the previous evening and she had told me that they had crossed into Zambia without further incident. Of course that meant nothing. In Africa a border is more of a notion than a fact and they were just as much at risk in Zambia as they had been here, but it made me feel better to know they were on the other side of the border.

The convoy ground to a halt and I climbed stiffly out of the SUV, stretching to ease the kinks out of my back. I was still suffering a little bit from my bike ride. The heat struck at me and sweat started to run down my spine before I had taken two steps. Another perfect day in Africa was about to begin.

* * *

The first film was in the can within the hour. Just as the filming schedule was drawing to a close the crew were starting to get themselves organised more efficiently, but I had been warned that it would be the case.

The cameras and lights were packed up and the convoy headed back down the road to the second location, which we had passed earlier in the day. The schoolchildren stood in front of the low schoolhouse waving us goodbye and I checked my notes for the second location, a small village much in need of a new sewage system. This one wasn't a cheat, we only did that when necessary. This time we would be shooting inside the houses of the villagers, showing how they try to keep things clean and tidy. Then we would film outside, to show the sewage running in the street from the broken pipes. "Sounds like my local swimming baths when I was growing up." Was all that Dareen had said when she had been told about it.

Dareen invited me to ride with her. "I'm not comfortable being alone. I grew up in a big family. Lots of noise all around me all the time." I was happy to accept. It's not often I get to spend time in the back of a car with a leggy and attractive pop star.

I knew that something was up even before the convoy had drawn to a halt. On the way out the villagers had stopped what they were doing to shout out and wave as we drove through, telling us to hurry back. There should have been the usual crowd of women and children waiting for us. The men always hung back, their dignity stronger than their curiosity, but the single dusty street was empty.

Jan De Kok's men stepped out of their vehicles and fanned out into a protective screen. I could see their eyes darting from side to side as they looked for signs of life. Jan himself walked along the line of cars until he reached ours. I climbed out so that we could talk face to face, carefully closing the car door behind me so that Dareen wouldn't get spooked by anything we might say.

"I don't like the look of this, Mr. Mirren. I'm African. I know how country folk behave and they don't hide away in their huts when strangers come to town."

"That was what I was thinking. Should I send Jacob to see if he can find someone to talk to?"

"That would be a good idea. I'll send one of my men with him, just to keep an eye on him."

I was grateful. I didn't want to risk Jacob's safety. I watched patiently as they moved from hut to hut, banging on the hut wall then sticking their heads inside, before moving to the next hut to try again. After a few minutes Jacob came back to report to me.

"No one here boss. No sign of anyone."

"What about the huts? Are they occupied?"

"Everything that should be inside is inside. A few bits of furniture, cooking pots, clothes; all as it should be. Just no people."

"What do you think?" I turned to Jan.

"I think we should move on, as quickly and quietly as possible. This isn't right and when something isn't right in Africa then it's because there's something really badly wrong." It took me a few seconds to translate his broad Afrikaans accent and work out what he meant but when I'd succeeded I had to admit he was right. The filming would have to be abandoned.

"OK. We head back to the city."

The words were hardly out of my mouth when I saw movement out of the corner of my eye. Jan must have seen it as well because I sensed his body stiffen.

"There's…." but I got no further.

"I know." He whispered into his lapel microphone and I saw his men draw their weapons.

"No guns." I started to protest.

"Mr. Mirren, you're paying me a lot of money to protect you. Please let me do my job my way." He whispered into his microphone again and hurried along the line of cars. "I suggest you stay and look after Miss Debussy." He shouted back towards me.

I scanned the nearest huts for signs of danger but could see nothing. The movement that had caught my eye hadn't been repeated. A hush had descended on the village, broken only by the low mumbling of the vehicle exhausts as they idled, keeping the air conditioning working and the vehicles' occupants cool.

I became aware of a growing noise. I'm not a country boy so it took me a few moments to recognise the lowing of cattle and then the shuffling of their hooves and the rattling of their horns clashing together as they moved towards us. The commotion was coming from the far side of the vehicles from where I stood, forcing me to turn and stand on tip toe to see over the top and identify what was happening. From between two huts I saw first one, then a second and then a crowd of pushing, shoving cows. These aren't the nice black and white beasts with dainty little horns that you see in English fields. These were humped necked with a wide spread of lethally sharp horns to use against would be predators. The volume of noise had increased until it was an almost constant bellowing of distressed animals.

The cattle moved steadily towards the cars, driven on from behind. I could now hear shouting above the sound that the animals were making. Men's voices. It was children, boys, who herded cattle in Africa, not men. This was no routine movement of animals from one side of the village to the other. I would have known that even if we hadn't already been warned by the abandonment of the village.

Jan De Kok knew this too and he sent a couple of his men to try to head the beasts off, to divert them before they got in between the cars, but the animals paid them no heed. One of the men fired a gun into the air but it only served to make the animals move more quickly in the same direction. The vehicle I was leaning on gave a lurch as the first cow brushed against it. There was a gap between it and the car in front and two cows tried to get in between them at the same time. There wasn't enough room and one cow turned and tried to push the other out of the way, using its horns as a weapon. Blood spurted from the animal's shoulder and started to trickle down. Other cows caught the scent and I could see the look of fear and panic growing in their eyes.

With a log jam in front of them the cows behind started to spread out to both sides, eddying around the small convoy as they sought a way forward. I could see at least thirty by now, possibly more. Dust rose around them and hid the ones behind. There could have been thirty, but equally there could have been three hundred.

A man, one of De Kok's security team, climbed up on top of our SUV. Cows milled around and if the man fell he would surely be trampled, but he was light on his feet and rode out the tilting and swaying of the vehicle as the cows pushed against it. From his elevated position he could obviously see something that the men on the ground couldn't and he was speaking frantically into his radio. I saw Jan speaking back just as frantically.

"Get into the car, Sir." The man on the roof commanded. I hurried to obey before I was trapped and trampled by the animals.

The cows were pushing the security screen further and further away from the vehicles they were trying to guard. Too late the plan became apparent. The guards were almost pressed against the sides of the huts, desperately trying to avoid being trampled underfoot. With a solid phalanx of cows between them and their charges they were helpless. I had managed to get the door to our vehicle open and squeezed inside just before the weight of a cow had slammed the door shut, almost trapping my fingers. Now I was starting to feel a little bit seasick as the vehicle bucked and heaved under the pressure of the massed bovine bodies.

On the side that the cows had approached from I could see that the forest of horns was starting to thin out, meaning that most of the heard had now passed. A few more moments of this and we would be safe, I felt sure. It was then that I heard the shot. Even above the roaring of the cows and the stamping of their feet the crack of it was quite clear.

It was just one, but it didn't need to be more. The security man on top of the SUV fell onto the back of one of the cows. It bucked in protest and his body slid off and was lost to view. I hoped he was already dead, because if he wasn't he was entering a world of pain from which there was no hope of escape.

"It's like the film Zulu." I shouted above the noise, hoping to calm Dareen.

She looked at me quizzically. "In the film Zulu a herd of cows get out of their corral and between the attacking warriors and the defending soldiers. It stops the warriors from pressing home their attack and a lot of them are killed by the cattle."

"Well, I certainly wish I'd seen that film." I quickly realised that I might not be helping matters.

Before I could share any more of my knowledge of African based cinema the driver's door swung open. Dareen's driver, Michael, put out his arms to fend off whoever was trying to get in. The intruder was hidden from my sight by the bulk of the driver's seat and the door post.

A shot banged loudly in the interior of the car. Michael's blood spattered across the windscreen in a fine mist. His body was grabbed and pulled out to be replaced by the assailant. I didn't need to be told he was one of Akeem's men. I was just about to force the door open on my side so that I could pull Dareen to safety when the door beside her jerked open and another figure forced his way in, brandishing a gun at the pair of us.

Dareen threw herself towards me in panic, her arms hugging my neck and her weight pinning me to my seat. Any hope of pulling myself, and her, to freedom was gone.

Gears clashed and the car jerked forward, swerving around the HUMV parked just in front. It didn't quite make it and there was a loud bang and a jolt of a collision. There was a high pitched screech of tortured metal then our SUV broke free. The car lurched as it bounced off the side of a panicked cow and then there was open road in front of the windscreen.

The man with the gun pressed it hard into my temple and I didn't have to speak Swahili to get the message.

"Stay calm, Dareen. We'll be OK." I patted her shoulder but kept her head turned into my chest so she couldn't see the angry look on the gunman's face. My clothing stifled her frightened sobs. I wish I could have let my own emotions show so freely, but just as with the ivory poachers, someone had to keep a semblance of calm if we were to avoid both of us falling apart.

The gunman stole a glance through the back window and his mouth opened in a gap toothed smile. I suspected that there was no pursuit, or at least none that offered a threat. The car bumped over something hard and I saw black top road appear in front of us. There was no hope that one of the HUMVs would catch us now. They were slow in comparison to our BMW SUV and by the time they extricated another of them, assuming the cows hadn't damaged them beyond drivability, it would already be too late to follow.

I leant back in my seat, patted Dareen's shoulder once again, and resigned myself to a period of captivity at the hands of Akeem. The driver turned to give me a satisfied smirk and I realised it was the giant from the brothel, the bruises Jacob had inflicted still visible on his face.

Oh shit, I thought.

Eighteen - Primitive Conditions

Akeem didn't believe in offering his guests any sort of home comforts. We were sat on the hard floor of a bare room. The walls were unpainted concrete, as was the floor, and the only light came from a window set high in the wall, just below the ceiling. I had boosted Dareen up to it and she had gloomily reported that there were bars set into the concrete on the outside.

The door looked flimsy. I knew I would be able to kick it apart easily enough, but that would serve no purpose. If they hadn't thought to put a guard outside the door there were other people in the building. We had heard their voices as they laughed and argued. The noise of the door being kicked would bring people running.

The room's sole furnishing was a stinking bucket which neither of us talked about but we had worked out a modus operandi for its use without causing too much embarrassment to each other.

So we just sat on the floor and immersed ourselves in our thoughts, making the occasional conversational gambit to keep each other's spirits up, but we weren't fooling each other. Unless Jan De Kok and his team could track us down there was no hope of rescue, so until a ransom was paid we were stuck here.

Dareen placed her faith in a police investigation finding us. Her record company would no doubt post a reward for information leading to her rescue. But I knew better. The police would meet brick walls of silence in the shanty towns and the reward wouldn't encourage anyone to come forward. After the reward was paid whoever claimed it would still have to live here, with Akeem's people looking for them. Their chances of survival wouldn't be high and any potential informants would know that.

I also didn't place much faith in our chances of survival if a ransom wasn't paid. Keeping us was a risk under those circumstances so we would be disposed of. I doubted if Dareen would be treated in a chivalrous manner before she died, though I didn't say anything to her about my fears.

The thought must have communicated itself though, because I frequently heard her break down in sobs, in the dark when she couldn't be seen or when she thought I was sleeping. Every guard that entered the room gave her a leer that spoke volumes. You could almost feel the amount of self-control they were having to exert. No doubt Akeem had threatened dire consequences for anyone that dared to damage the goods. Dareen could only hope that those threats continued to be sufficient.

The main problem was having nothing to do. With nothing to occupy our hands or our minds all there was left to do was talk or think. We did both, of course, but there was only one thing we really wanted to talk about; our prospects for release and we had pretty much exhausted that as a topic within our first few hours of captivity.

Somewhere, someone switched on a radio. As luck would have it, it was one of Dareen's songs. One of the up-beat pop tunes that are her hallmark. I wondered if it had been deliberate. Perhaps it wasn't a radio at all, perhaps it was a CD player.

"I sold two and half million copies of that worldwide." It was the first thing Dareen had said for several hours. "Another four million copies of the album it was on. The album was called Right Back Atcha. I didn't really like the title. The studio came up with it. Said it would help sales in the U.S."

"You're pretty big in the States, so I guess it worked." If it helped Dareen's mood I would talk about pig farming if that was what she wanted to talk about.

"Yeah. I was due to start a tour there today. Or maybe it's tomorrow. I'm not sure. I've lost all track of time."

"We've been here three days." I said, helpfully.

"In that case tomorrow. I was doing studio rehearsals right up until the day I flew out here, then I was going to go back and do more, then fly out to Chicago to start doing stage rehearsals for the first show."

"Where was the first show?"

"Steinbrenner Field. That's in Florida."

I hadn't known that but I didn't want to admit it. Dareen seemed to be in the mood to talk and I didn't want to do anything to discourage her.

"It's where the Tampa Yankees play." She added helpfully. "They're a baseball team."

"I'm more of a rugby man."

"You don't look big enough to play rugby."

She was right, of course, though she didn't actually have to point it out. "Not playing, just watching."

"Who do you support?"

"Northampton Saints."

"Where do they play? Sorry, silly question, Northampton obviously. What ground?"

"Not so obvious. London Welsh used to play in Oxford, London Irish play in Reading and London Wasps moved to Coventry last year, But you're right, Northampton Saints do play in Northampton. Franklins Gardens to be precise."

"The only Saints I know are St Helens."

"Same game, different code. They're Rugby League. My Saints are Union." I went on to tell her the differences between the two codes of rugby, though she didn't appear to be taking in what I was telling her. A different song came on the radio, it must have been a radio I now realised.

"I quite like this one." I commented. "We tried to get him to do the telethon but he was too busy."

"Lucky him. It could have been him sitting here instead of me. I could do with a drink right now."

"What would it be, if you could have what you want?"

"Back in the day, when I was still Dareen Gallagher, I drank Bacardi Breezers, but now it's only the best for Dareen Debussy. Cristal champagne and Grey Goose vodka. What about you?"

"Normally whatever throwing lager they have on the pumps, but if I could afford it then a nice malt whisky. Glenlivet for preference. A nice 18 year old special reserve perhaps. Mind you, I'd need a pay rise first.

Having tortured ourselves we fell into another period of silence.

"I'm putting on weight." Dareen said, after a short while. "It's all the stodgy food they're feeding us." I had to agree that the diet wasn't particularly balanced. The main item on the menu was some sort of porridge made from maize. The guard referred to it as pap. It was bland but edible.

"Maybe we should do some exercise. You know, sit-ups, press-ups, star jumps, that sort of thing."

She considered the idea for a long while. "If we're here for another day then yes, we'll do that."

I wasn't sure what difference a day would make, but in the end it did make a lot of difference.

* * *

We were just discussing what sort of exercises we might do when Akeem arrived. I hadn't seen him before and he cut quite an impressive figure. He was tall and slim with a muscular looking body. His aquiline nose and paler skin spoke of Arabic blood, but that was quite common in the coastal regions where the Arab slavers had once rampaged. He was dressed in a designer tee-shirt and jeans, gold hanging around his neck and wrists. A heavy, expensive looking watch bulged, but what caught my attention the most was the gun hanging loosely in one hand; not threatening as such, just obvious.

The expression on his face was quite neutral, but it was his eyes that bothered me. There was something about his eyes that said that this man was dangerous. No, more than that, he was barely under control. They flickered from side to side, as though he was expecting to be attacked at any moment and so he had to constantly look out for his attackers. I could see the effort of will it took for him to finally bring his gaze to rest on Dareen.

"They won't agree your ransom." He grunted at Dareen, not bothering with any form of introduction. He didn't need an introduction, the entourage at his back provided that for him. He also didn't tell us who 'they' were but I assumed it was Dareen's record company, or the insurance company that carried Dareen's policy.

"You speak to them and tell them. They don't pay I start cutting pieces off you and FedEx them to London." His accent was thick and a little difficult to decipher, but his attitude filled in the gaps. He pulled a phone from his pocket and thumbed the buttons to dial a number. He passed the phone to Dareen, whose eyes were wide with fear. She fumbled it and it almost fell to the floor before she could recover herself.

"Hello, hello." She stuttered as she raised the instrument to her ear. There was no response, so she looked at the phone's display in puzzlement.

"There's no signal." She offered the phone back. Akeem snatched it from her and examined the display for himself. He let out a curse in Swahili, well, English actually as most of the really bad swear words used in that language were borrowed.

"Outside." He used the gun to metaphorically propel her through the door. Dareen hurried to obey. The entourage trooped after

Akeem, keeping a respectful distance behind him. I was left standing in a corner, unimportant and forgotten.

With the door hanging open I couldn't resist a small peek. The corridor stood empty. I ventured out and tip-toed my way along to the end. Looking to the left I could see the crowd around Akeem standing in the bright sunlight. I blessed the thick concrete walls, with their steel rod reinforcements, that had blocked out the phone signal.

I turned back and hurried along the corridor in the other direction, hoping against hope that there was another exit. At the back of my mind a flicker of guilt began to grow as I realised I would be abandoning Dareen, but I couldn't see any alternative. If I could get help she would be free that day. If I stayed where I was then she might die, or at least have her body disfigured by Akeem as a way of making the insurers meet his demands. Besides, I might yet get caught myself and I had no illusions about my value to Akeem. I was a make-weight, like an extra sausage that a butcher might throw in to keep a customer happy.

I reached the other end of the corridor. There was second corridor running at right angles, doors giving access to rooms. But at the far end, the opposite side of the building to where Akeem and his men were gathered, I could see light. There was a door, or at least a large window. I set off towards it.

Half way along I froze. A shadow was thrown across the passage, indicating movement inside one of the open doors. I took a cautious peek around the edge of the door frame and into the room. There was a woman standing beside a pot, stirring something. The smell told me that it was the ubiquitous maize porridge that would be our lunch. It had also been our breakfast and our dinner the previous evening.

Her back was towards me so I risked stepping past the doorway and continued along the corridor, more cautious now that I knew the building wasn't entirely empty. At last I reached the source of the light, a door to the outside world. It opened onto a compound. Tufts of parched grass broke up the earth that had been packed tight by the passage of feet. Junk littered the area. I could make out what was left of a rusting car engine, the frame of a bicycle and an old wash tub, all with weeds sprouting around them and through them.

Around the compound ran a wall, about six feet high. It would be a stretch for me to reach the top and pull myself up. I'm not really a physical sort of person and the last time I had tried to do a pull-up I had abandoned the attempt before I got half way. I scanned the small area for an alternative.

My eyes lit up when I spotted a stack of abandoned drums; Vegetable oil cans, each once holding 25 litres of the liquid, according to the peeling labels. I scurried over and placed two cans side by side, then climbed up. They wobbled under me but didn't fall. I reached the top of the wall, my chin brushing the coping stones. With my elbows and upper arms I heaved myself upwards, my toes scrabbling for purchase.

I managed to get the toe of one, by now, very scuffed Marks and Spencer shoe onto the top of the wall and that allowed me to drag my body upwards. I felt the harsh concrete cutting into my palms, breaking the skin and knew that there would be a stinging pain to follow, but I did my best to blot it out. At last my whole body was lying along the top of the wall. From that position I could see other houses on either side, but to the rear there was nothing but open scrub land littered with bits of metal, wood and plastic, the detritus of the shanty town left where it had fallen or been blown.

I dropped to the ground, feeling a sharp twist in my ankle as I did so. I grunted with pain but managed to prevent myself crying out. Gingerly I tested it, gradually applying my body weight. Nothing broken, it seemed, but it would slow me down. I hobbled my way up to the top of a low ridge and then started to descend more steeply down the other side. Once my prison was fully screened by the ridge I stopped to allow time to get my bearings. To the right the scrub continued, unbroken, out into the savannah, but to the left there were more houses, well, make-shift huts really. In front there was another low rise, but from beyond it I could hear the sound of engines. Engines working at high revs, suggesting a road. I limped towards it. As the ground rose it brought me into view of the concrete building once again. I looked back and saw a head appear above the wall. It cried out in triumph as I was spotted and the head was followed by shoulders and a body as the man clambered over.

I stumbled on, my twisted ankle a searing point of agony. Fear gave me wings as I realised what might happen to me as a punishment for escaping. They didn't need me. I could be killed as a warning both to Dareen and her insurance company.

The ground began to fall away towards the road once again. I saw a car, an old and battered looking Ford, slow down and pull into the side of the road barely fifty yards from where I was. A man climbed out and sauntered around from the driver's side to the passenger side. There, shielded by the bulk of his car, he started to undo his fly, his intention pretty obvious.

He saw me approaching but he continued to do what he was doing. He was too far into the process to abandon it now. Besides, it was a common enough practice in a country where the concept of a public convenience is almost unknown. As I passed him he gave a smile and a small nod of greeting, but I ignored him. The sounds of pursuit were growing louder and this was no time for idle pleasantries.

I used the body of the car to lean on and take the weight off my ankle for a moment as I sidled around the back and along the side closest to the road. The driver's door was lying open, so I slid inside and let out a sigh of relief as the frayed upholstery of the driver's seat took the weight off of my ankle.

The engine was still running, bubbling away with a slightly irregular beat. A tiny bit of my mind wondered if one of the spark plugs wasn't firing properly.

The man realised what I was doing and called out a protest, hurrying to tuck himself away, but he was already too late. I pressed down the clutch, put the car into gear, lifted my left foot as I pressed down hard with my right, my ankle shrieking a painful protest as I did so. The car lurched forward and the driver's door slammed shut under its own weight.

I realised the handbrake must still be on so I fumbled with it, managing to get it free from its ratchet before the engine stalled. With that small amount of restraint eliminated the car flew forward like a horse that's been slapped on the rump. In the rear view mirror I saw the man run into the middle of the road, shouting ineffectually for me to stop.

He was joined by two more men, raising their arms to point guns at my fleeing vehicle. Smoke bloomed from the barrels but I didn't hear the sound of any bullets hitting home. In the mirror I saw their figures dwindling in size until they were mere dots and then the road curved and they were gone.

Nineteen - Night Raid

"Can you get them out?" I gave Jan De Kok a look which I hoped was appealing, but may just have made me look like a sick sheep.

"It's a police matter, Mr. Mirren." He'd said it half a dozen times already, but I had reminded him that it was his men providing security when Dareen Debussey and I had been snatched and that stung him, I could tell.

"Do you believe the police will try a rescue?"

"Probably not. They'll wait for the insurance company to pay a ransom."

"And then what will they do?"

"Raid the shanties, bust a few heads, and then things will return to normal."

"And Akeem will walk away with the ransom money."

"That's the way it works sometimes. The police don't want trouble in the shanties. The government doesn't want trouble in the shanties and the criminals don't want trouble in the shanties. It's people like Akeem that make sure that the police and the government don't get that trouble."

"It would be better if the shanties didn't exist." I observed.

"In a perfect world they wouldn't, Mr. Mirren, but this isn't a perfect world. This is Africa and you know perhaps better than I do what poverty is like in Africa, even in quite prosperous countries."

"And what are the chances of the ransom being paid?" I dragged us back onto the subject again before he could side track me any further.

"I've spoken to the negotiator that the insurance company have sent. He's an old pal of mine from back home. He says the demand is too high. It's more than the insurance policy covers and he's having trouble talking Akeem down to the level where the company will pay. Trouble is the internet is alive with rumours and some of those rumours are saying that the insurance is worth millions more than it actually is."

"Can no one explain that to Akeem?"

"That's what the negotiator is trying to do, but Akeem isn't listening. He's not used to this sort of crime. Oh, he's kidnapped people for ransom before, but they've been the children of local business people. He's had some idea of what sort of ransom he can ask for. This is new to him and he's getting his sums badly wrong. If the negotiator can keep him talking for long enough he's bound to reduce his demands, but at the moment....."

"And if the negotiator can't keep him talking? What if Akeem runs out of patience?"

Jan refused to meet my eyes or answer my question. That in itself gave me my answer.

"You have to do something, Jan. I saw this Akeem. His eyes told me that there's something not right in his head. He could snap at any moment."

"I have to admit I've heard stories about him. He once beat a man to death just because he spilt his drink. It didn't even splash on his clothes. I think in pretty much any other country he'd be locked up in a secure mental hospital."

"You see! A man like that could snap at any moment. We have to get Dareen out now, today, before he goes off the rails."

Jan stood and paced over to the window of my hotel room. He gazed out of the widow at the street below, giving himself time to think the matter through. Still staring out the window he spoke again. "She might have been moved by now. If I'd had a prisoner escape I'd move my other prisoners before the police traced the escape route back."

"And maybe she hasn't been moved. You need to send someone to take a look."

"As it happens I already have. I'm just waiting for him to report back to me."

That took me by surprise as Jan had argued strongly against any sort of rescue attempt. I said as much.

"It does no harm to do a reconnaissance, Mr. Mirren. Things can change fast and it's useful to be ready." At that his phone rang and he turned back to face the window again as he took the call. It was very one sided. Plenty of talk coming down the line to Jan, but only grunts and the occasional yes or no going back the other way. He finished the call with "OK, get back here and you can brief us all together."

Turning back to face me he walked to the centre of the room so that I no longer had to shield my eyes from the glare or view him in silhouette. "Well, Mr. Mirren, it appears that Miss Debussey is still in the building where you left her. There are guards crawling all over it and the only reason Akeem would use so much manpower would be to guard something very precious. As much as anything that rules out an assault by the police. They don't tangle with heavily armed criminals if they can help it."

* * *

We had borrowed one of the hotel's meeting rooms to hold the briefing. Jan De Kok's team were there, as was Jacob and his boys. The meeting started with Jan's scout, Mosi, telling us what he had seen.

"There are guards on the outside of the compound. I could see three of them. While I watched I saw the police arrive in a car, two officers only. They got out and they spoke to the guards. The guards were armed but they didn't threaten the police and the police didn't seem bothered by the guns. They talked and I heard laughing."

"Do you think that the police know that Dareen is inside?"

"I can't answer that, but I don't think they were there by accident. I think they have been given a job and were not too bothered if the job was done or not."

"I think we can assume that Akeem is protected. Maybe not by the officer in charge of this case, but that doesn't mean that he will intervene either. They won't act if they think a ransom will be paid." Jan put the scene in context for my benefit. "Mosi, please continue the brief."

Mosi had drawn a plan of the building onto a flip chart. The building was made up of two wings arranged at right angles to each other, with the perimeter wall, the one I had climbed over, joining the ends of the two wings to complete a square footprint. The front door was on the left of the horizontal wing as it was drawn on the chart, the one that faced onto the shanty town, and the rear door was at the top of the vertical wing.

"It was built as a clinic but for some reason it was never used. For a while it was locked up and abandoned but one day Akeem broke in and claimed it as his own. Now it is used to house some of his men and their wives, mainly low level gang members. As well as the three guards at the front I think I saw guards in the compound at the back as well."

I got up and took the marker pen from Mosi and drew the interior layout, as best as I could remember it. The interior corridor running along the middle of the horizontal wing, parallel to the front wall and the other corridor running down the middle of the side wing to get to the rear door. I then added in the rooms that I remembered passing, finally placing an X where I thought Dareen would be; the centre room on the rear side of the corridor of the horizontal wing.

"Thanks for that Mosi. Thank you, Mr. Mirren. The fact that extra guards have been put in place suggests Akeem is concerned that someone might attempt a rescue, and it's not the police he is worried about. So, any suggestions how we get past the guards?" Jan's eyes scanned the room, inviting us to contribute.

"Over the back wall and overpower the guards." One of Jan's men suggested.

"Nay man," another replied. "Too much risk of the alarm being raised before we got in."

"OK, then take out the guards at the front and walk in the front door." He tried again.

"What with?" Asked Jan. "We can't make any noise. We can't be sure how many more are inside."

"Drug their food?"

"Only if we can get into their kitchen and that's on the inside, but I think we're on the right lines here. Anyone else?"

"Send them a present. A bottle of something nice, but spiked. They take a drink, fall asleep and we walk in." I couldn't believe it was my voice that was speaking.

"I can see I'm going to have to keep my eye on you Mr. Mirren. Mosi, do we have anything that could do that?"

"I have friends at the hospital. I'm sure I could get hold of something."

"OK," said De Kok, "so we've got two or three people inside. There may be a guard outside the door where the hostage is being held." I noticed he didn't refer to her as Dareen or Miss Debussey. Was it a deliberate omission to dehumanise her in case things went wrong? I hoped not.

"Silencers on our guns." Mosi suggested.

"If we kill anyone the police would be justified in charging us with murder. This isn't the wild west. We can only use guns in self-defence.

"OK then, tranquilizer darts."

"Now that is a good idea. But they have to be quick acting."

"I know someone in the game department." Jacob volunteered. "They use dart guns all the time to capture wild animals. Something that will bring down a rhino in a few minutes would bring down a man in seconds, I'm sure."

"OK, Jacob. I'll leave that with you. I think we have the basis for a plan, gentlemen."

"Can't we use the darts on the guards outside as well?" one of the other men asked.

"No. We'd have to fire three darts at once to make sure that none of them managed to raise the alarm. We'd also have to be very accurate with the shots, in the dark and at an unknown range. It's all too risky. We'll find another way to get the drugs into them. I think I have an idea about how to do that. OK, gentlemen, let's get busy."

"I'm coming with you." I was surprised to hear myself say it and Jan was equally surprised.

"Do you think that's a good idea?"

"I have to. I ran out on Dareen. I have to be there when that door opens."

"You can't beat yourself up over that, Mr. Mirren. You did what you had to do. If you hadn't got out we wouldn't know where they were holding her and we wouldn't be here discussing this now."

"I know, but that might not be the way she sees it. I just need her to know that I didn't run out on her just to save my own skin."

Jan shrugged. It wasn't his concern if I wanted to walk back into the lion's den. "OK, Mr. Mirren, but if you get caught I won't be risking any of my men to go back and get you. You understand?"

"Yes. I understand. If it makes you feel happier I'll stick like glue to whoever you tell me to."

He turned to address Jacob. "Now, I want my men to be free to cover the entry and the escape, so can your boys do the driving?"

"Sure Mr. De Kok. They'll do more if you want."

"We'll keep it to driving for the moment, but make sure they can take care of themselves, if you get my meaning."

Jacob beamed a smile and I turned a diplomatic blind eye to what was being suggested.

* * *

The night was dark and a light drizzle was falling. In the small hours of the morning there was no one moving in that part of the shanty town, though we could hear music playing some distance away. Probably a shebeen still open for the night owls and those with nowhere else to go.

The HUMVs had been parked a distance away from the old clinic and we had approached on foot so as not to raise the alarm. Along the way three of Jan's men had peeled off to go around the back of the old clinic and provide cover, just in case we needed to get out that way. They would keep the guards in the rear compound busy while we climbed the wall.

Now we stood in the deepest shadow we could find, with our backs pressed against the side wall of a nearby house waiting for the next bit of the plan to be executed.

Lights swept across the building as a vehicle approached. A taxi bumped across the uneven ground to pull up next to the guards. They immediately straightened, hands hovering over the butts of their hand guns like three cowboys getting ready for a gun fight. The taxi's rear door opened and a girl staggered out. She was dressed in the skimpiest of skirts, tottering on high heels. Even from the distance from which we were observing it was clear that she was drunk.

She approached the guards, brandishing a bottle. They argued with her and she argued back, gesticulating towards the inside of the building. Whatever she was saying the three men were having none of it and they adamantly refused to admit her.

"She's good, isn't she?" Jan De Kok whispered into my ear. "She's our receptionist. She's been nagging the arse off me for years to let her do something in the field."

I wanted to tell him that he was letting her take a hell of a risk, but he probably knew that already. She was a volunteer and no doubt the risks had been explained to her. She was playing the part of a drunken prostitute to a tee. She would have fooled me and I was in on the plan. The men didn't seem at all surprised to see her. They were just doing what they had been told and refusing to admit her to whoever inside the building was supposed to have called her up.

The argument drew to a close and the woman gave in. She handed the bottle over with instructions for its delivery, then staggered back to the taxi. The door slammed shut and the car drew away, the driver, another of Jan's men, apparently hurrying to get out of a dangerous part of town.

The three guards gathered into a huddle and examined the bottle. I knew it was locally made whisky, the best that could be bought without having to pay for the genuine, imported article. Imported whisky was too expensive, well beyond the purse of a prostitute and would have made the guards suspicious.

There were a few moments of discussion but Jan knew his targets. The drink was too much of a temptation to be resisted. The man holding the bottle twisted the cap off and raised it to his lips, taking an experimental sip.

He obviously liked what he tasted because he tilted the bottle again, this time taking in more of the fiery spirit. Satisfied, he passed the bottle to the next man and for the next twenty minutes or so the bottle continued its small circuit until it was finally tilted to the vertical to extract the very last drop. Even without the drugs each man had drunk enough to send him to sleep. The drugs would just make sure that they didn't wake up any time soon.

One by one they felt the drink and drugs combination begin to take affect and they staggered to the wall of the building, leant on it then slid down into a sitting position. Their heads drooped. One slid sideways to lie prone on the damp ground.

Jan sent one of his men over to check on the sleeping figures. Pointing his gun at them he gave each of them a sharp tap with his foot, then a second, before signalling to tell us that all was safe. With a rush we crossed the open ground between the house and the old clinic and gathered in the shadows at the side of the building. The pain from my swollen ankle slowed me down, but I was just about able to keep up.

The man who had gone ahead tried the door. A bright rectangle of light shone out as he swung it open, then beckoned us forward.

Jan left two men to stand guard, just in case anyone approached or the drugged men started to stir, then led myself and two more of his men inside. After the darkness of the night the bright interior of the corridor hurt my eyes and I had to shield them while they adjusted to the fierce glare of the overhead fluorescent strips. Jan took a cautious look around the corner and along the corridor. He pulled his head quickly back and held up a single finger. One guard outside the door of Dareen's prison.

A bulky air pistol was passed to him. It was far bigger than any such weapon I had ever seen, but it had to be to contain the tranquilizer dart. Jan stepped out into the corridor, raised the weapon and fired, all in a single fluid movement.

The guard let out a small shout of pain as the dart struck him in the chest, piercing the thin material of his brightly coloured shirt. He turned towards us, surprise growing on his face at seeing an intruder. His hand went to the waistband of his trousers and he felt under the bottom of his shirt for the butt of his gun, but already his movements were uncoordinated. He staggered forward for a couple of steps then went down onto one knee. He tried again to move but the tranquiliser drug was now rushing through his bloodstream and into his brain. He managed to get half way to his feet again then just collapsed in a heap.

The two men behind me moved forward and walked carefully and quietly towards the now recumbent figure, their handguns held ready for action. One gave the guard a prod with his foot then the pair of them dragged him to one side so that he wasn't blocking access to the door.

"OK, Mr. Mirren, You're on." Jan whispered in my ear. It was the first word to be uttered since we had left the relative safety of the shadows of the house where we had hidden, waiting for the woman in the taxi to arrive and perform her pantomime. I stepped forward. The slapping of the soles of my shoes on the bare concrete sounded deafening to my ears, but it was no louder than the footsteps of any of the others.

I reached the door and tried the handle. It didn't turn. I tried harder and this time it moved a fraction. I was being too careful, scared to make a noise in case it raised the alarm. I gave the handle a firm downward push and the door opened a fraction as the latch came free of the striking plate. Taking a deep breath I eased the door open to its full extent and stepped across the threshold.

Sparks exploded painfully in my brain and I was knocked backwards against the doorframe as something clanged against the side of my head. I smelt a foetid odour and my befuddled senses worked out that I had been hit by the slop bucket, the only weapon that the room held. A body pushed hard against me and squeezed into the corridor.

I turned, holding my aching head, just in time to see Jan grab hold of my assailant and force his hand across her mouth.

I put a finger to my lips to urge Dareen to stay silent and not to fight. In her panic she didn't seem to be grasping what was going on. How long had she stood there in the dark, the bucket held in her hand, waiting for the door to open? How frightened had she been when she had swung the bucket at my head? No wonder she was confused.

Her eyes adjusted to the light and she tensed and snarled as she recognised me and saw the faces of the grinning security men. I was taken aback at her reaction before I realised that she must have thought I had been recaptured and was being returned to the prison cell. I leant forward so that I could whisper into her ear. Not that making a noise would make any difference. The clanging of the bucket against my head must have woken someone else by now.

"It's OK. We're here to get you out." I hissed at her. She relaxed and turned to see who was holding her and was relieved to see Jan's face looking back.

I could hear voices coming from around the corner. Sleepy voices, not alarmed as far as I could tell, just curious. Jan pointed at the guard still sleeping on the floor and his two team members gathered him up and bundled him into the now empty cell, pulling the door closed. Once that was done we were able to make our way quickly along the corridor and out of the front door to freedom.

Twenty - Responsibility And Accountability

Fortunately for me I arrived back in Britain at the start of the Easter holiday weekend, which gave me time to gather my thoughts and prepare myself.

I could hardly argue that my trip to Africa had been a resounding success. There had been two kidnappings of three very high profile pop stars as well as a gun battle with ivory poachers which we were lucky to walk away from with our lives. I could hardly hope that MOF was going to vote me a civic reception and reward me with a pound from the poor box. The terse e-mail summoning me to Greg Jones' presence first thing on Tuesday morning was the last one I had read before boarding my flight home.

All that was aside from the diplomatic repercussions of carrying out an armed paramilitary raid on a government building. It turned out that the government still owned the disused clinic and had turned a blind eye to Akeem squatting in it. The police's embarrassment at not being 'able' to locate Akeem's hideout was buried under a mountain of bluster and protest over the actions for which I was held accountable. I was lucky not to have been thrown into prison (a proper police one) or escorted onto the plane in handcuffs.

We were fortunate that Akeem had decided to cut his losses. With Jan and his men stalking around the corridors of the hotel and the police showing a highly, if somewhat belated, visible presence on the outside Akeem was discouraged from trying to recover his prize. In the last twelve hours or so hours before we left we saw no more of him or his men

The only people who appeared pleased with me were the insurance company, who agreed to foot the bill for Jan and his team in recognition of the fact that he had saved them several millions of pounds.

After clearing away several weeks' worth of junk mail around the door of my small flat in Lewisham, turning on the heating and ventilating the room to get rid of the stale air, I settled myself down in front of my laptop and started writing my report. I hadn't been told to do so, but I had no doubt that someone, at some time, would ask for a written account of what had happened.

The first kidnaping I could lay at the door of Ded NuronZ and their megalomaniac PR woman. I had acted promptly to recover the situation without involving the police, which meant there would be no adverse publicity for the charity. All the publicity that followed could be laid squarely at the door of Vicky Mitchell.

The incident with the ivory poachers I could also dismiss. That whole expedition had been organised by Charleese Morgan, with only a little bit of input from me, and no doubt what happened would still have happened even if I hadn't even been there. In fact my presence had been a material factor in us all getting out alive. I was an innocent bystander and was placed in as much danger as everyone else. It was an unfortunate incident but unforeseeable in any real sense.

The last incident, the kidnapping of Dareen Debussy, however, was all down to me. I had known there was a danger and I should have cancelled the filming and got her out of the country before leaving myself and taking the producer, Lionel, with me. OK, London didn't offer any advice on the subject, but as the man on the ground I would be held responsible for what had happened.

I described the events in as plain terms as I could, not seeking to excuse myself. When I read the report back I had to conclude that I would fire me for negligence, so I wouldn't be surprised if that was what Greg Jones did. I had one ace up my sleeve to play if I chose to do so. I closed the report file and opened up my dossier on Metro TV.

It wasn't complete, not by a long chalk, but there was enough there to make Greg sit up and take notice. Very little of it would stand up in court. The only cast iron case I had was against the set designer, Gary Larkin. Unless he spilt the beans on the rest of the fiddles the big fish would escape the net and I didn't want that to happen.

Would it be enough to save my job?

Come to that, did I really want to save my job? I had aged ten years during the few weeks I had spent in Africa. I had been shot at and had spent time imprisoned as a hostage, not being sure if I would be released. I had been in the middle of a cattle stampede, and I had dealt with both Vicky Mitchell and Cherry Versace-Laboutin, managing to walk away without throttling either of them. Maybe I would be better off just resigning.

But I loved my job, really. I was making a difference to the lives of millions of people just by doing it. Despite Igor Kasnisky and Helen Spencer's frauds and fiddles the telethon would raise a huge amount of money and most of it would be spent on improving the lives of people who otherwise wouldn't get any help, or at least not as much help as they needed. That was important and I wasn't going to throw that away.

I carefully copied the Metro investigation files onto a memory stick and slipped it into a padded envelope. Rooting through the kitchen drawer I came up with more than enough stamps to cover the postage. I carefully wrote my mother's address onto the envelope and scribbled a note asking her to look after the memory stick and not to give it to anyone else. I decided against adding a melodramatic request to hand the stick to the police if anything suspicious happened to me. My mother wasn't stupid. If anything suspicious happened to me she would know that the memory stick was important, otherwise I wouldn't have bothered sending it to her.

The next time I went home I could look forward to an interrogation as skilled as anything that the KGB would be able to offer.

When I got back from posting the small package, the phone was ringing. My heart skipped a beat when I recognised Charleese Morgan's voice.

"Hi there Andy. How's it going over there?" Her Tennessee drawl sent shivers down my spine. I clearly wasn't yet over my crush on her.

"Er, OK I guess. Things have been pretty hectic."

"I know. I've seen the internet. Trouble just seems to follow y'all round like an old hound dog, don't it."

I chuckled at her fake hillbilly phrasing which I knew she had put on just for my benefit. "Well, I do seem to get more than my fair share."

"Is there anything I can do to help?"

"Well, a call to my boss to tell him not to sack me might help."

"Consider it done." She laughed.

"How are things your end?"

"Oh, pretty good. We've got barely two hundred miles to go now. Four more days if things go to plan."

"Any more trouble with ivory poachers or the like?"

"Funny you should say that. It seems that the army have been conducting an awful lot of exercises recently, both before we crossed the border and since. Hardly a day has gone by when we haven't seen some sort of military activity. Last night we got a visit from the local Zambian military commander, complete with a field kitchen to cook us a grand dinner."

"Sounds like you're getting the full VIP treatment."

"Yeah. I'd be happier if they'd spend the money on their own people, but like you told me when you were out here, you gotta work with these people or they'll end up working against you."

"That's lesson number one when it comes to aid work in Africa."

We chatted for a while longer, catching up with what we had both been through, then Charleese reminded me that she still had a lot of hard cycling to do so I had to let her end the call.

On the spur of the moment I rang Cassie and invited her out. She wasn't free until Sunday so I promised her dinner and a movie if she spent it with me. Laughing, she told me I was a tough negotiator but she agreed to the proposal.

As I hung up the phone I was feeling in a slightly more up-beat mood. Perhaps Easter wouldn't be too bad. After all, there were worse ways to spend it; Just ask Jesus.

Twenty One - Low Profile

The street outside the MOF offices was crammed with reporters and TV news crews. I had been a bit naïve to suppose that I might have arrived back in Britain entirely unnoticed. We had managed to avoid most of the circus in Africa itself as we were in such a remote area, but back on home territory the sharks were circling, scenting blood in the water.

I ducked back round a corner before being spotted, grateful that no one had yet found out my home address. But I knew the area better than they did and it was a small matter to navigate a couple of back streets and enter the building through a fire escape door used by the smokers for their fag breaks. I was under no illusions, however. Someone inside was bound to Tweet news of my arrival and by the time I left my escape route would be covered. But that could wait for a couple of hours.

I trudged up the stairs to Greg's office. There was a perfectly good lift but I was in no hurry to get there. Besides, I was early for my appointment. There seemed to be no point in sitting on a hard backed chair outside his office door like some errant schoolboy waiting for the Head Teacher to admit me.

I entered his office in response to his bidding. He was engrossed in something on the screen of his PC and I suspected it was the copy of my report, e-mailed before I left home.

"Welcome home, Andy. You managed to avoid the scrum outside, I see."

He didn't offer to shake my hand, something he always did when I visited the building. I explained how I had entered undetected and he offered me a seat, though there was no offer of coffee.

"This has caused a lot of bad publicity, Andy."

"I always thought there was no such things as bad publicity." I had promised myself I wouldn't be defensive.

"Don't be flippant. This is a very serious matter. Can you give me one reason why I shouldn't dismiss you on the spot?"

"How about the fact that the charity is being ripped off for hundreds of thousands of pounds by staff at Metro TV and I have the evidence. If you sack me that evidence goes straight into the hands of the first of those reporters outside the front door to catch my attention."

It was nice to see that I had caught him off guard. Stunned didn't seem to be an adequate word to describe him. His jaw dropped, though he hurriedly closed his mouth again. He was at a loss as to what to say, but I wasn't.

"Igor Kasnisky and his girlfriend, Helen Spencer, have been systematically ripping off the charity by putting business through their own companies which often results in this charity being charged twice for the same work." I paused and took a breath before continuing. "We pay once to pay staff at Metro TV and again to pay for the company that does the actual work. The companies are owned by nominees, but there is circumstantial evidence that Kasnisky and Spencer are linked to those companies. Give me a few more weeks and I'll provide the tangible evidence of those links." I wasn't actually sure I could do that, but of course Greg wouldn't know that either. "Sack me now and you'll never get it. Instead you'll get a scandal which will damage the fundraising programme for years; perhaps permanently. What happened in Africa will be nothing by comparison."

"You can't threaten me, Andy. That in itself will get you sacked."

"I'm not threatening anyone, least of all you. I'm stating facts. You can accept them or ignore them. It's entirely up to you."

He was off balance and struggling to regain his equilibrium. I pressed home my advantage.

"We both know you're not going to sack me, Greg. It's too close to Cuddly Toy Day and you haven't got anyone to take over my job. If you had I probably wouldn't have been offered the job in the first place. You might sack me afterwards, but you aren't going to do it today. But if you let me finish my investigation you'll end up saving the charity from a scandal that could destroy it."

"Does the senior management at Metro know about this?"

"Helen Spencer is senior management, but if you mean the Board or the Chief Executive then no, at least I don't think so. It seems to be a personal scam. They've seen an opportunity and taken it. The Cuddly Toy Day team are pretty much autonomous within the company because we pay all the bills. No one asks too many questions so long as the telethon keeps generating profits for Metro."

I noticed that all talk of dismissal, or even disciplinary action, had been forgotten.

"Tell me how this scam works."

So I did, and for the next hour I took him through my dossier, showing him the web of companies and billing arrangements that all led back to a handful of people who I was sure were the nominee directors of companies actually owned by Kasnisky and Spencer.

"I need a copy of this?"

"Of course. It won't be much use, not yet. There's nothing there that would stand up in court."

"This can never go to court. The damage this would do to us, to our fundraising. No it's unthinkable."

Much as I hated to admit it, Greg was right. Kasnisky and Spencer would go free at the end of this. "So what will you do?"

"Well, I agree with you, we need the smoking gun. The proof that Kasnisky and Spencer are directly profiting from this. Then I'll take it to Metro. They can deal with the pair of them."

"This is actually a great opportunity for the charity." I offered my opinion.

"How do you mean?"

"It's too late to change production companies for this year's Cuddly Toy Day, so we have to carry on as if nothing is happening. But that doesn't stop us, or rather you, from opening up negotiations with one of the other TV companies, perhaps one of the big boys. We have a proven model and the financial capability. We don't need to go cap in hand begging to any of them. We can get a new deal on better terms."

"Metro won't like that."

"Metro should have had better oversight of the show. If they'd spotted what was going on we wouldn't be talking about this now. Also Metro have benefited from a growing budget and never once offered us better terms. Has the renegotiation been successful?"

Greg shook his head. He had to admit I was right. Credibility is a delicate flower and Metro's lack of care had crushed their credibility as far as I was concerned and I could see that Greg felt the same.

"You're sure you can find the smoking gun?"

In truth I wasn't at all sure, but I wasn't about to say that to Greg.

We talked over what I planned to do, how I would manage my investigation and how I would report back to Greg. Now that he knew about the scam he wanted to keep a firm hand on things, just in case anything went wrong. We eventually exhausted the subject.

"What are you going to do about all the press outside, Andy? They won't go away until you give them a story."

In truth I had hoped that the charity would look after that for me. They had their own press office and were used to dealing with the media. I said as much to Greg.

"Oh, we can issue a statement, but it's your story they're after Andy. You're the man who rescued Ded NuronZ and Dareen Debussey. You were with Charleese Morgan when she was attacked by ivory poachers. You're a big hero Andy." I was sure I heard a note of sarcasm in his voice, but I let it go.

I let my brain work on the problem for a moment before I answered. I had the germ of an idea.

"Maybe we can use it to make money for the charity." I suggested.

"How so?"

"The Press Office makes it clear that I won't do interviews and won't make any off the cuff statements. They can say that I'm traumatised by the whole event. But I will attend a press conference and will make a statement there and answer some questions. But, and this is where the charity benefits, each newspaper, wire service or TV company that wants to attend will have to make a five thousand pound donation to MOF. That should net at least a hundred grand, probably more."

Greg steepled his fingers and pressed them against his lips. His eyes were gleaming and I could see he was taken with the idea. "Wait here." He said at last, getting up from behind his desk. He disappeared along the corridor and I guessed he was going to consult with the other directors and the Press Officer. He returned half an hour later, a beaming smile on his face.

"OK. We'll do it. The PO is sending the invites out to the papers and TV stations now, then she'll sit down with you and draft your statement. She'll babysit you during the press conference as well, and if things start getting out of hand she'll close it down. But that won't mean it will go away. You could do with avoiding your flat for a few days. Is there anywhere you can go?"

I didn't think there was. I could go home to Essex and stay with my parents, but I didn't really fancy that. Mum and Dad were great, but a little of them went a long way. Besides, if the press tracked me down it would mean their home being placed under siege. A thought crossed my mind but I dismissed it. Then I let it cross back again. It was worth a try, at least.

"I also want to announce that Ded NuronZ will no longer be associated with Cuddly Toy Day." I might as well press home my advantage while I still had it.

"Why's that?"

"First of all, thanks to their irresponsible behaviour we didn't actually get any film of them in Africa. It means they'll get their free publicity if they go on the show, but we'll be out of pocket on the deal. Secondly, I also intend setting the record straight. Their version of events will be discredited, their lies, well, Vicky Mitchell's lies, will be laid bare for all to see. They'll be a millstone round our necks if we keep them on the show. Finally, it will set down a marker for all the other celebrities who use the telethon to promote themselves. Nothing and no one is bigger than the charity."

"Quite a speech, Andy." I shrugged. I saw no reason why Ded NuronZ should profit from something that had caused me so much stress and which had placed my life, and that of Jacob and his colleagues, in so much danger.

Greg went into one of his silent, contemplative poses and I knew I had won. If he was going to oppose me he would have done so immediately. This was his way of telling me that he was giving my proposal serious consideration, weighing up the pros and cons before he caved in, sorry, before he accepted my advice.

* * *

With the lunchtime news, and my press conference appearance in particular, occupying the attention of the staff at Metro TV, watching on one of the several large screen TVs in the open plan office, I managed to sneak quietly in, work my way round the back of the throng and to my desk.

Sitting squarely in the middle was a gift wrapped cylindrical box. The attached card told me it was from Dareen Debussey, 'With thanks and I'll never forget what you did'. Several x's were inscribed under her name. I tore at the wrapping paper in anticipation.

"Should I be jealous?" I looked up from my appreciation of the carton encasing the bottle of 18 Year Old Glenlivet and into Cassie's sparkling blue eyes.

"You have to be emotionally engaged in a relationship to be jealous when someone receives a present." I answered noncommittedly.

"Very clever, Mirren. Let's suppose I was 'emotionally engaged' as you said. Would I have reason to be jealous?"

I gave her my best, reassuring smile. "Not of Dareen Debussey. It's true that I know far more about her than is healthy for a casual acquaintance to know and I'll never be able to hear her sing without certain images intruding on my pleasure, but we were forced together. That's all."

"What about Charleese Morgan then? I've heard Igor on the 'phone to her and her people. Your name featured quite a lot."

Now there she had me bang to rights. I did have, or rather I'd had, a crush on Charleese and could hardly deny it. But it was over. What happens in Africa stays in Africa. No it doesn't. If that were the case then there would be no Cuddly Toy Day. But my relationship, if I had ever had one, with Charleese had definitely stayed in Africa. I thought I would try a little bit of obfuscation.

"She's going to invite me to her wedding. Does that answer your question? She says I can take someone but we'd have to share a room." I left the idea hanging in the air to see what sort of reaction I'd get. Cassie's folded arms told me I wasn't yet off the hook.

"Well, you're back and seemingly none the worse for wear."

Personally I reserved judgement on that one. I suspected that the mental health industry might yet make some money out of me in the form of counselling, but I didn't want to dwell on that possibility. We'd talked about my experiences while eating dinner on Sunday evening, but it had been in an abstract sort of way. More about what had happened and less about how I had been involved, and in particular how closely I had been involved with the female participants. It had obviously been praying on Cassie's mind since then.

I changed the subject.

"Actually I've a favour to ask. I need to keep a low profile; avoid the press, that sort of thing. Could I crash on your couch for a few days?"

She gave me an appraising look, obviously trying to decide if my request was worth the investment in her time. She let her lips form a half smile.

"OK, but no funny business. My bedroom door is closed and stays closed."

I hurried to assure her that I would be the perfect gentleman and also the perfect house guest, starting with the preparation of dinner for two that evening. Cassie gave me a list of foods to avoid, nothing too demanding, and then flounced off back to her desk.

The crowd around the TV was breaking up and Martin spotted me and drew the whole pack towards my desk. I was pressed back against the wall as I tried to fend off the mass of questions that flew around me. It was half an hour before order was restored and I could start my real day's work. Even then I found myself the subject of curious glances every time I looked up from my work.

Later in the afternoon I saw Ded NuronZ' agent, Damian Ellis, stalking towards Igor's office. His face was like thunder. I caught his eye and his lip curled in anger. He paused and I thought he was going to change direction and come charging across the room to attack me, but he just mouthed something and continued towards his destination. The summons to Igor's office followed almost at once, delivered by a smirking Sonia.

"Shall I pack up your things?" She asked, mocking what she saw as my predicament. Well, I already knew I would have the last laugh so I let the jibe go and sauntered across the office in what I hoped looked like a relaxed manner, but probably made me look as though I was in urgent need of a toilet.

I knocked and entered without waiting for an answer. Ellis was sat in one of the comfy arm chairs. I waited patiently to be invited to sit but instead Igor went straight on the offensive.

"What's all this nonsense about Ded NuronZ not being allowed on the telethon?"

"MOF considers that their conduct while they were in Africa wasn't in keeping with our code of ethics. We have therefore decided that the group should have no further involvement in this year's telethon." It was my announcement to the press conference, delivered word for word.

"You can't do that." Spat Ellis.

A few months ago I would have quailed under a verbal assault such as that, but once you've been shot at you tend to find verbal assaults less daunting.

"Actually we can. Under the terms of the contract any artist that fails to complete the scheduled filming can be removed from further involvement."

"But it was you who stopped them from doing the filming." Igor reminded me.

"Yes. For their own safety. Their prior behaviour had placed them in danger and to keep them in country would have been to place them at further risk. You don't have to take my word for it, you can ask their insurers. They removed their cover."

Igor had to concede that point, but Ellis wasn't finished with me yet.

"They only did that because news broke about them being kidnapped. If you had kept quiet no one would have been any the wiser."

"I said nothing to anyone other than to report events back to my employers, as I was duty bound to do. All the press coverage was as a result of Vicky Mitchell, your employee, announcing the whole thing to the world to try to get a press frenzy going. It worked. She even suggested to me that you had approved it."

Ellis's jaw started going up and down like a stranded fish, but no sounds were coming out. But Ellis wasn't yet finished. "You'll regret this. We'll blitz you with PR that blames you. Their fans won't donate a penny to your charity and lots of other people may decide not to donate either."

"Please don't force me to release the recordings."

"What recordings?" He started to look nervous.

"You don't think I would talk to Vicky Mitchell about what happened without taking adequate precautions to make sure my side of the story was properly recorded, do you?" In fact that was exactly what I had neglected to do, but Ellis didn't know that. I wasn't actually lying. I didn't say I had recordings of my conversation with Vicky Mitchell, I just said I had recordings, which I did have. Lots of recordings of Charleese Morgan singing songs with African school kids.

"You're bluffing." He tried to sound confident but I could hear a nervous tremor in his voice.

"I'll tell you what. You go and organise your PR blitz and I'll send my recordings to the newspapers and TV and we'll see who's bluffing." It's me, it's me, I'm the one who's bluffing. My brain was screaming so loudly that I thought the whole outer office must hear it, but Ellis fell silent.

I should play professional poker, I decided.

"It wasn't my decision to get rid of Ded NuronZ," I said, turning back to Igor. A half-truth, it may not have been my decision but it had been my idea, "That decision was taken by the board of MOF. If you have any issues with it I suggest you take it up with them."

"So how do we replace them?" Igor accepted defeat without admitting he had been defeated. Maybe he just decided it wasn't his battle.

"Now look here, Igor, you promised me you'd get Ded NuronZ back in the show."

"I promised I'd try. Now that Andy has told me the circumstances I'm afraid I have to go along with MOF's decision. At the end of the day it's their show, not mine." I noted the way he had passed the buck so smoothly.

I ignored Ellis's stuttering protests to answer Igor's question. "We have quite a lot of background footage." Igor's office door slammed against the wall as Damian Ellis stormed out. I pretended not to notice despite Igor's wince. "I think if you approach Suite 2X we can probably cobble something together that will look convincing. We have an outreach centre and hostel here in London that helps African migrants who want to return home. It's not a major project but if we film the girls chatting to some of the hostel residents and play some of the footage in the background to show the severity of the choices these people have to make we can strengthen the message about how important our work out there is."

"A sort of anti-immigration message." Igor nodded his head approvingly. I cringed. That wasn't what I had meant, but to explain that to Igor would take too long. I decided to say nothing, but to pay close attention to the filming to make sure that the message wasn't the one Igor was suggesting. "OK. I think I can sell that. I know the group's agent quite well. I'm sure she'll get the girls to do it as a favour to me."

I crossed back towards my desk reasonably happy with the way things had gone. On the way I stopped at Sonia's desk. "I hope you haven't packed my stuff up." My face was a picture of innocence, "It seems I'm not going anywhere after all." I sauntered off, feeling the daggers she was throwing at my back but not caring a jot.

Twenty Two - The Smoking Gun

My short stay with Cassie was quite painless, even though she was playing things quite cool. I think she suspected more had gone on in Africa than I had told her. She was right, up to a point. I hadn't told her of my crush (infatuation?) on Charleese, but she seemed to be far more suspicious of the time I had spent with Dareen Debussey. I guess it was the fact that we had been locked up together for several days. Maybe she thought we had found some interesting ways to pass the time.

In truth I hadn't been attracted to Dareen that much. Sure, she was a gorgeous looking woman, but I hadn't found much in common between us. Once the glamour image had started to wear thin, which doesn't take long when you're sharing a bucket for toilet, she was just a nice girl who might become a good friend, but that was as far as it went. Cassie, however, wouldn't be persuaded.

I insisted on cooking for the two of us. Cassie had once admitted that the most challenging thing she found to do in the kitchen was open a tin, whereas I enjoyed cooking and liked to serve up something tasty in the evening. After that we watched TV or downloaded a film. Going out was out of the question. I was supposed to be keeping a low profile and it only needed one person to recognise me and Tweet my location for that plan to fail.

I tried to avoid talking about work, but it was unavoidable that the subject would raise its head. After one glass of wine too many on my last night with her I vented my frustration over not being able to get any further with exposing Igor's frauds.

The next day, at work, Cassie beckoned me into the small communal kitchen where we all made our hot drinks. Carefully watching the doorway to make sure we weren't disturbed or observed, she passed me a slip of paper, at the same time pushing my hand towards my trouser pocket, indicating that I should conceal it before anyone saw me with it.

"What is it?" I whispered, rather enjoying the intimacy of the situation.

"You'll see. Just make sure no one can see you when you look at it." She saw someone approaching and pulled away from me. "How do you take your coffee?" She asked in a loud voice; rather too loud, I thought.

Martin entered the small space and wriggled his way past me to the sink, where he splashed water into his mug. "You two should get a room." He simpered at us.

Cassie flounced out while I just played along by giving him a blokish nod and a wink, before leaving. I realised that Cassie hadn't made the coffee she had inquired about and I hoped Martin hadn't noticed.

I tried to stop myself running towards the gents toilets. If Cassie was giving me something that she considered to be highly secret then it had to be important. I locked myself in a cubicle and retrieved the slip of paper.

There wasn't much on it, just a username and a password. I could tell that the username was for an e-mail account, but not the one provided by Metro TV. The name itself was just a jumble of numbers and letters, as was the password.

I took out my 'phone and keyed in the address of the popular e-mail provider that made up the second half of the username. Carefully I tapped in the username, and then the password. I held my breath with anticipation. The in-box seemed to take an age to download, but as the phone was connecting via the office Wi-Fi system it was actually faster than usual.

At last the display filled with e-mails. The senders names were a mixture of the familiar and the unknown. I was just about to select one and open it when I stopped myself. The text was dark in colour, meaning it hadn't yet been read by its intended recipient. If I read it then I would be betraying the fact that I had hacked the e-mail account.

I paused for a moment. Was I breaking the law? I know that journalists had been prosecuted for doing this, so I must assume that I was. I had to tread very, very carefully. I scrolled down the page until I found the start of the e-mails with paler coloured text. These were the ones that had already been read.

I tapped my finger onto my selection and the e-mail opened up. I drank it in like a man who had spent weeks in the desert without any water.

"Hi Igor,

Just about ready to sign the contract for the catering. I've managed to push the price up to £10.50 per head for the proles and £17.50 per head for the VIPs, plus VAT of course. Not bad for some dried up sandwiches and a sip of supermarket wine! For the after-party we'll be charging £35 per head. I've done a deal for some really cheap fizz. We'll be pouring it behind the scenes so I doubt if anyone will spot the difference. By the time the party starts everyone will be too pissed to notice.

It's going to be pretty profitable this year.

Regards

Hazel"

It seems I had hit pay dirt. Hazel Delacourt was on the Board of Directors of one of the companies that provided services to Metro TV for Cuddly Toy Day and here she was bragging to Igor about how much money they were going to make out of the deal.

Hazel, I had already established, was Igor's sister, so the bragging was explainable to a degree. A clever lawyer would find a way of explaining it as some sort of sibling rivalry. Metro TV and Cuddly Toy Day weren't even mentioned in the e-mail, so any assumption that I made would be blown out of the water quite easily, but I knew I had what I needed. This was just one e-mail. There were hundreds in the e-mail account and some of them would reveal much, much more than this one.

I checked my watch and noticed it was lunchtime. I vacated my cubicle, washed my hands and returned to the office. I picked up my jacket and announced to the room at large that I was going to the pub if anyone wanted to join me. It was a fairly normal occurrence. Friday afternoons tended to be quiet and passed more quickly with a couple of pints of beer and a sandwich to help cushion the routine.

Martin accepted the invite and once he had spoken Cassie felt she could join me without attracting undue comment. The three of us headed for the lift.

We had to use the basement exit just in case there were still any reporters hanging around the front door, but once outside we made our way round the corner to The Greyhound.

"If I'd known we were coming here I'd have stayed behind." Martin grumbled. It wasn't his sort of place.

"I like it. It's a good old fashioned London boozer."

"Precisely why I don't like it." Martin waved his hand airily. "If I wanted to mix with the hoi polloi I'd go to football matches."

"Don't be such a snob, Martin." Cassie scolded him. "Besides, it's cheaper than that wine bar you usually go to."

"If I wanted cheap I'd go to the canteen." Martin wasn't to be appeased.

"No beer in the canteen." I reminded him. We had arrived at the doorway and I put myself in front of him. "Anyway, it's free if you're not paying, and I'm buying."

This did the trick and Martin finally gave in with good grace. He found a table for us and started reading the bar menu. Cassie sat alongside him while I made my way to the bar.

I wasn't bothered by Martin joining myself and Cassie; without him she probably wouldn't have come for fear of being seen to be too cosy with me and I needed to speak to her before she went home at the end of the day. The problem now was going to be getting rid of Martin so I could talk to Cassie in private.

As it happens, the ever resourceful Cassie came up with the solution. Returning from the bar with a second round of drinks she 'stumbled' and spilt enough over Martin's trousers to send him scurrying for the toilets muttering about cleaning bills and cack handed women. He didn't return.

Cassie moved from her side of the small round table to huddle together with me on the bench seat beneath the widow. She giggled like a naughty schoolgirl. I liked the way things were developing, but business first.

"That username you gave me is dynamite. How did you get it?"

"You like? It wasn't easy, so you owe me big time, Mirren. Actually it was quite easy. Sonia keeps a notebook with all Igor's usernames and passwords in case he forgets them. She left the book on her desk this morning when she went off to the loo. Silly bitch even left it open at the right page. Igor had needed to change his password for the company intranet so she had just written down the new one."

"Are any of the others any use?" I asked hopefully.

"Not so far as I could see. There was his Facebook and Twitter accounts, his company intranet, like I said, company e-mail and a couple of others. I think one might be a bank account username but I can't be sure."

"That would be useful, if you can get your hands on it. Maybe his intranet password as well. He will have access to areas that I haven't been able to get into."

"OK. I'll see what I can do."

"But don't take any chances. I don't want you losing your job over this."

"Or tipping Igor off." She smiled mischievously at me.

"Or tipping him off." I agreed, I took a long sip at my beer. "I've enjoyed being at your place the last few days."

"And I've enjoyed you being there. I forgot how nice it was to have a flatmate."

"Was that all I was, a temporary flatmate?"

She ducked the question by asking one of me. "Are you sure it's safe to go back home?"

"Yes. I rang my neighbours across the hall. They haven't seen any reporters since yesterday morning. They're pretty sure they've given up and gone to look for another story elsewhere."

"And they haven't been seen outside Metro today, so maybe you can stop sneaking in and out through the loading dock."

"Actually that wasn't too bad. The entrance is closer to the tube station."

A silence fell over us as we both contemplated my move back to my own flat. I sipped at my beer and Cassie sipped at hers and we both finished at about the same time, firmly placing our glasses on the table with gentle thuds.

"Well, now that I'm not your landlady any more, why don't we go back to my place and celebrate." She smiled shyly at me under her eyelashes and I thought I detected a slight blush, but maybe that was just the effect of the alcohol.

"Do you mean….."

"I mean I have a bottle of cheap champagne in the fridge and a pizza in the freezer."

"Oh, well OK. How I could I refuse an offer like that."

We stood and I followed Cassie out of the pub.

We finished the champagne but the pizza remained in the freezer until the following day and we ate it for Saturday brunch.

Twenty Three - Confrontation

After leaving Cassie's flat the following morning I made a hasty return to my own flat and started to work my way through Igor's private e-mails. I had been right. This account was used only for his illicit e-mail traffic. There wasn't a single personal message amongst them, other than the odd familiar greeting at the end of a few of the messages.

Not only did I have my smoking gun, but I was also able to place a smoking gun into Helen Spencer's hands thanks to a swathe of messages from her that firmly implicated her as being a co-conspirator. All I now needed was proof that all the transactions referred to had resulted in money changing hands and I had Igor and Helen bang to rights, as the Sweeney have probably never said.

I had arranged to meet Cassie for dinner and as we ate I filled her in on what I had found.

"I think I've got enough now to take this back to the charity, but It would be nice to tie it up in a nice ribbon."

"How do you mean?" Cassie licked ice cream from her spoon in a way that sent a shiver running down my spine.

"Follow the money, they say in all the best movies. All the evidence points to Igor and Helen having links to almost all of the businesses that have contracts with Cuddly Toy Day, but none it proves that either of them are gaining anything financially. There's no reference to any payments to either Igor or Helen."

"Is that important?"

"It is if we want to get fraud charges out of this."

"Is that what you plan?"

"I doubt that the charity would want to go that far. It would be bad PR if people knew that the charity had been ripped off. People might not want to donate in case it happened again. But I think we need the insurance policy, so to speak."

"I'm guessing that Metro will lose the contract for Cuddly Toy Day."

I could hear a note of concern in Cassie's voice. Would this cost her, her job?

"That's going to happen, I'm afraid. It's not just what Igor and Helen have been doing. It's the way the clean money has been spent. The over-staffing, the free lunches and goodness knows what else."

"That's great. Thanks a bunch Andy. So I'm going to be out of a job in a few weeks."

I saw the anger building in Cassie's face. When she had started out to help me it had just been a bit of a lark, a bit of payback for the hurt that had been done to her friend Mellissa; perhaps also a bit of personal revenge against Igor. I still hadn't got to the bottom of that. Cassie hadn't anticipated how it might all end up.

"I'm sorry. Look, whoever takes over the contract is going to have to set up a new team. I'm sure I can put in a good word and get you a place with them."

"Wow! Thanks Andy. I'm so grateful for the crumbs from your table." The sarcasm and hurt dripped from Cassie's lips.

"I'm sorry Cassie. I didn't mean it like that. But you know I have to do this."

"It's for the greater good. I know. It's what people always say when they are about to wreck other people's lives." She dropped her spoon into the table with a clatter that made other customers stop and look around at us. "But your precious charity will survive, won't it?"

"It's the only reason I'm doing this."

"Yes, very noble. And what about you? What's going to happen in your little world, Andy? A big fat promotion to show how grateful the people of Africa are for you saving them." I could see that she was fighting back tears. Cassie wasn't the sort of girl that would want a man to see her crying.

"Cassie, it's not like that. I don't care…." But it was already too late. Cassie had grabbed her handbag and was heading for the door. I rose to go after her but a waiter expertly intercepted me. I suspected that a few bills had gone unpaid in the past because of women running out of the restaurant being pursued by their apparently distraught boyfriends.

By the time the waiter had printed the bill and I had settled it there was no sign of Cassie outside. She had vanished into the Lewisham night.

I tried phoning her but all I got was her voicemail. With tears in my eyes I wandered back to my flat.

On Monday morning I viewed the wreckage of both my flat and my life. There wasn't a surface that didn't have a beer can standing or lying on it. A half-eaten takeaway pizza lay next to the sofa. I staggered into the bathroom and took a wary look in the mirror. It was as bad as I had feared. The figure that stared back had a heavy layer of stubble below red rimmed and bloodshot eyes. There was a bit of pizza crust in my hair. I felt that if I sniffed hard enough my reflection would smell as bad as I knew I smelt.

My phone was ringing. It took me a several minutes to track it down beneath the sofa, during which time it had stopped and restarted a couple of times. Someone wanted to speak to me and they weren't going to be fobbed off with voicemail.

"Andy Mirren" I eventually manage to croak at the device.

"I want you in my office in an hour, Mirren." It was Helen Spencer's voice and it felt as though she had taken a razor to my skin.

"I'm sorry. I'm sick." I burbled back at her. I checked the time on my watch and saw it was almost eleven a.m. on Monday morning.

"Don't give me that, you little shit. If you aren't in my office in an hour I'm coming over there to drag you out. Got it?"

I was certain she would carry out her threat. Helen Spencer's temper was legendary at Metro. It seemed to be in inverse proportion to her small build and it was rumoured that even the Chairman was frightened of her.

"OK, OK. Look, I'm in Lewisham. I can't get to you in an hour, at least not if you don't want to have to disinfect your office afterwards."

She didn't ask me why I needed so much time, for which I was grateful. "One o'clock then. Not a minute later. You understand me?"

"Yes, I understand. Look, you're clearly upset." My befuddled brain was starting to clear and was trying to make sense of this sudden summons. "What…." I tried to formulate the sort of question which would suggest that I had no notion of why she might be upset. "What have I done wrong?" It was the best I could come up with.

"I'm pretty sure you know, Mirren. I know what you've been up to. I hope you have a good explanation for yourself."

The line went dead and I considered what she had said as I made my way back to the bathroom.

She knew something, but what exactly did she know? I gave a guilty glance towards my laptop. Its blank screen told me nothing but I noticed that there was a flashing light on it that told me that the hard drive was being used, so the machine was still switched on.

With a guilty start I threw myself at the machine and woke it up. There, on the display, was Igor's clandestine e-mail account. I scrolled up to the top of the e-mail list. There were two unread e-mails, both received that morning according to the transmission times. But below them were several that had been received the previous evening. The shading of the text was light, indicating that they had been read.

I lowered myself onto the sofa and held my aching head in my hands. What had I done?

* * *

It was a different snooty receptionist that welcomed me to the executive floor, but the welcome was no warmer than on my previous visit. She directed me to my destination, which of course I was familiar with, and I dragged my heels through the expensive carpet, making my way to Helen Spencer's office as slowly as it was humanly possible without actually growing moss during the journey.

I knocked on the door and it was answered with a snarl that would have made a Rottweiler envious.

The scene was familiar, Helen Spencer sat behind the polished gleam of her empty desk, with no chairs present for me to sit on. The only addition was Igor, sat in a chair at the side of the desk that placed him firmly in Helen's camp, languidly picking at a finger nail.

Helen glared at me with the sort of stare that would have turned nitrogen into a liquid. I tried to make myself appear the picture of innocence but I knew that I wasn't fooling anyone.

Helen didn't waste any time with greetings, or welcoming me back from Africa. She didn't even ask me why I had been off be sick.

On my journey into the office I had been trying to work out what she might know and, more importantly, how she knew it. Even if I had opened those e-mails Helen Spencer couldn't have known it was me that had read them. There could only be one answer. To get back at me Cassie had ratted me out. It was hard for me to accept, but it was the only explanation that worked.

"OK, Mirren." Her voice dripped venom. "What have you told the people at MOF?"

"I have no idea what you're talking about." I lied. Deny, deny, deny. It was the only tactic I could think of until I had more information to go on. What had Cassie told her? Was it the whole story, up to and including the hacking of the e-mails? Or was it only a little bit of the story, just enough for them to know I was on to them but not enough to betray her involvement. That seemed more logical. But if it was only a little bit, which little bit was it?

"Don't come the innocent with me. Mirren. We know you've been meddling. We know that your precious charity is looking for someone to take over the Cuddly Toy Day contract."

Ah, so that was the bit they knew. That made sense. That was the bit that affected Cassie the most.

I felt myself starting to shake then, all of a sudden I was back in that bare concrete room in Africa with Akeem holding his gun casually in his hand, his cold dark eyes telling me with absolute certainty that if I did anything he didn't like he would kill me. The shock of the image at first startled me and then reassured me. I suddenly knew Helen Spencer for what she was: nothing but a playground bully, using her position to terrorise those she saw as being unable to defend themselves. Igor, of course, was her acolyte. The weak boy who fawns around the bully in order to protect himself from being bullied and who gains power as well as protection because of his position.

I pulled myself up to my full height. It wasn't much, but it made me taller than Helen Spencer, and for some reason I felt that was important at that moment.

"I did what any loyal employee would do." To my own surprise I managed to keep the tremor out of my voice. It encouraged me to continue. "I reported back on all the money that was being wasted here: the overstaffing; the free lunches and the rest. You had a chance to recover the situation. All you had to do was renegotiate the contract."

Greg had told me that Metro's negotiating team, led by Helen Spencer, had played hard ball and wouldn't shift an inch on the price of the contract for Cuddly Toy Day. That had figured. She wouldn't have wanted to derail the gravy train.

"So MOF has put out feelers to other production companies to take over the contract. It's what any sensible organisation would do." I finished what I had been saying.

Helen looked as though I had physically assaulted her. Whatever she had been expecting from me it hadn't been defiance. Out of the corner of my eye I noticed Igor stand up and walk casually towards the window, as though suddenly interested in the spectacular view across the river towards South London. It didn't need a genius to work out that he was putting physical space between himself and Helen, just in case.

"What do you mean, loyal employee?" She exploded. "You've given away Metro's commercially confidential information."

"May I remind you, Helen, that I don't work for Metro TV. My loyalty is to MOF and for all the people they are trying to help."

"You little shit!" She advanced around the desk like a tiger about to launch itself at its prey. I honestly thought she was going to hit me. "MOF! There would be no MO Fucking F if it wasn't for Metro TV." She stopped inches from me, her face glaring up at me from about three inches below my nose. I could smell her perfume, heady and expensive. It reminded me of who was paying for it.

"That may have been true twenty years ago, Helen, but we're one of the biggest charities in the country now. Thank you for doing that for us, but it doesn't give you the right to rip us off. Do you know how many of your people work for us? About half of them!" It was an old joke but it made its point. "Now, if you'll excuse me I've got work to do trying to save some of the money you're wasting."

It sounded sanctimonious even to me, but I had to get out of there.

"Clear your desk." Helen barked at me. "You're no longer welcome here."

That stopped me in my tracks, but only for a moment. I reached round and pulled my wallet from my pocket and carefully withdrew a card from one of the slots.

"If I leave then this leaves with me." I waved the card in front of Helen's face and then realised it was my Nectar Card, not the MOF credit card. I ignored it, hoping Helen hadn't also spotted the error.

"Whoa. Let's not be too hasty here, Helen." Igor had spotted the danger and decided to intervene. She turned on him with a look of surprise, then spotted the warning look on his face.

"Yes, Igor's right." I took the opportunity to seize back the initiative. "If I leave then MOF won't appoint another liaison. I'll just work from our offices instead of yours. But I won't need the charity's credit card. If you want to get payments made you'll have to submit invoices." I paused for effect. "Itemised invoices."

If I had vomited on her Manolo Blahniks Helen couldn't have looked more disgusted. "What do you know?" It came out as a hiss, like the threat of a cobra about to strike.

"I know what I can see with my own eyes." It was a suitably enigmatic reply. At least I hoped it was. "Or is there something else I should know?"

As soon as I said it I knew I had overreached myself. The question had been too arch. I wasn't cut out to be Machiavelli.

Helen gave me a shrewd look, almost respectful, as though one criminal mastermind was sizing up another.

"Nothing. You know all there is to know." She replied eventually, slowly retreating behind her desk. Her eyes bored into me, searching for answers. Igor's eyes swivelled between us as though someone had hit him on the back of his head with a baseball bat and his brain had gone 'tilt'. He hadn't kept up with what had just happened between Helen and I.

"Now, I believe I was quite ill before you so rudely dragged me from my sickbed." I turned on my heels, not waiting to be dismissed. I knew who now held the power in our little triangle of relationships. Igor started to say something but Helen signalled him to shut up.

I stepped out through the office door and pulled it closed behind me, stopping while there was still a small open crack. I made sure I was out of any eye lines and waited. I wasn't disappointed.

"He knows." Came Helen's lowered voice.

"Knows what? Oh, you mean he knows. Shit. What are we going to do?"

"We're going to do nothing, not here anyway. Get your coat, we're going for a long lunch."

"But I've had lunch." Igor protested. I couldn't see Helen's expression, of course, but I could almost feel Igor withering under it. I hurried away from the door and took refuge in the toilets before Igor could emerge.

* * *

On my way out of the building I stopped off in the main office, looking for Cassie. I found her in the kitchen washing coffee mugs. She turned to look at me as though butter wouldn't melt in her mouth.

"I'm sorry…" She started to say, but I didn't let her finish.

"Thanks for grassing me up." I kept my tone even, not showing her the upset that I really felt. "I've just had a very tough ten minutes with Helen and Igor. I'm lucky to still be here."

"But....but," was all she could manage before I turned and stalked away. As soon as I was sure I was out of sight I let my shoulders sag and my head drop. I could understand Cassie's reasons, of course. She and I were just getting to know each other. Our relationship might crash and burn at any moment. She had to at least hang onto her job, if that were possible. But all the same......

Perhaps I shouldn't have shilly-shallied about. Perhaps I should have made it clear just how I felt about her before I left for Africa. Even while I was in Africa I hadn't suggested anything in my e-mails and phone calls that might hint to her that I was growing very fond of her. That was my silly schoolboy crush on Charleese, of course. Well, that was that. Cassie and I were now history. It had taken just one weekend for me to wreck things between us. That was a record even for me.

Twenty Four - Following The Money

I was pouring over Igor's e-mails, seeing if I could glean any more information from them, when the knock came on the door of my flat. Well, it was more of a thud really. I went to answer it and found Cassie standing on the doormat.

In one hand she held a bottle of wine and in the other a four-pack of beers. I wondered how she had knocked on the door and remembered the thud. She had obviously kicked it. I looked at her feet and saw the soft pumps she was wearing and guessed that she might have hurt her foot. Serves her right, I thought, rather ungraciously.

"I don't think we have anything to say to each other." I was just about to slam the door in her face when I saw that she had been crying. Her eyes were red lined and there was a dribble of snot at the corner of her nose. At once I felt ashamed of being so callous.

"Look, Andy, I don't know what you think I've done, or said, but I promise you, I haven't done anything. Please, let me in so we can talk."

"You grassed on me to Helen. She knows that MOF are looking elsewhere for someone to run Cuddly Toy Day."

"I promise you Andy, I have no idea how she found that out, but it wasn't from me. Please, let me come in. I have beer?" She held the cans aloft and gave me an appealing smile. Cassie does appealing very well. I never stood a chance.

There was something about how she had said it that made me believe her. She could, of course, be here on Helen's instructions, trying to find out more, but I doubted it. Cassie might have betrayed me, in anger or out of self-preservation, but I was pretty sure she wouldn't spy on me.

I stepped back and held the door open. She stepped inside and waited for me to show her the way into the sitting room. She could have guessed, of course. It isn't a very big flat, but she was on my turf and wanted to play things by my rules. I pointed towards the door to the living room and then went along the short corridor to the kitchen to get a corkscrew and glasses. By the time I returned Cassie had already removed the screw top cap from the wine, looking slightly smug as she saw what I was holding. She was sitting on the small sofa. It was the only comfortable place to sit in the room. I had a choice: sit next to her in close proximity or use one of the hard back chairs at the small table where I ate and, as now, worked. I chose the hard back chair.

Cassie rose and took the wine glass that I was holding, exchanging it for a can of beer. I pulled the ring and poured half of it into my own glass. Cassie sat back on the sofa, leaning forward slightly, her elbows resting on her knees, her wine glass held between the fingers of both hands as though she was fearful that she might drop it.

"OK. It's your nickel, as the Yanks would say." The silence was becoming oppressive and someone had to say something and after all, it was her who had sought me out.

"Andy, I didn't say anything to Helen, or to Igor. I was upset at the thought of losing my job. It's only natural, isn't it? But I just went home and went to bed. I can't say I slept much, just tossed and turned all night, but by the morning I had realised that you didn't have much choice. It can't go on, what they're doing. It isn't right for your charity and it isn't right for Metro TV either." She took a small sip of her wine before continuing.

"I was going to call you yesterday, but I thought I'd let you sweat for a bit, just to let you know you weren't getting everything your own way." She gave me a small, sad smile. "Then you didn't come in to work this morning and I didn't know what to make of that. Your diary on the intranet didn't show you having any appointments, so I waited and I waited but you still didn't show up. Then Igor started running about like he'd been stung by a wasp and I knew something was wrong and it didn't take a lot to put two and two together and work out your absence and Igor's panic were linked."

"Actually they weren't" I interjected. "I just had one hell of a hangover." She gave me a curious look, inviting an explanation.

"After you ran out on me on Saturday night I went on a bit of a bender. Well, 'went' would be a bit of an exaggeration. I stocked up on beer, locked the door and drank till I passed out. Then when I woke up I drank some more until I passed out again. The original lost weekend."

"Oh. I'm sorry. Perhaps I should have phoned, just to let you know that I wasn't angry any more.

"It's probably a good thing that you didn't. In my state I might have said something stupid."

"Instead you waited until you were sober and then you said it."

Neat trick. She had turned the tables on me and put me in the wrong.

"Now hang on…" I started then realised that if I challenged her then it would only make matters worse. Besides, we were straying from the point. "Oh, never mind. So, if you didn't tell Igor and Helen then who did?"

Cassie shrugged. "Igor and Helen know a lot of people in the business. Perhaps they got a tip off from one of the companies that MOF have approached."

I had to admit that it was a possibility. Old friends, even old enemies, stay in touch and it would be easy for one to let something slip, either by accident or design. It was even possible that there had been a leak from inside MOF.

"Look, Andy, I can understand how you might think that I had told Igor, but I promise you I didn't. Even if I didn't love you I wouldn't have given Igor the satisfaction." She stopped herself, realising what she had just said. I saw a blush start to colour her cheeks.

"Did you just say…"

"Yes I did." She cut across me. I took the hint and stopped talking. Cassie took a big sip of her wine; bigger than is normal in polite company. I took a more modest pull at my beer. We sat in uncomfortable silence for a moment and then both tried to speak at once.

"Cassie, I…

"Andy, Don't say….." We fell silent again.

At last Cassie made a decision. She stood and placed her empty wine glass on the table next to my elbow. "I think I'd better go."

I looked up into her clear blue eyes and held her gaze. "If you leave now I'll have to follow you all the way back to Stockwell."

"I'll take a taxi" She said, half-jokingly.

"I know where you live. I can be there in an hour. I'll stand on your doorstep all night if I have to."

"You mean it, don't you?"

"Cassie, I was wrong to jump to conclusions, but it was the only logical explanation I could come up with. I should have trusted you and I'm sorry."

She gave me a long look, appraising me as though she was trying to decide whether or not to buy me. After a moment she sat down on the sofa again.

"Can we get past this, Andy?"

"We can start again, if that would help."

"Tell me how."

"I take you out for something to eat and then put you in a taxi home. Tomorrow we meet up at work and see how we feel. If you still lov…"

"Don't say it, not now."

"OK, if you still have feelings for me then we take it from there."

"And what about you. Do you have feelings for me?"

I confessed to her that I did.

"OK," she said after a moment's reflection. "Let's cut out the time delay." She stood up and crossed to me, placed her arms around my neck, bent her knees so her face was on the same level as mine and kissed me. Gently at first and then more passionately. After what seemed like a glorious age we broke from our clinch and she stepped back.

"That settles it, I think." She patted her hair back into place as it had become a little dishevelled. "Now, I didn't only bring you beer and wine."

She fished around in her handbag and produced a slip of paper. "I wasn't going to buy my way back into your affections, but I got this for you." I took the paper and unfolded it. It was another username, but this time with two passwords. "Igor's bank account access details." She explained.

"And if we hadn't……"

"I might still have given them to you, as a parting shot. Made you feel bad."

It would have done; that much I knew.

"How did you get it? For that matter how did you find out where I live?" I had just realised that I had never told Cassie my address. I was going to invite her back with me on the Saturday but we hadn't got as far as that before she ran off.

"You're not the only amateur sleuth, Mirren. The username and password I got from Sonia's notebook again. She left it on her desk when she went to lunch, silly mare. Your address I blagged from

MOF. I told them I had a package that I needed to get to you and was going to send it by courier but didn't have your address. They fell for it."

I had to admire her determination, as well as her guile.

"Do you want to take a peek?" I asked her.

"You bet your life. It's Simpson and Yardley's Bank. Very posh but also very discreet."

I found the website and entered the username and the first password. The website took me to another screen with drop down boxes where I had to select specific letters from the second password. A little circle rotated and then, on the screen in front of us, were Igor Kasnisky's bank statements. Cassie had pulled the only other hardback chair close to mine and we sat huddled together in front of the screen, her arm draped casually around my shoulders as I worked.

I scrolled back through time scanning the pages of financial information until I found what I was looking for. At last, three months earlier, I found what I had been hoping to find: A credit payment of slightly over ten thousand pounds. The reference column showed it to be share dividend payment from a company called Elite Event Catering Ltd. A company fronted by Hazel Delacourt, Igor's sister and which had the catering contract for Cuddly Toy Day.

"Bang bang." Cassie murmured into my ear.

"Yes, as smoking guns go that's just about the best we could hope for."

Cassie leant towards me and poked her tongue into my ear and within microseconds I had forgotten all about Igor's bank account.

* * *

Cassie and I agreed that we should keep our relationship low key while we were at work. Any hint that she was close to me could cause her a lot of grief. They couldn't fire me, but they could fire her! So she left my flat early while I tidied up the place and then followed later.

Martin caught up with me just before lunch, perching himself on the edge of my desk and engaging me in a gossipy sort of tone.

"So, tell me all about you and Cassie then."

I looked up at him with what I hoped was an innocent gaze. "What are you on about? Cassie's a mate, that's all."

"Oh, come on. You can do better than that. Sherlock Martin is on your case. Let's review the evidence, shall we? Igor goes into a flap on Monday morning and you don't show up for work. When you do arrive you go and find Cassie in the kitchen and speak to her for a microsecond and she spends the rest of the afternoon in and out of the loo in floods of tears, or so the girls in the office have been saying. Then she goes off at five, still in tears as far as I can tell and then shows up this morning in the clothes she was wearing last night. Now that would be a dead giveaway by itself, but Cassie has been wearing the sort of look that only comes when a girl is in love, and you have been giving her lustful glances whenever you think that no one is looking. Now tell me I'm wrong!"

It was true that I had been stealing glances at Cassie all morning but I deny most strongly any suggestion that they were lustful. Loving, perhaps, but not lustful. But I didn't say any of that to Martin. Any admission of guilt would be around the office quicker than an e-mailed video clip of a cat playing the piano. Deny, deny, deny; that was the best way to deal with it, I decided.

"I have no idea what you're talking about, Martin. OK, Cassie is still wearing the same clothes as yesterday, but that doesn't mean she was with me last night." I decided I could live with that statement. It was factually correct, even if it was also ambiguous.

"It doesn't mean she wasn't, either." Martin was quick to jump on my obfuscation. He gave me a long stare which I tried to avoid by focusing my attention on my PC monitor. "So what are you doing for lunch today?"

"Cassie and I are going to lock ourselves in the stationery cupboard and have rampant sex." I laid the sarcasm on thickly. "Oh, no, it appears we aren't going to do that after all." I nodded towards Cassie's end of the office where she and two of her female colleagues were heading for the lifts. Their coats suggested they were leaving the building.

"Very funny. OK, shall we head for the canteen?"

I agreed, logged off my PC and joined the general exodus that usually started at about that time of day.

* * *

The first sign of trouble was when I followed Martin across the canteen towards the empty table he had spotted. It could have been an accident, of course, but people usually exchange apologies or trade insults after that sort of accident.

Half way to the table I noticed someone heading towards me on a collision course. I made a slight course correction but so did he. I tried again but again he changed direction to match me. I had no alternative but to stop in my tracks and let him go round me, which I did. He came on, barged into me and sent my tray flying, then headed off towards the lift without a backward glance. I turned to stare at his retreating back, but he just kept on walking, as though the incident hadn't occurred.

Martin turned back and came over to help me clean up. My frothy coffee was spread across several square yards of mock marble floor tiling and the mug it came in was broken, as was the plate that had held my sandwiches. I was just about to retrieve those, safe in their wrapping, when a large foot was placed on them, crushing them flat, before they were kicked across the room. I looked up from my kneeling position straight into the eye of a suited executive type. Young, as many Metro executive types were, but his suit cost as much as I earned in a month.

"Oh, sorry. I seem to have spoilt your lunch. Good job it was free." He drawled, before turning and walking away.

"What was all that about?" Martin asked, helping me to my feet.

"I'm not at all sure. Do you know him?"

"Only by sight. He works for Helen Spencer, I think."

"That makes sense." I muttered, almost to myself. But Martin had caught it and gave me a curious look.

"And what have you done to upset la Belle Helen?"

"Nothing." I know said it too quickly and too emphatically which just made Martin more curious.

"More secrets? I'm starting to get a bit of déjà vu, you know."

"What do you mean?"

"Your predecessor, Mellissa. She suddenly started having 'accidents' like that, not long before she went off on one of her periods of sick leave."

"Did she?" I asked, with a 'butter wouldn't melt in my mouth' expression.

"Yes. We didn't know why at the time, but I always thought she had something dirty on Helen and Igor. I never found out what it was, though."

"What has that to do with me?"

"Nothing. Nothing at all. Just a bit of a coincidence, that's all."

"No, just a couple of clumsy bastards with no manners." I tried to dismiss the incident, but I could see that Martin wasn't buying. It was a good thing he didn't see what happened later.

* * *

It was a classic 'school bullying' approach: get the weak kid when he's on his own and when he thinks it's safe.

I recognised the first one straight away. It was the one with the feet big enough to crush a prawn mayonnaise sandwich. I suspected the other was the one who had caused me to drop said sandwich in the first place. They were lounging against some railings on my route to the underground station.

I spotted them well in advance and considered what I should do. The sensible thing would be to turn around and walk the other way. I could get a bus (well, three buses actually) home if need be. But I was damned if I was going to allow myself to be intimidated. In my head I heard the crack of AK-47 bullets fired by ivory poachers and I set my shoulders.

They straightened up and stepped away from the railings, blocking my path. On the street side of the pavement I was hemmed in by parked cars. I could step through a gap between the vehicles, but it would mean turning my back on them and I had no intention of giving them an easy target.

"We've been waiting for you." Sandwich crusher issued his challenge.

"I'm sorry, someone should have told you, I'm straight." I quipped. His face darkened. I was two paces away when I was forced to make a choice between stopping or trying to force my way between them. I decided to stop.

He launched himself and grabbed the lapels of my coat, trying to turn me so that I was pushed against the railings.

There is a subtle difference between a professional thug, who beats people up for a living, and an amateur bully. It is that the thug is ready for his prey to fight back, while the bully is so confident he doesn't entertain the possibility of his prey turning on him.

I forced my knee upwards with as much power as I could muster. I didn't have much room to build up any momentum, but I got lucky and my patella made solid contact with his not so solid testicles. In a movie his eyes would have crossed as he doubled over in agony. I was pleased to see that the movies had got it right for a change.

He released his grip and sank slowly to his knees. I quickly turned towards his partner in crime in case he fancied having a go, but he was already retreating. He held his hands up in a pacifying gesture and continued to back away. When he had gone about five yards he turned and ran.

Feeling moderately safe I turned back to my assailant and helped him to his feet. He was still clutching at his genitals as though he was afraid that they might have become detached. He had also vomited copiously and I smelt gin. I suspected this was as a result of the Dutch Courage he had consumed before accosting me. I almost felt sorry for him. He would have trouble explaining his injury to his girlfriend.

I made a pretence of dusting off the lapels of his designer suit. "Now, you tell Helen Spencer that if she tries anything like this again an e-mail will go to Metro's Chief Executive telling him all about Acclaim Design. And if I ever see you anywhere within kicking distance of me again I'll finish what I started." I patted him on the cheek the way I had seen TV hard men do it and continued along the street as though I didn't have a care in the world.

I wasn't too worried about revealing what I knew about Acclaim Design. Gary Larkin's fraud was so obvious that I was surprised it hadn't come to light already and now I knew that Igor was getting 'share dividend' payments from the same company.

I turned a corner so that I was out of sight of my assailant. I almost collapsed against the wall of the nearest building as I allowed relief to wash over me. I may have to take up a career in acting if I ever decide to leave the charity fundraising sector. I fought down the feelings of nausea that had nearly caused me to vomit before sandwich crusher had even laid hands on me. I just stood there, waiting for the adrenalin to subside and my heart beat and blood pressure to return to less dangerous levels.

After a few minutes I was calm enough to take in my surroundings and I realised I was only a few yards from The Greyhound. I half staggered and half walked to its welcoming doorway and made my way through the early evening crowd to the bar.

"Large Scotch." I stammered, only belatedly adding a 'please'.

* * *

I met my neighbour, Bill, in the entrance to our apartment block. Bill was a nickname, of course, short for Wilhelmina and I'm not surprised that she had adopted it. We chatted as we climbed the stairs and it was Bill who first noticed the door to my flat lying open.

"I think you've been burgled, Andy." She observed, a little unnecessarily. "Let me go in first."

Your first thought might be that it was unchivalrous of me to allow her to go ahead of me, as she suggested, but Bill is an instructor in Tae Kwon Do and I had once seen her demolish a six foot man in a demonstration bout - and he was a black belt in the art. I hoped that anyone inside my flat had good medical insurance. Then I thought fuck 'em. They shouldn't be in there.

As it happened my flat was empty. I noticed that the door had been forced open using a crow bar or something similar. It wouldn't have taken much effort, as I had thought on many an occasion. What greeted us was a scene of destruction. Broken furniture, picture frames, glass and electronics lay strewn around the floor. My pride and joy, a forty two inch TV set, had been reduced to a jumble of broken plastic and circuit boards.

"I hope you've got good insurance, Andy." Muttered Bill. "Have they stolen anything?"

I doubted that they had. This wasn't a burglary, this was a message. I wondered if my designer suited assailants had anything to do with it, then concluded that this was something that would have been sub-contracted.

"I don't know." I whispered. After the shock of my earlier encounter this was a little bit too much for me to take in. Bill went through into my bedroom and returned in a hurry, pulling the door closed behind her.

"You do not want to go in there." She placed herself in front of the door to make sure I didn't try to enter.

The ever practical Bill pulled out her phone and made a call to the police. I knew that the chances of catching whoever had trashed the place were minuscule. As it was, several hours passed before a harassed looking Community Police Support Officer arrived to take my statement and make a record of any stolen property. I knew there was no chance of a more thorough investigation. Anyone who lived in Lewisham would expect no more.

As it happened there was little that had been stolen. The TV had obviously been too large to be carried away, but my PS4 had gone, along with the small amount of cash that I kept in a tin in the kitchen to pay for takeaway deliveries.

Bill and her partner Coral worked alongside me through the night to get the place habitable again, carefully noting each piece of damaged property so that I could claim for it. Bill also arranged for a builder pal of hers to come around and fit a new door and door locks for me. The bill for that would go to my landlord. At four in the morning they tucked me up on the sofa and left me to toss and turn for the rest of the night, my bed being in need of a new mattress before it could be used again.

As dawn crept around the edge of the curtains I swore a dire revenge on Helen Spencer and Igor Kasnisky. But I would wait. The time wasn't yet right.

Twenty Five - Show Day

'Show Day' was what it was all about. The culmination of a year's worth of effort all ending up in the organised chaos of a TV studio. Electricians were trailing cables across the floor to trip up the unwary; carpenters hammered in the last nails to stop the set from collapsing, Floor Managers and their assistants scurried here and there, consulting clipboards and talking into the microphones of their headsets. Everyone seemed to be doing something except for me. All of a sudden I had nothing to do.

I had checked the dressing rooms to make sure that everything that had been specified in the celebrities' riders were as agreed. I carefully placed the 'goody bags' of donated gifts on the tables beneath the mirrors and laid the good luck cards on top; each one signed by the trustees of the charity, thanking the celebrities for giving up their time to help raise money for the poor people of Africa. The Press Officer at MOF had done well this year and each goody bag held a bottle of designer perfume or cologne, a pair of gold earrings or a signet ring, an invitation for dinner for two at a trendy new restaurant and a few other shiny things. In return for their largesse, the donors would get their company names flashed across the bottom of the nation's TV screens several times that evening.

Now it was the turn of Metro's personnel to take over. They would do the 'meet and greet' and escort the pampered guests to their dressing rooms and, later, to the Green Room where refreshments would be served. This, of course, was in addition to the stocks of alcohol that formed the majority of the riders.

Rehearsals would start at 10 a.m. exactly, when the show's host, Dave Desmond, would go through his opening routine for the benefit of the cameras and crew. There would be three rehearsals in all, two for the Director and crew to plan the camera positions and adjust the sound and lighting and a final one, the dress rehearsal, for the celebrities themselves to perform their routines and work out their 'spontaneous' banter with Dave and the other co-hosts.

While the telethon itself would run for five hours the rehearsals were much shorter because so much of the show was made up of the pre-recorded film we had shot in Africa and other locations, as well as recorded routines from some of the soap opera casts, newsreaders, weather presenters, and all the others who gave up their time to look silly in support of the charity.

I wouldn't be present for the show itself. I would be answering the phones and taking pledges at MOF's offices in Southwark, but I would be returning for the after-show party. I knew that I would be as welcome as a wasp at a picnic, but I had earned my right to be there so be there I would.

There had been a continuation of the campaign to intimidate me. I had expected nothing less. It was all very low level and sneaky, so I did my best to ignore it. Word must have got out about the loss of the contract because staff in the office started to glare at me and make snide comments. Even the normally irrepressible Martin had started to give me a wide berth.

"Nothing personal, Andy, you did what you had to do." He explained, "but if I'm seen to be on your side they'll make my life a misery as well. Besides, I've got a chance to join another production team so I have to be seen as a loyal company man."

I understood. In his shoes I might have done the same.

Only Cassie remained loyal to me, if only in private. At work she also had to be seen to be loyal to Metro TV, but that helped in a lot of ways as she was able to keep me abreast of what was going on behind the scenes, especially with Igor and Helen.

I don't think Igor spoke directly to me again after the bust up with Helen. If he had to communicate with me at all he used Sonia as his mouthpiece, or sent me e-mails. Short, very terse e-mails.

I made my way back to Metro TV's offices from the rented studio. It was unusually quiet, even for a Friday. Like me, many of the staff would be answering phones for most of the evening so they had been given the day off. Either that or their presence was required at the studio to run errands on behalf of their superiors. Cassie was one of the few who was present, left behind to answer Sonia's and Igor's phones. She gave me a conspiratorial smile but said nothing, just in case she was overheard.

I opened up my e-mails to find one from Greg Jones telling me that a deal had been agreed with a new production company to take over the running of Cuddly Toy Day. A meeting would be held with the board of Metro TV on the following Monday to formally announce the severing of ties. The message warned me to keep the information to myself, but I knew it was already an open secret that Metro had lost the contract. My treatment by my colleagues in the office was evidence of that.

I zapped the e-mail across to Cassie and was surprised to get one back within seconds. I smiled to myself as I read it. Cassie had won the job of Executive Assistant to the woman who would be the new producer of the show. Effectively she was getting Sonia's job in the new organisation. I would have liked to have claimed credit for helping her, but she hadn't even told me she had applied until after she'd attended the interview. "If I get the job I want it to be because I'm the best candidate." She had explained. "Not because someone pulled strings for me."

I stood up and saw her smiling across at me. I blew her an extravagant kiss. She stood and walked across the room towards me, draped her arms around my shoulders and gave me a long, slow kiss in return.

"Aren't you worried by what they'll think?" When I came up for air I nodded towards the only other people in the office, who were now staring at us with astonished looks on their faces.

"Not any more. I won't be working here as of this evening. Have you seen these?"

She held up an envelope bearing the logo of Metro TV. I noticed that there was one on almost every desk.

"It's a redundancy notice, effective as of tonight I am no longer employed by Metro TV. I think that Igor is trying to sabotage the fundraising. People will find them when they arrive for work this evening and I suspect most of them will turn right around and go home, or go to the pub."

So, Igor and Helen were getting their retaliation in first. It didn't surprise me. I knew that Helen was spiteful and Igor would do whatever she told him to do.

"I'm not going to be very popular around here, am I?"

"Only with me. What will you do about getting the phones answered?"

"I'll let the office know. They'll just about have time to round up some more volunteers and put them on stand-by, just in case."

"Do you think Igor will trash the show?"

"No. He wouldn't want to look unprofessional and nor would the acts that are performing. It might reflect badly on them and they would take it out on Igor, not the charity. He won't want to risk that. He has to try to stay in work in this business."

"Helen has had to fight with the Board to keep his job here."

"How do you know that?"

"Sonia told me. She took the minutes at one of the meetings that were held. It was looking bad for Igor until Helen showed up. She made him sound like a cross between Albert Einstein and Mother Theresa."

I grunted. It helped to have friends in high places. Igor would need them again pretty soon.

"Is Sonia staying?"

"Of course. She and Igor are like that, remember." She held up her hand and crossed her fingers to demonstrate how close Sonia was to her boss. "Besides, if Igor tried to get rid of her she'd be up the stairs to tell Helen all about their relationship before Igor had time to zip up his flies."

"I thought Helen knew about Igor and Sonia."

"Apparently she doesn't, at least not according to Sonia. I know that Helen lets him use sex to get what he wants out of people. Helen does it as well, but that's business. Sonia would be seen as pleasure and that's a whole different ball game."

I marvelled at the way some people were able to manipulate others. I hoped I would never be like that. In fact I swore I never would be.

Cassie stopped talking and gave me another kiss. She then grabbed hold of my lapel and pulled me across the room towards Igor's office. Three pairs of very curious eyes watched us as we went. "There's something I've been dying to do since the day we met." She explained, closing the office door behind us. For the next twenty minutes we did something very unprofessional on top of Igor's shiny desk.

* * *

As we had suspected the majority of Metro's employees picked up their redundancy notices and turned round and walked out of office in tears or raging at the behaviour of the company, whichever was their personal preference. That left the phones to be answered by the volunteers that had been hurriedly recruited. It made things easier for me, of course. It meant that I didn't have to face them. I turned up to provide the volunteers with some hasty training and then stayed on to oversee the operation after Greg Jones asked me to. Cassie came along to support me, which I was grateful for.

After polishing Igor's desktop we had adjourned to Cassie's flat. It was nearer than mine. Ostensibly we were getting some rest in preparation for the evening's work, but resting had very little place in our plans at that time.

Of course it was only discomfort delayed. After spending the evening in the local wine bars most of the staff would be at the after-party, swilling down as much free wine and beer as they could before it ran out. I could have avoided the after party, of course, but I saw no need to do that. It was my party as much as anyone else's. Besides, MOF was picking up the tab. I hoped I'd be safe from the worst of the spite if I hung around with the MOF executives, but I couldn't avoid all of the Metro crowd.

The party was held on the studio floor, starting as soon as the Director gave the all clear at the end of the telethon. A small army of caterers moved in and started erecting trestle tables and laying out canapés, while others set up a bar on one side of the room. On the recently vacated centre stage area of the set a band started to set up to provide music. They were supposed to be a small part time group but, as usual, Igor's finger was in the pie and they were actually an up and coming band signed to an agency that he had shares in. That made them expensive. Fortunately they produced a good sound and were able to keep people dancing.

Most of the celebrities and performers had hung around, making inroads into the alcohol that had been included in their riders and staying just out of camera shot, hoping to be seen when the cameras panned to the audience. Even if the alcohol hadn't been provided they would simply have brought it into the studio with them. From the glassy eyes and loud voices I suspected that it wasn't just alcohol that had fuelled the mood of some of them.

Cassie and I arrived a little late. I'd had to wait until all the volunteers had taken their final calls. Back at MOF a small band of other volunteers would continue to work through the night as slower responders decided to make their pledges, but the mass of the calls fell away as soon as the end credits for telethon started to roll.

I hadn't been to one of these shin digs before but Cassie was able to fill me in on the form. Once everyone of importance arrived, that is to say the Board of MOF and their opposite numbers at Metro, there would be speeches of gratitude and ritual back slapping on both sides before the party got too advanced. The executives would then hang around for about another half hour before making a discreet withdrawal and leaving the field clear for the real revels to begin.

As usual MOF spoke first so I missed our CE, Martha Vine, give her speech. Not that it mattered too much. What came next was what I was most interested in. What would the Chief Executive of Metro have to say? Cassie and I arrived just in time to find out.

As the band stood looking bored and tried to resist playing with guitar strings and drum sticks, the CE took the microphone and tapped the end of it. The lead signer winced and muttered something, no doubt derogatory, about the unnecessary strain being put on his expensive equipment.

"Good evening, ladies and gentlemen." He started, trying to speak over the conversations that had had started up as soon as Martha Vine had stopped talking. There were still some angry glances being thrown in her direction. I assumed that she hadn't made any announcement about the loss of contract, but of course when staff have been made redundant they didn't need to hear the reason said out loud. I doubt that there had been more than a smattering of applause, and that only from the MOF employees.

"Good evening." He tried again. The drummer gave a frustrated roll on his snare drum followed by a clash of symbols and the noise faded into silence.

The CE seized the opportunity to make his speech. He started predictably enough with congratulations for the production and thanks to all the staff for their hard work. He reiterated the final total raised that evening, which had once again broken records and thanked the various celebrities and performers for their contributions. Then he came to the bit I had been waiting for.

"Of course it has come with great sadness that we have recently found out that we will no longer be the production company for Cuddly Toy Day. After twenty long and successful years the contract has been awarded to one of our competitors."

He was interrupted by a smattering of boos, but he quietened the crowd with a wave of his hands.

"We fought hard to retain the contract, but the cost structures were such that we simply couldn't reduce the budget to a level that was acceptable to MOF. Quite frankly we are amazed that the new company can do it for the price and maintain the same level of quality." He looked meaningfully at Martha Vine, who was trying manfully (or womanfully) to look in any other direction.

"They can do it because they'll only charge once for the work to be done."

The voice echoed across the room and I looked round to see who had spoken, before realising that the voice had been my own. There was a murmur of whispers and I stepped forward. I felt a hand on my arm and looked round to find Greg Jones trying to prevent me moving towards the stage.

"Yes, Greg. They have a right to know why they've lost the contract." He gave me another appealing look but relinquished his grip and let me go. I took a few steps forward until I was standing in front of the band.

"Do you want to know why you're losing the work? Losing your jobs?"

"Judas." Someone called. The insult was repeated, along with a few other more choice names.

"You may think that, but it wasn't me that caused this."

"Please sit down, young man." The CE tried to drown me out with his amplified voice, but I had captured the crowd's attention.

"Let him speak." Someone shouted from the protection of the crowd. Others echoed the call.

"I don't know how he can know why we set our budget at the level we did, but if that's what you want."

I saw Helen Spencer hurry forward to try to stop me being handed the microphone but she was too late. It was in my hand now. She couldn't countermand her own CE. She gave Igor a helpless looking shrug and turned back to the safety of the crowd of Metro executives who were gathered near the front of the stage. I noticed with some pleasure that a space was made around her. The protective bodies weren't so protective any more. I wondered if some of her senior colleagues knew more than they were letting on about her and Igor's financial affairs.

"I'm sorry that anyone here has lost their job. I wish it hadn't been necessary." There was some more booing and cat calling and I waited for it to die down before proceeding.

"Several months ago I brought to the attention of MOF that I thought that the budget for Cuddly Toy Day was too high and that it had been artificially inflated. The more money that was raised the more money Metro TV was paid to provide the show. The sums didn't match up and that worried me. MOF approached Metro TV to request that the contract be renegotiated. Metro agreed and Helen Spencer was appointed as chief negotiator for Metro."

Curious glances were directed in Helen's direction but she pretended to ignore them, feigning indifference to the implied criticism.

"After weeks of talks Metro hadn't offered to reduce costs by a single penny. I can now tell you why that was."

The large studio space was so silent you could hear a pin drop. I could even hear the barely audible background hum made by the band's amplifiers. Out of the corner of my eye I saw Igor moving backwards through the crowd, trying to make himself as invisible as possible.

"The costs were inflated in various ways. In some cases Metro TV was paying a member of staff to do certain work and then paying a second time, as that work was sub-contracted to another company. Take this evening, for example. Why is there an external company catering this party instead of Metro's normal caterers?"

The Metro CE looked up, surprised, then turned towards Igor. "Yes. I think I'd like to know the answer to that one, Igor. Igor, where are you?"

The crowd shuffled aside to reveal Igor just about to exit through the studio doors. He stopped, realising that he couldn't avoid answering the question.

From where I was I couldn't hear Igor's reply, but from his body language he was obviously denying any knowledge.

"Perhaps I can answer my own question, Mr Goldburg." The CE nodded his head for me to continue.

"In many cases the outside contractors were companies owned by Igor Kasnisky, along with Helen Spencer."

"Is this true?"Goldburg challenged Helen. Her face was white with shock as she saw her world starting to crumble around her. But she wasn't going without a fight.

"It's complete nonsense. I have no idea what he's talking about. But what he said is slander and I shall sue."

"It's only slander if it isn't true." I responded from the stage. "Sue me if you like but I'll produce everything I have in front of a court."

"What have you got, young man?" Goldberg signalled Helen to be quiet once again.

"E-mails, copies of bank statements, orders and invoices signed by Igor."

"So, all that means is that Igor is guilty. It doesn't mean I knew anything about what was going on." I smiled as Helen threw Igor out of the lifeboat.

"Some of the e-mails are from you to Igor and some from him to you. They make it very clear that you are in it together."

"Well Helen?" Goldberg turned back to her.

"He's lying."

"It's all on here." I brandished a memory stick. "By my calculation Helen and Igor will make about half a million pounds out of this year's Cuddly Toy Day. If you don't believe me we can go and find a computer and check what's on this stick."

"Shall we do that?" Goldburg turned to ask Helen Spencer.

Helen glared at me. She must have worked out that I'd had access to Igor's bank account but if she challenged me on that she would have to reveal that I knew about some very incriminating financial transactions, including some to accounts in her own name.

"This is a farce, a kangaroo court. I'm having nothing to do with it." Helen turned and stalked from the room, her back ramrod straight as she struggled to maintain a dignified air. Igor followed behind her, throwing frightened glances back over his shoulder.

I raised the microphone to my lips again. "If Helen Spencer and Igor Kasnisky hadn't been so greedy Metro TV would probably have been able to renegotiate the contract with MOF. Some of you might still have lost your jobs as the Cuddly Toy Day team was grossly overstaffed, but many of you would still be employed. Their greed robbed millions of people of the money they need to keep them alive. That's why I had to act." I handed the microphone to the band's lead singer.

I hadn't expected a round of applause and I wasn't disappointed. As the band struck up the opening chords of their next song most of the people present went into huddles to discuss what I had just told them.

I saw Jesse James and Dareen Debussey crossing the floor towards me, but first I had to talk to Goldburg. I headed towards him and they followed in my wake.

"I'm sorry about that, Mr Goldberg. But these people had the right to know why they were losing their jobs."

"How did they know that, anyway?"

"Igor's last act before today's show was to send out redundancy notices."

"I only signed his new contract this morning, the little worm. Is it as bad as you said?"

"Judge for yourself." I handed him the memory stick. He laughed.

"I thought that was just a bit of theatre. It's really all on here, is it?"

"Every sorry bit of it."

"And the meeting on Monday was to hand this over, was it?"

"It was, well, a copy anyway. Our Board will want to know what you intend doing about it."

"Yes, of course they will. And what do you think I should do about it?"

"Bad publicity will damage next year's telethon fund raising. Why should the people of Africa suffer because Spencer and Kasnisky got greedy? Isn't that why we're here tonight, after all?"

"Good point, young man. I'll bear that in mind. Now, if you don't mind, my weekend has got off to rather a poor start, so I'd like to go home and try to enjoy what's left of it."

He turned and stalked away. I also turned and nearly walked into Dareen Debussey.

"So, that was what it was all about. All that fuss about our entourages and our riders."

"Everyone had their snouts in the trough, even some of your agents. Some of them paid Igor backhanders for getting their acts on the show"

"Mine?"

"No, not yours. She'll protect you like a mother grizzly protects its cubs, but as far as I can tell she's honest."

"What about mine?" Jesse James asked.

By way of answer I nodded towards the band, now into some heavy dance music which was starting to fill the floor as people started to get over their shock at what had happened.

"They have the same agent as you."

"Ah, I see. Just like the caterers then?"

"I'm afraid so."

He shrugged. "No matter. I've had several agents sniffing around me for months. Maybe it's time for a change. I won't suffer." I smiled and he draped an arm around my neck.

"Come, on. It's a party. Let's get drunk." Dareen hooked her arm through mine and we marched across the studio towards the bar. Cassie caught up with us and managed to squeeze herself between myself and Dareen. Dareen gave a knowing smile and gracefully gave up her place.

I was handed a glass of the second rate champagne that Igor had arranged for the caterers to provide and grimaced as I took a sip. Jesse went further and spat his back into the glass.

"Come on, you three. I've got some really good stuff back at my pad. Raid the buffet table while I get us a cab." Our small party left the studio after liberating a bottle of Jack Daniels and some cola from one of the dressing rooms. After that things got a bit hazy.

Twenty Six - Tennessee Waltz

Cassie and I leant on the white painted fence rail and admired the crimson sunset taking place behind Mount Clinch. From behind us, inside a gargantuan marquee, came the sounds of an energetically performing country and western band that were blasting out loud music as they struggled to make themselves heard above the boisterous crowd.

"Enjoying it?" I asked, taking a sideways look at Cassie. She looked wonderful in her electric blue dress. It seemed to make the sparkling blue of her eyes shine with life.

"Yeah, it's been great."

"You seem pre-occupied." I had noticed that Cassie had seemed to be in some way absent for the last hour or so.

"Weddings do that to me. They're great to start with, everyone having fun, cheering on the happy couple then, oh, I don't know, I start to feel as though my turn will never come."

"Is that a hint?"

She gave me a long look. I could sense that she had something she wanted to get off her chest. Should I push the issue or hope that she would come to it naturally? I decided to go for it.

"You know, I have been thinking along the same lines….."

She pressed a finger to my lips to silence me. "I'm not pushing you into proposing to me, Andy."

"It wouldn't really be pushing. I really have been thinking about it."

"So why haven't you said anything up until now?"

I took a small sip of my champagne, not so much to give me courage but more to wet my mouth which had suddenly gone very dry.

"I didn't know how you would react. We've been together a year now and things have been going so well. I didn't want to spoil things. Let's face it, we only moved in together three months ago."

It was true that it had taken my second trip to Africa for us to see sense and save my rent money by arranging for my meagre possessions to be stored at Cassie's so I could vacate my flat. I'd hardly spent any time in it for months as Cassie's place was so much more convenient for both of us. Bill and Coral had wept buckets as they helped me load the rented van. When I got back to London I stayed the night with Cassie and then just didn't bother to go flat hunting in the morning.

"It's been good having you with me." Was all that Cassie said.

"Just good?"

She turned and gave me a mischievous grin. "You're fishing for compliments now, aren't you." I blushed in acknowledgement of the accusation.

I decided to take the plunge. Going down on one knee I hoped the tuxedo rental store in Nashville wouldn't charge me if I got grass stains on my trousers. I took her left hand and lifted it until it was almost touching my lips.

"Cassie, will you marry me?"

"On one condition." My heart sank. What sort of condition could she be demanding?

"Oh, erm, OK. What is it?"

"We don't have a honeymoon in Africa." She beamed at me.

"You can choose where we go. Anywhere you like."

"In that case, Andy Mirren, I will marry you."

I practically sprang off my knees and into Cassie's arms. It was a long time before we stopped kissing.

We were interrupted by a discrete cough behind us. "You know, I did provide you with a room for that sort of thing."

We turned to see Charleese standing behind us, resplendent in her oyster coloured wedding dress, flowers woven into her flowing blond hair. She couldn't have looked more beautiful if she had been created in an artist's dream.

"Sorry, Charleese, we were, well we were just celebrating something." I wondered why Cassie didn't tell her that we had just got engaged, then I understood. The sensitive Cassie didn't want to intrude on Charleese's day. We could 'come out' in the morning when the wedding was over.

Charleese gave Cassie a curious look and then swivelled her head to give me one as well.

"There's something you two aren't telling me, and I think I can guess what it might be. Come on, out with it."

"Honestly, it's nothing, really. We were just taken by the moment and the sunset and everything." I nodded towards the horizon where the sunset was now just a red smear, but lights had been strung through the trees to provide illumination.

"Well, it is a very romantic spot, which is why I chose to have my ranch built here. OK, I'll let it go for now, but I'll get it out of you before you leave. Now, let's go party some more." She took the two of us by the hand and pulled us close to either side of her, drawing us back towards the marquee. The band were playing the opening chords of one of Charleese's own songs and I suspected she would be cajoled into singing for her guests before long.

It had been a long and very big year and was about to get bigger.

On the Monday after Cuddly Toy Day I had been called into Greg Jones' office. He introduced me to Sarah McVey, the new producer of Cuddly Toy Day.

The contrast between Sarah and Igor couldn't have been greater. Sarah was one of those fifty something women who don't care too much about their appearance. She was all chunky cardigans, rumpled tweed skirt and no-nonsense brogues. Her hair was a steel grey explosion around her head with a pair of spectacles peeking out from the top like a nesting owl. If half a dozen miniature dachshunds had been circling her feet I wouldn't have been surprised. As I shook her hand she shifted her position slightly and I spied Cassie perched on a chair behind her, note book in lap and ready to take notes if needed.

"This is Andy Mirren, of whom you have no doubt heard." Greg introduced me with a nervous look.

"There's hardly anyone in the business who doesn't know that name after Friday evening. Word gets around, young man."

I didn't know what to say so I decided that the best thing was to say nothing.

"Sarah is going to need a liaison for next year's telethon. We were wondering if you wanted to take the job on again?"

"I should declare an interest." I addressed myself to Sarah. "Cassie and I are going out together."

"So she told me in the taxi over here. I know I won't have any secrets from you, regardless of whether you're outside the tent pissing in or inside pissing out. After what you did to that slimy toad Kasnisky I think I'd rather you were inside the tent. So, do you want the job?"

It was an unexpected offer. I had been on my way back to my cubby hole in the basement when Greg had rung me.

"Why me? You know what I'm like. It might get a bit tense at times."

"Good. The budget MOF has agreed with us is tight. I need someone who isn't scared of challenging every penny that's spent. You've proved willing to do that at Metro, so I'd like you to do it for me. No doubt we'll have arguments, possibly even heated arguments, but I expect that and respect it. Now, do you want the job or not?"

I said that I did and Greg beamed at me and ordered cups of coffee all round as we started the first production meeting for the next year's show.

Later Greg called me back for a private chat.

"I can't say I approve of everything you did, Andy. Making waves doesn't make you the most popular person. There was even a time, for a while, when the Board were thinking of getting rid of you. You might have become a liability."

"To tell you the truth, Greg, after I came back from Africa I was considering jacking it all in."

"So why didn't you?"

"It would have let Igor Kasnisky and Helen Spencer off the hook, for one thing. The other was that it would have left the job half done. Both jobs in fact; the telethon and Kasnisky. I didn't want to do that; it didn't seem right."

Greg nodded his understanding.

"Do we know what's happening to Igor and Helen?" I asked.

"Rumour is that they'll be allowed to resign. Quietly of course. They'll struggle to find jobs with reputable TV companies after the revelations you made."

"I suspect they'll find something with someone who has a more flexible approach to morality. Someone with their own ethics, or rather lack of them."

"I think you're probably right. And of course we can't hope to keep everything out of the press. Someone is bound to blab. I think that our Press Officer is in for a busy time. Anyway, what I called you back for was to discuss your salary. I've been authorised to give you a pay rise. When you took the job last year we gave you a pay increase, but it was nothing like the salary we had paid Mellissa Sutherland. So now you're going to get the same package that she had."

He handed me a letter. It said 'draft' at the top but there was no doubting what it was, my new contract. I looked at the salary section and blinked.

Wow. With that amount coming in I could move out of my poky flat and..... And what? Had I just risked everything to reduce the costs for MOF just to start lining my own pockets? I handed the letter back to Greg.

"I'm very flattered Greg and it's a great gesture, but I can't accept it." I told him why.

"But Andy, you've earned this. Several times over in fact."

"I know Greg, but that isn't the point. I don't need it. Look, I'll make you a counter offer. I'll take a rise of 2% above inflation for the next three years and an extra week's holiday."

The pay rise was reasonable and much better than many people would be getting if the press was to be believed. The extra holiday wouldn't cost the charity anything.

"But you have to take more than that. It wouldn't be right otherwise." Greg was clearly flummoxed, not used to people turning down huge salary increases. "I'll tell you what. How about we give you a bonus?"

That got my attention. A bonus was a just reward for saving the charity money. But not a big bonus. I wasn't greedy. I'm not a banker.

"OK. How about half a percent of what I saved the charity on last Friday's show? At the end of the year I'll take the same again on any additional savings I'm able to make on this year's budget."

Greg did some quick calculations in his head and then broke into a smile. "I'm happy with that, Andy. I like the idea of paying by results. I'll get the new contract drawn up and you can take a look at it. If you're happy then we have a deal."

And that was that. The rest of the year was something of a blur as Cassie and I immersed ourselves in the planning for the next telethon. I went to Africa again, of course, but this time steered well clear of anywhere where we might run into Akeem and his men. It had actually been a bit boring and I had missed Cassie so much it had hurt.

Which brought me, eventually, to Tennessee and Charleese's wedding day. We would have loved to have spent more time in the States, Cassie wanted to see New York, but the telethon was only weeks away and we couldn't afford to take the time off. So the next evening would find us back at Nashville International Airport for our flight back to London via Chicago.

The evening was getting late and the band had toned down the music to a waltz beat. There were only a handful of people left who, like us, were Charleese's house guests. Cassie and I held each other tightly as we moved in time to the music.

"Do you want a long engagement or a short one?" I whispered in her ear.

"Oh, short. If my Dad has time to think about how much a wedding costs he'll probably emigrate."

I chuckled. That was something else of course. Meeting Cassie's parents. I realised that I knew hardly anything about Cassie's family. Would they like me? She spoke very fondly about them and joked about her Dad, but they obviously had a good relationship.

"You'll have to meet my parents." I reminded her.

"I hope I'm good enough for your mother's little boy. Mothers don't like women stealing their sons, you know."

"They'll love you." I assured her. And they would, I knew it.

"I think it's time we went to bed." Cassie murmured.

On our bed I found a bottle of champagne, tied with a ribbon and bearing a hand written card which said.

"You two can't fool me. Have a wonderful life together."

--- The End ---

Author's Note

I would like to remind readers that this is a work of fiction. I have no reason to believe that any TV company involved in telethons has ever behaved in the way that I portrayed in this story. From this book it would be easy to assume that all charity fund raising was subject to fraud or that money was being wasted. I would like to assure readers that I don't, for one moment, believe that.

In my research, I studied the annual reports and accounts of the largest charities that use telethons to raise funds. It's something that you can do for yourself if you visit the Charity Commission website: https://www.gov.uk/government/organisations/charity-commission I was quite satisfied that, as far as I could tell, the money they raised was spent wisely and wasn't wasted. Unfortunately, it costs money to raise money, so all charities will incur some costs but there is no reason to believe that those costs are excessive.

Celebrities give their time freely to help raise money. OK, sometimes their efforts are not as altruistic as they would like us to believe, but if they weren't present on telethon night the amount of money raised would be considerably lower and that would help no one. The resulting income is worth any free plug that a performer might get for their record or their tour. Many performers and celebrities are more deeply involved and their participation, freely given, helps to make the evenings a success.

The characters Igor Kasnisky and Helen Spencer exist only in my imagination. I do, however, hope that there are few Andy Mirrens out there somewhere keeping an eye on things.

I have been accused of not portraying a very positive image of Africa and Africans and I apologise if you get that feeling. The necessities of storytelling sometimes require authors to concentrate on the needs of their story and neglect other aspects of life.. I have no reason to suppose that, in general, African people are any better or worse than their European or American counterparts. There is good and bad in all societies and it is unfortunate that for the needs of my story I have had to focus on some of the bad.

The world is an unfair place and it's easy to forget that a sizeable proportion of the world's population lives in a constant state of struggle with fear, poverty, hunger, hardship and disease. Some of that comes about through natural causes but a lot is a result of man's inhumanity to man. Now that you have finished this book, please consider doing something, however small, to help relieve the suffering of others. A portion of the royalties I receive for this book is being donated to charities that work in Africa and to Help For Heroes here at home.

Next

Robert Cubitt takes another direction completely for his next work and launches himself into the world of sci-fi and "space opera".

Below is a short extract from Robert Cubitt's next book, "The Magi", the first part of a nine volume Sci-Fi epic adventure to be published in 2016. The author hopes that you enjoy this short extract.

One - The Out Of Place Android

The door of the shuttle craft hissed downwards and An Kohli stepped out along the ramp it formed. Two younglings stared at her with interest, but when they saw that she wasn't carrying goods to barter or sell they lost interest and scuttled off about their own business.

Such was the nature of the galaxy these days; not even the arrival of a shuttle craft attracted any interest. She doubted that the younglings would even mention her arrival to their parents. That suited her for the time being. She wanted to find the one she was looking for and then get off this useless lump of rock and never see it again.

Dust swirled around her and she wrapped her neck-cloth around her face in a vain attempt to keep it from entering her mouth and nose. Already she could feel the grit between her teeth. She looked at the hand held tracker. The steady pulse indicated that her target was about one hundred li to the north, if this lump of rock actually had a north. OK, she admitted to herself, north was a concept not an actuality; her target was about one hundred li diagonally to her left. It would feel like double that in the heat and dust of this shitty rock.

She wished she'd landed the shuttle a little closer but she hadn't wanted to let him know she was coming. He was the type that always ran first and asked questions afterwards.

An Kohli took a deep breath, regretting it at once as she inhaled a mouthful of dust, and strode forward, skirting past some mud built houses. She passed the same two younglings struggling to pull a bucket of water from a well and then pour it into a small tank mounted on wheels. When the tank was full it would need both of them to drag it home. Again she puzzled at the nature of a galaxy where the arrival of a shuttle craft from an orbiting space ship could attract so little attention, but where the inhabitants of the planet still drew their water from wells. She gave a mental shrug. The galaxy was a big place and she had encountered stranger things than younglings at a well.

The dust continued to torment her as she crossed the open ground. Across the rock strewn plain she could see the building she was heading for. There were draft animals tethered outside and a crude sign announced its purpose, though she couldn't read the alien script. She corrected herself angrily. Here it was she who was the alien.

She pushed open the door and ducked under the low lintel into the dim room. Bars across the galaxy all seemed to conform to a type, she mused. The darker the interior the more shady its clientele and there was no one shadier than the one she was looking for. Now for the fun part.

He was a shape shifter, which meant that he could be any one of the occupants of the bar. There was a trick to identifying a shape shifter, though. Stare at him, or her, for ten seconds or more and he, or she, was bound to reveal themselves. They hated being stared at. The problem was that if you stared at people in this sort of bar you were likely to start a fight, which was why shape shifters liked bars like this one.

Her arrival had caused heads to turn. Her tall, slender figure always attracted attention. One look at the powerful Menafield Pulsar holstered on her hip suggested that there was nothing to look at here and that it was a good idea for people to just go about their business. She stomped her way to the bar, her thick souled boots making the floor vibrate. Sly looks still came her way, admiring her good looks and the waves of glossy purple hair that framed her face perfectly. She ignored them and focused on the task in hand.

An ancient droid bartender creaked towards her and offered her a drinks menu. She knew that this was a pretension and that whatever she ordered would numb her taste buds for days, but she made a show of looking at it before pointing to the glass of the man standing nearest to her and saying "I'll have one of those."

The droid creaked away to get the drink and she scanned the room quickly, not allowing her eyes to rest on any individual for more than a few seconds. Those that been watching her covertly looked away quickly, but not quickly enough for her not to notice.

So which one was he? Not the two men sat at the back of the room. They were clearly having an argument, perhaps over the rather frightened looking female that sat between them. It wasn't the female either. Shape shifters can't change sex, though they can make themselves appear in female form if you don't get close enough to find out which bits haven't been changed. She was showing plenty of the bits that a male shape shifter would have to simulate by stuffing a bra with socks.

Not the two men sitting opposite each other in silence, staring into their drinks. They were the defeated, worn down by years of scratching a living out of land that was only fit for growing rocks. Scattered around the room were half a dozen more men, drinking by themselves, each with an attitude that suggested it wasn't worth bothering to talk to them. Two more of them she dismissed as being in the same defeated category, which left four that might be her quarry. The droid returned and placed a foaming glass in front of her.

An Kohli took a tentative sip and narrowly resisted spitting the liquid out. She was not the sort of person who spat in public. The liquid was a sour tasting beer. The man whose drink she had copied raised his glass and took a large mouthful. An acquired taste, An Kohli concluded. She returned her attention to the four men she thought might be him and tried to stare at them without appearing as if she was staring. A difficult task as any lovelorn teenager who has ever tried staring at a pretty girl would be able to testify.

The first one was easy enough. He was the one further along the bar, standing with his back to her, though the way he twitched his head suggested he sensed he was being watched. Just as he started to turn An Kohli switched her attention to another man on the far side of the room. He was sat sideways on but the glazed look in his eyes suggested he wouldn't notice if the roof fell on him. She counted off ten seconds; nothing. She shifted her gaze again, across the room. A young man in dirty work clothes. Not likely, the one she was looking for had never done a day's manual work in his life, but a disguise is a disguise. Nothing.

The final possibility suggested someone from off-planet. He was well dressed in a modern style which she recognised but couldn't quite place. Not local, she concluded. He met her gaze directly but didn't react to it. Again, nothing. She checked her tracker. The light pulsed steadily and indicated she was standing within a few met of him. She heard the droid creak towards her again and then it hit her. She turned and levelled her gaze at it.

After ten seconds the droid slammed it's fist onto the bar in frustration, making heads turn. Yes, she was right. A backward planet like this wouldn't have the technology to build droids. This one was old and badly maintained and the know-how to maintain it wouldn't exist here either. She doubted that they had even developed as far as steam power.

"Fuck you." The droid said, its voice wheezy and crackling.

"You can drop the disguise, Den."

"Not in front of the natives." he wheezed. "Don't want to scare anyone. How did you find me?"

"Female intuition." She smiled a mischievous smile.

"You bitch. You planted a tracker on me, didn't you?"

"That would be telling." She continued to grin broadly.

The droid figure let out a wheeze of anger, like a hiss of steam from a leaking pipe. "Well, now you're here you better tell me what you want."

"How do you know that I'm not just looking for a bit of company?"

"Quit fooling around. We both know you didn't cross a hundred parsecs of space just for the pleasure of my company, so spit it out."

"I've found them." She whispered.

"Found what?" His jaw dropped with a clang as he realised what she was talking about. "Oh. *Them*. So where are they?"

"Well, when I say I've found them I really mean I know who has them and I have a rough idea of where she may be."

"Oh, so you haven't found them then. Not really."

"OK, Mr Pedantic, maybe not *found* found, but at least I know where to start looking."

"So who has them?"

"Su Mali."

The droid figure nodded its head, making a noise like fingernails on a blackboard. "Makes sense. She could crack the vault of the Bank Of The Universe if she could get past the guards. So why do you need me?"

"You know that one person couldn't take on Su Mali. She's too clever and too good a shot. Beside, she's one of yours. Only a Gau can recognise another Gau at first sight."

"You know, An Kohli, I have a long lived desire to die peacefully in my bed surrounded by a bevy of Sutran beauties. If I go with you the chances of that happening are reduced to about zero. Not only would Su Mali be out for my blood, our blood, but the Fell would send every unlicensed bounty hunter in the galaxy, and a few other galaxies, to track us down and kill us. That's not a job you would apply for if you saw it on the galactic vacancies board."

"It's worth a lot of money."

"If I was interested in money I wouldn't be working here for 10 nuks a day. After the last caper I decided that there was more to life than the pursuit of money."

"Wow, you've changed Den. I never thought I would hear you say you weren't interested in money."

"When you've had your genitals held in the very tight grip of a Norian warrior you start to re-evaluate your life a little. You can't make love to a Sutran beauty if you don't have any genitals."

An Kohli spotted her opportunity. "OK, how about the women. There'll be plenty of those if we recover them. They'll be throwing themselves at you."

"Will you be one of them?"

"Only in your dreams."

"That's what I thought. I'll stick with the Sutrans. No deal."

Once she might have considered a relationship with Den Gau, but not after coming back on board her own ship to find him in a very compromising position with her co-pilot, Gala. An Kohli had forgiven Gala but kicked Den Gau off the ship. She had been sorely tempted to eject him from the airlock without a space suit but had relented when Gala had pointed out that Den Gau still owed her money. While An Kohli might be prepared to forego any debts Gala would rather be repaid in full. Some chance of that, An Kohli had thought at the time.

"OK, There's fame and glory." That would surely appeal.

"You remember Malik?"

"The Sentinel who rescued Gib Dander?"

"That's him. Well that rescue got him fame and glory. He's dead now. His body is spread across three star systems. That's what fame and glory gets you. No deal."

That was a bitter blow. She had liked Malik. He was one of the good guys. If Den Gau turned her down she had been going to go to Malik next. Sentinels were expensive, but they were the best. To be honest Den Gau was far from her first choice but he had the sole advantage of being both a Gau and available; if he could be persuaded.

"What about Bubar?"

"In hospital last I heard. Lost an arm. It's taking time to grow back"

"Linder?"

"On permanent retainer to Gib Dander now, along with Harker and Elway. You won't find any other Sentinels willing to take on the job, not for what you can afford to pay and not on this side of the galaxy.

She chewed the inside of her cheek, a habit she had when she was deep in thought. "Ok." She said, finally. "What will it take to get you on board."

He was about to reply that wild fiju couldn't get him to take the job, but then he had an idea of his own.

"Get me into the Guild".

An Kohli's eyes opened wide with surprise. She hadn't expected that. With Den Gau's reputation it was unthinkable.

"You have to be joking." She struggled to keep the scorn form her voice. She couldn't afford to upset him, at least not at the moment.

"Never been more serious."

"But they'd never take you."

"With you recommending me they might."

"Flattering, but I think you over estimate my influence within the Guild.

"Not if you recover the Magi."

She shushed him and quickly scanned the room to see if anyone had heard him use the M word. "Careful what you say. If anyone gets wind of this we could be screwed before we even start."

"But you see what I mean." Den Gau continued, knowing he had the advantage. "If finding the….them can make me rich, get me women and get me fame and glory, surely it can get me into the Guild, especially if you were the one who recovered them and I was the one helping you."

He had a point, An Kohli had to concede. But the Guild set high standards and they didn't, ever, work on the wrong side of the law which was more, much more, than could be said for Den Gau.

"Look, I can't make any promises…."

"But you can promise to try. Put in a good word for me. For crying out loud if we pull this off then we've…."

She cut him off again before he could blurt out what the effects might be. Who knew who was listening.

"OK, OK. I give in. If we succeed I'll do whatever I can to get you into the Guild, but I can't make any promises that they'll accept you."

"You're a Guild member. Your word is your bond so I'll trust you. Besides, if we don't succeed it won't matter anyway because we'll probably be dead."

"Good point." She extended her hand and the droid figure shook it, letting out another shriek of tortured metal that made the bar's occupants turn to look once again.

With her business complete An Kohli let her natural curiosity get the better of her. "How did you get the job here anyway? This planet doesn't have the technology for droids."

"You know me. I can sell snow on an ice planet. I turned up as myself and offered the owner a droid bartender for 10 nuks a day. All it would need is a storeroom at night where it could recharge. He said yes so the next day I turned up looking like this. Not only do I get a roof over my head I get 10 nuks a day and all the blash that I can drink. Not that any sane person would want to drink more than a glass of that stuff." He indicated the glass that sat untouched in front of An Kohli.

"What about food?"

"They sell food here as well. Well, food of sorts. I get the leftovers and with food of the quality they serve here there's always plenty of leftovers."

"I suppose you know all the regulars."

"We don't get many regulars. This is a drovers and traders bar. Most of the customers come in for a few drinks and are then back on the road as soon as they sober up. We get a few in from the village, but not many. They don't have a lot of cash round here for drinking."

"What about him? The one behind me with the smart cloths."

"I've been wondering about him myself. He turned up a couple of days back and has been in and out a few times. Looks like he's waiting for someone."

"Is there any reason that he might be looking for you?"

"You know me. Its more than a possibility. If he is then he hasn't made any attempt to make me show myself, which anyone who knew me would do straight away. Are there any other ships in orbit?"

"The ship's sensors didn't show any. I haven't seen any shuttles parked close by either."

"Well, he pays cash and he's not caused any trouble, which around here is always a good sign. Who knows, he might be hiding out here as well."

"If he was then he'd dress down a bit. Make more of an effort to fit in. He doesn't fit and that bothers me."

"You're paranoid, Kohli"

"An Kohli. You know I hate it when people don't use my full name."

"Whatever. So, what do we do now?"

"When does your shift end?"

"When we close tonight."

"Any reason why you can't leave then?"

"No. I'll leave a note for the owner of this dump to say the droid's broken down and has to go off planet for repairs. He'll have to manage by himself till this is over."

"You'd come back to this arsehole of a place?" An Kohli found the idea ludicrous.

"Believe me, If we pull this off we're going to need some out of the way place like this to hide out for a while, or we'll end up spread across three star systems just like Malik."

He was right. This job would make them some powerful enemies.

"So where is Su Mali?" Den asked.

"Not now. I'll give you the low down when you join me tonight. My shuttle is on the other side of the village. Meet me there when you've finished here."

With that she stood up and walked out of the bar. Several pairs of eyes followed her. Most were for the traditional reasons that men's eyes follow the swaying rear view of an attractive woman, but the well-dressed man appeared to have less salacious motives. He watched the empty door frame for several seconds after An Kohli had disappeared, before returning once more to his waiting.

And Now

Both the author Robert Cubitt and Selfishgenie Publishing hope that you have enjoyed reading this book and that you have found it useful.

Find Robert Cubitt on Facebook at https://www.facebook.com/robertocubitt and 'like' his page; follow him on Twitter **@robert_cubitt** You can also e-mail Robert Cubitt at **robert.cubitt@selfgenie.com**

Please tell people about this eBook, write a review on Amazon or mention it on your favourite social networking sites.

For further titles that may be of interest to you please visit the Selfishgenie Publishing website at selfishgenie.com where you can join our mailing list so that we can keep you up to date with all our latest releases (or maybe that should be 'escapes').

Printed in Great Britain
by Amazon

86069112R00159